Praise for Debbie Macomber's
Bestselling Novels from Ballantine Books

CHRISTMAS NOVELS

Mr. Miracle

"Macomber's Christmas novels are always something to cherish. *Mr. Miracle* is a sweet and innocent story that will lift your spirits during the holidays and throughout the year. Celebrating the comforts of home, family traditions, forgiveness and love, this is the perfect, quick Christmas read."
—*RT Book Reviews*

"[Macomber] writes about romance, family and friendship with a gentle, humorous touch."
—*Tampa Bay Times*

"Macomber spins another sweet, warmhearted holiday tale that will be as comforting to her fans as hot chocolate on Christmas morning."
—*Kirkus Reviews*

"This gentle, inspiring romance will be a sought-after read."
—*Library Journal*

"Macomber cheerfully presents a holiday story that combines the winsomeness of a visiting angel (similar to Clarence from *It's a Wonderful Life*) with the more poignant soulfulness of *A Christmas Carol* to bring to life a memorable reading experience."
—*Bookreporter*

"Macomber's name is almost as closely linked to Christmas reading as that of Charles Dickens. . . . [*Mr. Miracle*] has enough sweetness, charm, and seasonal sentiment to make Macomber fans happy."
—*The Romance Dish*

Starry Night

"Contemporary romance queen Macomber (*Rose Harbor in Bloom*) hits the sweet spot with this tender tale of impractical love. . . . A delicious Christmas miracle well worth waiting for."
—*Publishers Weekly* (starred review)

"[A] holiday confection . . . as much a part of the season for some readers as cookies and candy canes."
—*Kirkus Reviews*

"A sweet contemporary Christmas romance . . . [that] the best-selling author's many fans will enjoy."
—*Library Journal*

"[A] sweetly charming holiday romance."
—*Library Journal*

ROSE HARBOR

Love Letters

"[Debbie] Macomber's mastery of women's fiction is evident in her latest. . . . [She] breathes life into each plotline, carefully intertwining her characters' stories to ensure that none of them overshadow the others. Yet it is her ability to capture different facets of emotion which will entrance fans and newcomers alike."
—*Publishers Weekly*

"Romance and a little mystery abound in this third installment of Macomber's series set at Cedar Cove's Rose Harbor Inn. . . . Readers of Robyn Carr and Sherryl Woods will enjoy Macomber's latest, which will have them flipping pages until the end and eagerly anticipating the next installment."
—*Library Journal* (starred review)

"Uplifting . . . a cliffhanger ending for Jo Marie begs for a swift resolution in the next book."
—*Kirkus Reviews*

"Mending a broken heart is not always easy to do, but Macomber succeeds at this beautifully in *Love Letters*. . . . Quite simply, this is a refreshing take on most love stories—there are twists and turns in the plot that keep readers on their toes—and the author shares up slices of realism, allowing her audience to feel right at home as they follow a cast of familiar characters living in the small coastal town of Cedar Cove, where life is interesting, to say the least."

—*Bookreporter*

"*Love Letters* is another wonderful story in the Rose Harbor series. Genuine life struggles with heart-warming endings for the three couples in this book make it special. Readers won't be able to get enough of Macomber's gentle storytelling. Fans already know what a charming place Rose Harbor is and new readers will love discovering it as well."

—*RT Book Reviews* (4½ stars)

Rose Harbor in Bloom

"[Debbie] Macomber uses warmth, humor and superb storytelling skills to deliver a tale that charms and entertains."

—*BookPage*

"A wonderful reading experience . . . as [the characters'] stories unfold, you almost feel they have become friends."

—Wichita Falls *Times Record News*

"[Debbie Macomber] draws in threads of her earlier book in this series, *The Inn at Rose Harbor,* in what is likely to be just as comfortable a place for Macomber fans as for Jo Marie's guests at the inn."
—*The Seattle Times*

"Macomber's legions of fans will embrace this cozy, heartwarming read."
—*Booklist*

"Readers will find the emotionally impactful storylines and sweet, redemptive character arcs for which the author is famous. Classic Macomber, which will please fans and keep them coming back for more."
—*Kirkus Reviews*

"Macomber is an institution in women's fiction. Her principal talent lies in creating characters with a humble, familiar charm. They possess complex personalities, but it is their kinder qualities that are emphasized in the warm world of her novels—a world much like Rose Harbor Inn, in which one wants to curl up and stay."
—*Shelf Awareness*

"The storybook scenery of lighthouses, cozy bed and breakfast inns dotting the coastline, and seagulls flying above takes readers on personal journeys of first love, lost love and recaptured love [presenting] love in its purest and most personal forms."
—*Bookreporter*

"Just the right blend of emotional turmoil and satisfying resolutions . . . For a feel-good indulgence, this book delivers."
—*RT Book Reviews* (4 stars)

The Inn at Rose Harbor

"Debbie Macomber's Cedar Cove romance novels have a warm, comfy feel to them. Perhaps that's why they've sold millions."
—*USA Today*

"No one tugs at readers' heartstrings quite as effectively as Macomber."
—*Chicago Tribune*

"The characters and their various entanglements are sure to resonate with Macomber fans. . . . The book sets up an appealing milieu of townspeople and visitors that sets the stage for what will doubtless be many further adventures at the Inn at Rose Harbor."
—*The Seattle Times*

"Debbie Macomber is the reigning queen of women's fiction."
—*The Sacramento Bee*

"The prolific Macomber introduces a spin-off of sorts from her popular Cedar Cove series, still set in that fictional small town but centered on Jo Marie Rose, a youngish widow who buys and operates the bed and breakfast of the title. This clever premise allows Macomber to craft stories around the B&B's guests, Abby and Josh in this inaugural effort, while using Jo Marie and her ongoing recovery from the death of her husband Paul in Afghanistan as the series' anchor. . . . With her characteristic optimism, Macomber provides fresh starts for both."
—*Booklist*

"Emotionally charged romance."
—*Kirkus Reviews*

BLOSSOM STREET

Blossom Street Brides

"[An] enjoyable read that pulls you right in from page one."
—*Fresh Fiction*

"A master at writing stories that embrace both romance and friendship, [Debbie] Macomber can always be counted on for an enjoyable page-turner, and this Blossom Street installment is no exception."
—*RT Book Reviews*

Starting Now

"Macomber has a masterful gift of creating tales that are both mesmerizing and inspiring, and her talent is at its peak with *Starting Now.* Her Blossom Street characters seem as warm and caring as beloved friends, and the new characters ease into the series smoothly. The storyline moves along at a lovely pace, and it is a joy to sit down and savor the world of Blossom Street once again."
—Wichita Falls *Times Record News*

"Macomber understands the often complex nature of a woman's friendships, as well as the emotional language women use with their friends."
—*NY Journal of Books*

"There is a reason that legions of Macomber fans ask for more Blossom Street books. They fully engage her readers as her characters discover happiness, purpose, and meaning in life. . . . Macomber's feel-good novel, emphasizing interpersonal relationships and putting people above status and objects, is truly satisfying."
—*Booklist* (starred review)

"Macomber's writing and storytelling deliver what she's famous for—a smooth, satisfying tale with characters her fans will cheer for and an arc that is cozy, heartwarming and ends with the expected happily-ever-after."
—*Kirkus Reviews*

"Macomber's many fans are going to be over the moon with her latest Blossom Street novel. *Starting Now* combines Macomber's winning elements of romance and friendship, along with a search for one woman's life's meaning—all cozily bundled into a warmly satisfying story that is the very definition of 'comfort reading.'"

—*Bookreporter*

"Macomber's latest Blossom Street novel is a sweet story that tugs on the heartstrings and hits on the joy of family, friends and knitting, as readers have come to expect."

—*RT Book Reviews* (4½ stars)

"The return to Blossom Street is an engaging visit for longtime readers as old friends play secondary roles while newcomers take the lead . . . Fans will enjoy the mixing of friends and knitting with many kinds of loving relationships."

—*Genre Go Round Reviews*

October 2014

Dear Friends,

Like many others, I've always been fascinated with angels. My father saw an angel shortly before he died. The angel arrived in the middle of the night in human form, dressed in farm clothes, and helped my dad back to bed. Dad described the angel in detail. Angels among us isn't as far removed from reality as it might seem. Check out Hebrews 13:2 if you don't believe me. It was that verse that inspired *Mrs. Miracle* and now . . . drumroll, please . . . *Mr. Miracle*.

I owe a great deal to several people who made this entire project possible. First and foremost my agent, Theresa Park, and her incredible staff, Emily, Alex, Andrea, Abby, and Peter. And, of course, my two marvelous Ballantine editors, Jennifer Hershey and Shauna Summers, who encouraged and supported me through each phase of the writing process, along with my own amazing staff.

So now, my wonderful readers, it's your turn. I hope you enjoy the story of Harry Mills as he discovers the delights and pleasures of life on Earth along with its temptations and limitations. And then, of course, there's his mission with Addie and Erich . . . oh heavens (pun intended), there I go again. Okay, I won't say anything more. The story is for you to unfold by turning the page.

I hope that you're charmed by *Mr. Miracle* and that you, too, might find an angel or two in your own life.

Your feedback is important to me. You can contact me through my webpage at debbiemacomber.com or through Facebook. If you're so inclined you can write me at P.O. Box 1458, Port Orchard, WA 98366.

Merry Christmas and may God bless.

Debbie Macomber

Mr. Miracle

DEBBIE MACOMBER

Mr. Miracle

A Christmas Novel

BALLANTINE BOOKS · NEW YORK

2015 Ballantine Books Mass Market Edition

Copyright © 2014 by Debbie Macomber
Excerpt from *Dashing Through the Snow* by Debbie Macomber copyright © 2015 by Debbie Macomber
The Bride Wore Mistletoe by Christina Skye copyright © 2015 by Roberta Helmer

Published in the United States by Ballantine Books, an imprint of Random House, a division of Penguin Random House LLC, New York.

BALLANTINE and the HOUSE colophon are registered trademarks of Penguin Random House LLC.

Originally published in hardcover in the United States by Ballantine Books, an imprint of Random House, a division of Penguin Random House LLC, in 2014.

This book contains an excerpt from the forthcoming book *Dashing Through the Snow* by Debbie Macomber. This excerpt has been set for this edition only and may not reflect the final content of the forthcoming edition.

ISBN 978-0-553-39166-4
eBook ISBN 978-0-553-39162-6

Cover design: Lynn Andreozzi
Cover illustration: Alan Ayers

Printed in the United States of America

www.ballantinebooks.com

9 8 7 6 5 4 3 2 1

Ballantine Books mass market edition: November 2015

To Bill Abbott
in appreciation for his confidence
and faith in me

and in memory of Tommy
who really was Man's Best Friend

Mr. Miracle

Prologue

Well, well, well, Harry Mills mused as he glanced around the campus of Southshore Community College. *So this is Earth.* Students darted across the emerald-green landscape, scurrying toward their classes. The December sky was dark and overcast, threatening rain. Not uncommon weather for the Pacific Northwest, or so he'd been told.

This is exactly what I expected, he thought a bit smugly. Until now he'd had, shall we say, a heavenly perspective. Yes, he was an angel, but unlike his fellow angels and good friends, Shirley, Goodness, and Mercy, he had the ability to mingle with humans without suspicion. What he enjoyed most was the fact that the humans were completely unaware of who he was and the work he'd been given. Harry was on a God-given mission—a trial mission that was the opportunity of an eternity and one he hoped would become a permanent job if he performed well.

In preparation for his earthly visitation, Harry had carefully studied human behavior and had learned about ways to gently guide his charges. Of course, he knew all about free will, too, but frankly, he wasn't overly concerned. Just how difficult could it be to give a nudge to those in need of a bit of subtle direction? Naturally, he was required to work under certain parameters—restrictions, actually—but he didn't consider that a particular problem, either.

What did concern Harry was that he'd been assigned a mentor, which in his opinion was completely unnecessary. He didn't need anyone looking over his shoulder, watching his every move.

As the spiritual coordinator for this part of Tacoma, Celeste Chapeaux had been assigned to oversee Harry. Her powers were above and beyond his own. While his role involved the students in his class, her sphere of influence reached far beyond as coordinator of an entire area, including the campus and surrounding neighborhood. Harry knew he wasn't the only angel under her direction.

For now, Harry was willing to play by the rules in order to prove himself. In time, Celeste would realize an angel of his knowledge and intelligence was capable of managing assignments on his own without supervision.

Making his way across the campus, Harry was enthralled to see the brick walls of the three-story building with the ivy climbing to the top of the second floor. A more modern structure loomed to his left and housed the cafeteria known as the Hub. Celeste Chapeaux worked as a barista at the latte stand there.

Catching sight of her, Harry paused. She was young. Very young. Too young. She wore her hair so short it stood straight up on end and was dyed the color of a pomegranate. And she had a diamond piercing in her nose! He'd been assigned the body of a middle-aged man. Well, perhaps even a bit over middle age, wise and mature. This couldn't possibly be right. He knew that the bodies angels received were random, but still, it felt weird. He was expected to take direction from a woman barely out of her teens? This . . . this bejeweled, tattooed ruffian couldn't possibly be his lead.

She met his eyes, and it appeared that Celeste recognized Harry immediately. Her crooked smile told him she'd read his thoughts perfectly.

"Welcome, Harry," she said as she ground coffee beans. The scent of the roasted beans swirled around him. She pressed down the grounds and then twisted the small round container into the machine. She did this skillfully.

"Take a seat," she instructed, nodding toward the stool at the counter.

Still befuddled, Harry frowned and muttered, "I'd rather stand."

"Whatever."

He arched his brows. "Whatever what?"

"Whatever you want," she returned, with that same off-center smile.

The coffee machine made a horrendous noise, followed by a hissing sound that caught him unaware. Harry backed away before she set a freshly brewed Americano on the counter in front of him. He stared at the coffee, wondering what he was supposed to do with it.

"Take a sleeve; and be careful, it's hot."

"I don't need a sleeve." In fact, he wasn't sure what she was talking about. *Sleeve?*

She shrugged, again showing a decided lack of concern. "You have all the information on your assignment?"

He nodded, raised the cup to his lips, and tasted the coffee. The liquid had to be close to the boiling point and burned his lips, not to mention that the cup was uncomfortably hot to hold. Too proud to let her see, he set the cup down and then jerked his hand discreetly by his side a couple times to shake off the sting.

Celeste automatically handed him a paper sleeve, and, grumbling under his breath, Harry took it.

"You're stepping in, teaching the classic literature class."

Harry was well aware of his assignment.

"Have you read Dickens's *A Christmas Carol*?" she asked.

"Who hasn't?" he responded nonchalantly, wanting her to know he was well versed in human classic literature. Although he had reservations when it came to this particular story, especially the author's depiction of the afterlife.

"Who hasn't?" Celeste repeated. "Probably ninety-nine percent of the students in your class."

"That goes without saying. Anyway, you and I both know Dickens got it wrong. I have serious doubts about an author who so flippantly portrays heavenly spirits in such a manner. As far as I'm concerned, Dickens has taken far too much literary license. The description of Marley's ghost and the three spirits is beyond ridiculous. Someone needs to set the record straight. Humans don't actually believe—"

"Correcting misconceptions about heaven isn't part of your job," Celeste said, cutting him off.

Harry was tempted to argue, but changed his mind. He could see it would do little good. Clearly she was opinionated and most likely unable to see reason. He'd heard about angels like this, ones who were given an earthly assignment and lost their heavenly perspective. Sadly, they got caught up in the temptations of Earth. That wouldn't be a problem for him, of course.

Celeste leaned against the counter, resting her

folded arms there. "Am I detecting a bit of an attitude here?" she asked.

Rather than answer, Harry posed a question of his own. "How is it you're the one in charge?"

"Do you have a problem with that?"

"Ah . . ."

"Listen, Harry, while you were strumming away on a harp I was dealing with the likes of Columbus and Lewis and Clark. Do you have any idea how difficult it was to guide *them*?"

He didn't, and stared down at his coffee. "Playing the harp isn't as easy as it looks, you know."

Celeste grinned as if to say he didn't have a clue what he was talking about. "We need to work together, got that?"

He straightened. It hadn't been his intention to start off on the wrong foot. "Got it."

"Good."

The coffee had cooled down enough for him to take a cautious second sip.

"As I said, all the necessary paperwork has been arranged. Your story is that you've accepted a transfer from Oregon State Community College. For your first assignment, you're here to help Addie Folsom. She's made a few bad decisions but is back living at home now and has enrolled in your class. Addie is dyslexic and has some serious doubts about her ability to learn. She never did well in school and fears she won't be able to do so now. Your assignment is to show her that she's smarter than she thinks and can succeed in her desire to work in the medical field. Her father was a chiropractor and she would like to follow in his footsteps. And then there's her neighbor, Erich Simmons. As a young teen, Addie had a real thing for him. That relationship might require a bit of help on your end, but don't worry. Most everything leading up to their interaction has already been set in place. Addie is going to need encouragement and a bit of direction. This first student is a test to see how well you manage before you're given the more difficult tasks."

He nodded, having already familiarized himself with the young woman's history. "I'm ready for this," he assured his earthly guide.

"Excellent. If you have any problems, come straight to me—don't attempt to handle them on your own. That's why I'm here. And let me warn you, with a human body, you're about to experience . . ."

"No need. I've got this covered. There won't be any problems . . . I've been watching Earth for quite some time. I'm ready. Really, what could be so difficult about teaching a few eager students?"

Harry might have been wrong, but it seemed Celeste's eyes widened briefly as if she struggled to hold back a laugh.

"No one ever anticipates problems," she told him, taking her index finger and drawing circles on the counter as if she needed time to recover her composure, "but they do come up on occasion. I want you to know I'm here to answer your questions and help you maneuver through this foreign landscape. What you viewed from heaven is one thing; living among humans is entirely different."

"I'm sure I'll be just fine."

"We'll see," she whispered.

That almost seemed like a challenge to Harry. Perhaps he was being overconfident. He needed to remember that she was the one with experience.

"Any other words of advice you wish to pass along?"

She seemed both surprised and pleased by his question. "As a matter of fact, there are. Don't ever forget that the world is in a fallen condition. Humans, as attractive and awesomely created as they are, tend to believe that events occur in their lives randomly, with little or no meaning. They often overlook the obvious, that God is in control."

"In other words, their spiritual understanding is limited?"

"You got that right."

"I know that."

"Fantastic." Her smile was as bright as a 100-watt lightbulb.

"Anything else?" He was eager to be on his way, find his classroom, and get started.

"A word of caution: Do what you can to never cross Dr. Conceito."

"Who?"

"The college president. He won't cut you any slack. In fact, stay away from him entirely if you can."

"Okay. Is that it?"

"Remember, human understanding is limited, and furthermore, you're about to experience . . ."

"Yes, yes, I know."

She smiled again as if keeping a secret. "And whatever you do, unless it is an absolute emergency, you must not cross the line. You say you're familiar with the parameters of your mission, now prove it."

Harry raised his hand to stop her before she said anything more. "No problem." Really, this assignment—during the Christmas holidays, to boot—was going to be a piece of rum-soaked fruitcake. A real delight. He was absolutely convinced of it.

Rushing out of the Hub, Harry eagerly started toward his classroom. The meeting with Celeste could have gone better, he thought as he took a shortcut across the lawn.

"You!"

The sharp command in the man's voice caught Harry up short. He stopped and glanced up to find a distinguished-looking man, dressed in a coat with a starched white shirt and fashionable tie, his arm outstretched, pointing directly at him.

Harry flattened his hand over his chest. "Me?"

"Yes, you. I saw you walk across the lawn."

"Ah . . . yes."

"Did you read the sign?"

"The sign?"

"The do-not-walk-on-the-grass sign."

"Oh . . . I guess I overlooked it." Extending his arm, Harry introduced himself. "Harry Mills."

The other man frowned and ignored his hand. "Harry Mills from Oregon State Community College?"

Harry nodded and lowered his arm. "Yes, one and the same."

"Don Conceito, the college president. Come to my office. It looks like I'm going to need to review the campus rules with you."

Chapter One

This wasn't the way it was supposed to happen. Six years out of high school, Addie Folsom had envisioned returning home loaded and driving a fancy car. Instead, she was limping back in a twenty-year-old Honda with close to three hundred thousand miles and her tail between her legs.

So much for the great promise of moving to Montana and walking into a get-rich-quick opportunity. She'd left Washington State with such high hopes . . . and ended up living in a leaky trailer and waiting tables in a run-down diner. It took all six of those years for Addie to admit she'd made a very big mistake. Pride, she'd learned, offered little comfort.

Oh, she'd returned home for visits at least a couple times a year. When asked pointed questions about her work in the silver mine, she'd made sure her answers were vague.

Then, last summer, her chiropractor father had died unexpectedly of a heart attack.

Addie had adored her dad as a child, but the moment she'd hit her teen years, their relationship had deteriorated. She hadn't repaired things before he'd passed away so suddenly. In retrospect, she suspected she and her father were too much alike. Both were stubborn and headstrong, unwilling to admit when they were wrong or make the effort to build bridges.

They'd argued far too often, her mother stepping in, seeking to make peace between her husband and her daughter. How sorry Addie was for the strife between them, now that her father was gone.

For now, she was home for good. Addie parked in front of the single-story house where she'd spent the first eighteen years of her life. She loved that it had a front porch, which so many of the more modern homes didn't. Normally, the Christmas lights would already be up. Her father had always seen to that the Friday after Thanksgiving. This year, however, the two arborvitae that bordered each side of the porch seemed stark and bare without the decorative lights.

Her mother must have been watching from the living-room window, because the minute Addie climbed out of the car, the front door flew open and Sharon Folsom rushed out with her arms open wide. "Addie, Addie, you're home."

Addie paused halfway up the walkway and hugged her mother close.

Sharon Folsom brought her hands up to Addie's face and smoothed back her dark brown hair. Her mother's chocolate-brown eyes, a reflection of her own, held her gaze with an intensity of longing.

Addie found she couldn't speak. It felt so good to be home, to really be home.

Her mother hugged her even tighter this time. "You said you were coming back, and I'd hoped . . ." She left the rest unsaid.

"I'm not returning to Montana this time, Mom."

"Oh Addie, really? I couldn't be happier. So you decided you are definitely back to stay?" She wrapped her arm around Addie's waist and led her up the porch steps. "It's so wonderful to have you home, especially at this time of year . . . it's the first one that's so difficult, you know."

The first Christmas without Dad.

"I talked to your uncle Roy," her mother said.

"Yes?" Addie tried hard not to show how anxious she was to hear what her mother had found out.

"He's pleased to know you're interested in health-care. Your dad would have been so happy; that was what he always wanted for you. Roy said once you get your high school diploma, he'll do everything within his power to get you the schooling you need.

He's even willing to hire you part-time while you're in school and to work around your class schedule."

Addie hardly knew what to say. This was an opportunity she had never expected. More than she could ever hope would happen. Now it was up to her not to blow it.

"Aren't you excited?"

Again, her throat tightened and she answered with a sharp nod. She knew that no matter what she hoped to accomplish, she'd need her high school diploma. One class credit was all she needed. Why she'd dropped out when she was so close to graduation was beyond her. How stupid and short-sighted she'd been. Her one missing credit was in literature, so she'd found a class she could take at the local community college.

B-o-r-i-n-g!

As a high school sophomore, Addie had been assigned to read *Moby-Dick*. Because of her dyslexia, she was a slow, thoughtful reader, often using her finger on the page to help her keep track of the words. Then to be handed that doorstop and work her way through it page by excruciating page had been pure torture. Following *Moby-Dick,* she'd been completely turned off to reading in general . . . although lately, after her television had stopped working, she'd gotten a couple books at the library and enjoyed them immensely. Finding pleasure in reading had given her hope that maybe . . . just maybe she could return to school.

"I already signed up for a literature class. It starts this week, which I understand is a bit unusual; apparently, it was delayed until a teacher could be replaced." Addie had thought she'd need to wait until mid-February, when the second semester began. This class was perfectly timed for her.

"You enrolled already?" How pleased her mother sounded, and her face brightened with the news.

They were inside the house now, and after removing her coat, Addie tucked her fingertips in the back pockets of her jeans. Standing in the middle of the kitchen, she looked around and breathed in the welcome she found in the familiar setting. Her mother had placed a few festive things around the house to help celebrate the season. The Advent wreath rested in the center of the kitchen table. The first purple candle had been lit.

When she was growing up, it'd been a big deal to see who got to light the candle every night at dinner, Addie or her brother. Generally, Jerry was given the honor. Oh, how her brother had loved lording it over her. He lived in Oklahoma now, was married, and worked as a physical therapist for a center that trained Olympic athletes. He'd always been athletic himself, just like his best friend, Erich Simmons, who lived next door. The two had been inseparable; any mental image of her brother also conjured up his constant sidekick and the way she'd humiliated herself over Erich.

At one time Addie had thought Erich Simmons was the cutest boy in the universe. He was a star athlete, class valedictorian, and the homecoming king. Addie hadn't thought of him in a long time and didn't know why he'd popped into her head now. As a teen, she'd idolized Erich and hadn't bothered to hide the way she felt. He, unfortunately, found her hero worship highly amusing. Oh, there'd been the usual antics when they were kids. Her brother and Erich had wanted nothing to do with her, despite all her efforts to follow them around. It wasn't until she was fourteen and fifteen that she'd viewed Erich in a different light and sent him valentines and baked him cookies. It embarrassed her no end to remember what a fool she'd made of herself over him, especially since he treated her like a jerk.

"Addie?" Her mother broke into her thoughts. "You look a million miles away."

"Sorry, Mom."

"Bring in your suitcases. I've got your old room all ready for you."

It felt wonderful to be home.

Addie unloaded her car, which, sadly, took only a few minutes. Everything she'd managed to accumulate in six years was contained in two suitcases and a couple boxes. When she finished unpacking, she headed directly for the garage.

Her mother found her there ten minutes later. "Addie, my goodness, what are you doing here?" she asked. "I've been looking all over the house for you. Are you hungry? Would you like me to fix you something to eat?"

"In a little while."

"What are you doing?"

Addie stood in the middle of the garage, surrounded by several clear plastic boxes she'd brought down from the shelves. Her father had been a whiz at organization, a trait she'd inherited. "I'm looking for the outdoor Christmas lights."

"But Addie—"

"It won't feel like Christmas without the trees by the porch lit up."

"But Addie—"

"Mom, please, let me put up the lights." Her dad would have wanted her to do this for her mother, Addie was sure. She owed him this, even if things hadn't been so good between them when he died, or maybe because of that.

"Erich offered to put them up for me, but I said no."

"Good." Perfect Erich. She bristled at the mere mention of his name. He'd always been so thoughtful and kind . . . to others. But he'd tortured her at every opportunity. For one thing, from the time they were in first grade together, he'd insisted on calling her Adeline. Addie had always hated the name. She'd never even known the great-grandmother she'd been named after. Saddling her with that name had been her father's doing, no surprise.

Her mother moved a couple steps into the garage. "Um . . . there's a reason I didn't want Erich to put up the lights."

Addie straightened. Her mother's voice revealed hesitation and a bit of apprehension. "What is it, Mom?"

"I mentioned all those firsts without your father, remember . . . ?"

"Yes." It was one of the reasons Addie had returned home when she did. She didn't want her mother spending this first Christmas without Dad by herself. Jerry couldn't get away, but Addie could. Actually, she'd been more than ready to leave Montana. Although she'd come to love the state, everything else there had proved to be less perfect than she'd hoped. Her job at the mine had fizzled out after a few months, but pride hadn't allowed her to return home so soon after her grand departure. For a while she drifted from job to job, until finally settling in at the diner. She'd made friends and the tips were good. It was easy enough to coast through the next few years.

"I didn't say anything earlier when you called to say you were coming . . ." her mother said, interrupting her thoughts. Her mother wrung her hands.

"Mom, what is it?" Clearly there was something her mother didn't want to tell her.

"Please don't be upset with me."

This was all very strange. "Mom, please, don't worry. You're not going to upset me."

"You're sure?"

"Positive. Just tell me."

Her mother squeezed her eyes tightly shut. "I'm going on a two-week Christmas cruise with Julie Simmons."

It took a second for the information to sink in. "A cruise?"

Her mother still hadn't opened her eyes. "Julie's a widow. I'm a widow. We figured that we'd both get away this Christmas with a trip to the Caribbean. We booked a few days in Florida before the cruise as well. The sunshine and all . . . please tell me you're not upset with me."

"Of course not," Addie assured her, although her heart sank. This meant she'd be spending Christmas alone.

"Julie and I talked about it for months, and then right before Halloween we found this great deal from the cruise line and Julie said we should do it. If not now, when? I had no idea you'd be coming home, let alone for good, and . . . and, oh Addie, if you want I'll cancel the trip." Her voice became half plea and half regret.

"No way," Addie insisted, strengthening her resolve. "You're going on that cruise and you're going to enjoy every minute of it while I hold down the fort here."

"Erich offered to look after the house."

Of course he would.

"He's not married, you know, and neither is Karl."

Erich's younger brother.

As if she felt the need to keep talking, her mother continued. "Karl is dating a wonderful young woman and is spending Christmas with her family someplace back east. Neither Julie nor I have grandchildren yet, and being this has been such a difficult year . . ."

"Mom, please, you don't need to make excuses. I want you to do this. Please go."

"But you'll be alone."

"It's fine. I'll connect with a few friends and it won't be a problem. Don't worry about me."

"You're sure . . . ?"

"Absolutely positive."

"It's just that Julie and I have been so looking forward to this, and . . ."

Addie walked over and hugged her mother. "Stop. I wouldn't dream of letting you cancel this trip. It's perfect. You and Julie together on those warm sandy beaches. I'll be fine, I promise."

The relief in her mother's face was nearly palpable. Addie was sincere. She wanted her mother to get away for Christmas. "I still want to put up the outdoor lights," she said, returning to the plastic boxes her father had packed up the Christmas before and stored away.

"Oh sure, sweetheart, if that's what you want. Do you need me to help you?"

"I can do it." Among all the other valuable life lessons Montana had taught Addie, she'd learned resourcefulness. Though she'd never done it before, she'd figure out a way to string the lights on those two trees. It wouldn't feel like Christmas without them.

"I'll start dinner, then."

"Great. I'm starving."

After her mother left, Addie found the strands of outdoor lights and carted them to the front of the house. She needed a ladder, too. At five-foot-three, she wasn't nearly tall enough to reach the top.

She'd gotten everything set up when she heard the sound of a car door behind her. Standing halfway up the ladder, she glanced over her shoulder to see a bright, shiny, silver BMW parked at the curb behind her dilapidated, fender-rusting, once-blue Honda.

Erich.

Her heart sank. He was sure to make some derogatory comment about her car, right after he called her Adeline. He might even be so obnoxious as to mention her girlhood crush on him. Even before he spoke, her teeth were clenched.

"Adeline, is that you?"

Unbelievable! "It's Addie," she said coolly.

"Oops, sorry, I forgot," he teased, when clearly he hadn't. Then he had the audacity to laugh.

She brushed a long strand of dark hair away from her face.

"Need any help with that?"

"No, thanks," she said, as she continued to wind the strand around the bushy tree. She needed no help, least of all from him. It wasn't only the teasing she'd taken as a kid that contributed to her dislike of him—that was only a small part. Erich, Karl, and her brother had often ganged up on her. Being something of a tomboy, she'd followed them, hungering to join in their fun. Instead, Erich had teased her mercilessly. It'd gotten worse as she grew older and got braces. He'd called her "live wire" and poked fun at her until she'd run and hide in her bedroom. But that was nothing compared to the way he'd stepped all over her tender, young heart.

"You home for Christmas?" he asked.

"Something like that," she answered, without looking at him.

He hesitated, and when he spoke he sounded genuine and sincere. "Like I said when we spoke at the funeral, I'm sorry for your loss. I loved your dad."

"Yeah, me, too." The lump was back and she swallowed hard, determined not to let him see how his words had affected her. Funny thing was, she didn't remember speaking to him at the funeral. She'd been in a fog then, confused and grieving.

"Maybe I'll see you around."

"Maybe," she returned dismissively. At the moment, all she wanted was for him to leave her alone.

By the time she had the lights wound around the first tree it was pitch-dark. The only illumination came from the porch light.

A little while later, when Addie was half finished with the twin tree on the other side of the porch, her mother opened the door and called out, "Dinner's ready."

"I'm almost done," Addie promised, unwilling to quit now. She worked quietly, traipsing up and down the ladder as she moved the string of lights around the tree, stretching her arms as high as she could without losing her balance.

The Simmonses' front door opened. "Let me hand you the lights," Erich offered, crossing the yard and coming up behind her.

Addie's initial reaction was to reject his offer. She was more than capable of finishing this—she'd managed the first tree on her own. She'd rather avoid Erich's company.

"It's the least I can do to make up for calling you Adeline," he said.

"If you had to place lights on trees for every time you called me Adeline, you'd be decorating the entire Olympic National Forest."

"True enough. It's Addie from now on. I promise."

She wasn't sure she should trust him not to be a jerk, but she was tired and hungry. So while it dented her pride to accept his help, at this point, she was willing. "Okay." The second part took more of an effort. "Thank you."

His sigh was audible. "That wasn't so hard, now, was it? Come on, Addie, admit it."

"Harder than you realize."

Erich chuckled.

He continued to feed her the string of lights, and they didn't speak for several seconds. "I talked to Jerry the other day. We stay in touch on Facebook, but . . ."

Addie finished and hurried down from the ladder. "Listen, Erich. You don't need to make small talk with me. We've never really gotten along and there's no need to pretend otherwise." She guessed he felt a little sorry for her—back at home, having failed at her big adventure. In her sad, decrepit car . . .

"Fine." He held up his hands as if she'd pointed a gun at him. "You can't say I didn't try."

"Thanks for the help with the lights," Addie said, before heading into the house.

Harry watched the scene, standing beneath an ever-green tree, from across the street. Celeste stood next to him.

"What is it I'm supposed to do for these two again?" he asked, unable to hide his dismay. It had seemed like a piece of delicious rum cake earlier, but now that he saw the way Addie bristled around Erich, he was a bit more daunted. She was like a porcupine around him, defensive and unfriendly. And that was only a small part of what he sensed in her. She was full of fear, and trying desperately hard to hide her feelings of inadequacy.

"You'll find out soon enough. God has obviously crossed their paths for a reason. There must be something they need to learn from each other, don't you think?" she said, turning the question back on him.

"Just how am I supposed to help them find out what it is when they can barely tolerate the sight of each other?" he asked. He was an English teacher and Addie was in his class. There was only so much he could do while teaching her literature.

"As I explained earlier, circumstances have been set in motion."

"Yes, but—"

"Patience, Harry, patience."

"Do you have an idea about what's going to happen?"

"I do."

Harry frowned. "Don't you think you should fill me in, seeing that I'm going to be working with Addie?"

Celeste grinned. "All in good time."

Harry wasn't pleased. "Is there anything else you want to tell me?"

"Not yet," she said, and tucked her arm around

his elbow, shivered, and then glanced toward the sky. "Let's get back. The roads are getting icy."

Harry watched as Erich sped off in his shiny car. He had the distinct feeling Celeste had been trying to tell him something important.

Chapter Two

The last time Addie Folsom had stepped into a classroom it had resulted in an argument with the teacher and her being escorted to the principal's office. Later that same day, she'd walked out of Tacoma High School and never went back.

In hindsight, that hadn't been a smart decision. As a result of her dropping out of school she'd had an argument to end all arguments with her father, and the shouting match that ensued could be heard three neighborhoods away. She'd been grounded: Her father took the door off her bedroom, confiscated her phone, her television, her iPod, and her keys, and claimed she couldn't have any of it back until she returned to school. Addie adamantly refused. She was eighteen and headstrong. After weeks of fighting with her parents, she packed her suitcase, took back her phone and her driver's license, emptied her closet and her savings, and left home.

So it was with trepidation that she entered this classroom. Frankly, she didn't come with high expectations but was determined to give it her best shot and, God willing, pass the class and collect her high school diploma.

She hesitated only a few steps into the classroom, her heart beating fast and wild. The teacher locked eyes with her and smiled. His look seemed to be saying he'd been expecting her. Of course, it could have been Addie's imagination. The look of welcome might have been a simple gesture except that it stopped her cold. It almost seemed as if he knew her and she was the one he'd been waiting to meet.

"Addie Folsom?" he asked, approaching her expectantly, grinning broadly.

"Yes. How did you know?"

His eyes widened and he quickly glanced down, as if she'd caught him red-handed at something he knew he shouldn't be doing.

"Ah . . . you look like an Addie."

"I do?" Seeing how she felt about her name, this was depressing news.

"Oh yes. The minute I saw you, I said to myself, 'That young woman looks like an Addie.' You're going to do very well here."

She frowned. "How do you know that?"

"I . . . just do."

He wasn't making sense, but then she didn't have great expectations when it came to classes and teachers. Experience had taught her to quickly take her seat and keep her opinions to herself, especially if she wanted a passing grade, which she did. Her one desperate hope was that he never called on her to read out loud. She had nightmares about that from grade school.

He handed her a book, which was Dickens's novel *A Christmas Carol,* and Addie found a vacant desk toward the back of the room. A man dressed in fatigues who looked to be about her age sat in the farthest desk in the row behind. A mixed-breed shepherd lay by his side, his chin resting on his paws. The dog's gaze followed her closely. The name band on the front of the soldier's shirt identified him as Fairfax. He slouched in his chair with his arms crossed over his chest and his head down. He didn't appear to be any more pleased to be in class than Addie did.

"This seat taken?"

The question caught her by surprise, and she turned to find a large, muscular man with a huge tattoo on his neck. She didn't need to be an expert to recognize it as a prison tattoo. "No, feel free," she said, and gestured toward the empty desk directly across from her.

He slipped into the seat and slumped so far down that it was a wonder he didn't slide directly onto the floor.

Other students entered the class, and before long every desk was filled. A couple high school running start for college teens took the front desks and stared up expectantly at the teacher. The teacher took a marker and wrote his name across the whiteboard:

Harry Mills.

"Any alphabet soup go with that name?" the guy with the neck tattoo called out.

The high school students twisted around and stared back at him.

"Alphabet soup?" Harry reached for a sheet from his desktop and read it, as if that would supply the answer. "You're Danny Wade, right?"

Danny's eyes narrowed suspiciously. "Has my parole officer been talking to you?" he demanded.

"No, no," the teacher assured him with a dismissive wave of his hand.

"That's crazy. How do you know who I am?"

Again, the teacher looked flustered, as if once more he'd committed some error in professional etiquette. "Lucky guess?" he suggested on a hopeful note.

"Sh—"

"No bad language in the classroom," Harry said sharply, cutting him off. "Now, what did you mean by asking me about the alphabet soup?"

"You know," Danny continued. "Like Ph.D."

"Or CPA," another student suggested.

Danny chuckled. "Looks to me like he's got a degree in BS."

The professor appeared all the more confused and simply shook his head as if he wasn't sure how to answer.

"Say, just how long have you been teaching, anyway?" someone else wanted to know.

"Well . . ." Using his index finger, Harry pushed his glasses up the bridge of his nose. "A while now."

A few of the students snickered. The remaining students simply stared, Addie and the vet with his dog among them. Almost immediately, someone knocked on the door. The teacher looked relieved at the interruption as a security guard entered the classroom.

He was dressed in a campus security uniform and had a Taser gun strapped on his belt. His hand rested on the handle. "Everything okay in here, Mr. Mills?"

The teacher glared at the weapon. "Yes, of course. Everything is under control."

The security guy focused his attention on the class, removed his hand from the gun, and inserted his thumbs into his waistband, rocking back on his heels. "I just like to check in on things—hope that's okay."

He glared toward the back of the room, in Addie's direction. It took her a minute to realize he was focused on Danny Wade. Addie almost felt sorry for Danny. It wasn't hard to figure out that he was on parole. It didn't look like he was going to have an easy time of it, first with the teacher and now campus security breathing down his neck.

"Officer Brady Whitall at your service," he said, and bounced his fingers against his forehead, saluting Harry. "You have any problems and you know who to call."

"Ghostbusters?" Danny muttered under his breath.

Brady's arm flew out and he pointed directly at Danny. "I heard that."

Danny looked behind him at the shepherd lying contentedly on the floor, his chin resting on his paws, and shrugged as though he didn't know what the man was talking about.

"Thank you," Harry said, and quietly ushered him out of the room.

"Now, where were we?" he asked, looking back at the class.

Thankfully, the remainder of the sixty-minute class went considerably smoother. They talked about Charles Dickens, the author of *A Christmas Carol,* and Addie had to admit she was impressed. Harry, for all his discomfort earlier, seemed familiar with the author. He clearly knew the subject matter.

"Charles was the second of eight children," Harry said, "and he fathered ten of his own. He moved around quite a bit as a child and was forced to drop out of school to help support his family when his father was thrown into debtors' prison. It devastated poor Charles."

Danny sat up straighter. "His father did time?"

Harry nodded. "Those were bleak years for his family."

"Yeah," Danny mumbled. "Were they able to write him letters? Mail is everything to a guy in prison."

"Yes, but his mother and the younger children went to prison with his father."

"You mean he had conjugal rights?"

"Well . . . yes, I guess you could say that."

"Charlie went to live with a friend of the family," Harry continued. "He did what he could to help his parents and wrote them letters of encouragement. He was smart enough to make friends with a guard, and the guard snuck the letters in to his mother and father."

"How do you know that?" one of the eager students asked. "I never read anything about Charles Dickens knowing any of the guards."

"Oh . . . I can't remember exactly where I got that information, but it happened, I can assure you of that."

Harry certainly sounded convincing, as if he knew these facts firsthand.

"Dickens had to work in a shoe-blacking factory and he hated every minute. When his grandmother died and bequeathed money to Charles's father, the family was released from prison." The teacher's face sobered and he sighed. "It gives me no pleasure to tell you what happened afterward."

"What?" Danny called out.

It was clear Danny was going to be the most vocal member of their class. He seemed to have a comment or question for whatever the teacher said.

"Even with his father employed and the family back together, Dickens's mother left him with the family friend so he could continue to work in the factory under deplorable conditions. Sadly, he was never able to forgive her for not sending for him."

"My mother bailed on us," Danny said to no one in particular. "She was on crack and the state dumped us in a foster family."

"You forgave your mother, though," Harry said, with an approving look.

Again, how he could possibly know that was beyond Addie. This was one strange man. He must be psychic—that was the only thing Addie could figure.

The class ended and Addie was surprised at how quickly the hour had passed. She slid out of the desk and reached for her purse and book. They were assigned to read the first fifty pages before they returned to class on Wednesday.

She reached for her coat and slipped her arms inside. The vet with the dog stood and started out of the class.

"You left your coat on the back of the chair," Addie told him. He must not have heard, because he continued out of the classroom. Addie reached for the thick winter jacket and hurried after him.

"You forgot your coat," she said, louder this time, and touched his arm.

The vet whipped around, his eyes blazing fire, with a look so intense she gasped and automatically backed up, fearing he might reach out and strike her.

He blinked and immediately looked contrite. "I'm sorry . . . sorry." He grabbed his coat and hurried down the hallway, the dog trotting obediently at his side.

Addie pressed her hand against her chest in an effort to control her rapid heartbeat.

The security guard was making a fuss again, she noticed. He had a woman by the upper arm, and it seemed his hold was unnecessarily tight. The young woman looked as if she was part of the kitchen staff over at the cafeteria. She had on a white apron and wore a net over her hair. The school cop half dragged her toward the teacher.

"I found her standing outside your classroom, listening in on the discussion," he dutifully told Harry. "It's against regulations for her to be in this building."

Harry calmly spoke to the woman in Spanish. Her dark brown eyes widened and she adamantly shook her head. She answered in a flurry of her native language. The teacher listened intently, nodded several times, and then looked at Brady Whitall.

"It's not a problem. This is Elaina; she was simply curious about a few of the classes and decided to check them out."

Brady shook his head, dismissing the explanation. "College rules clearly state that the kitchen staff must remain in their designated area."

"Yes, but I think we can make an exception this one time."

Addie wanted to cheer. Harry Mills was something of a surprise. He made the class interesting, and yes, he was a bit odd, but he was willing to stand up to this overzealous school cop.

The security guard looked doubtful. "Did you clear this with Dr. Conceito? There are regulations about this sort of thing."

"Well . . . no, but I will."

Brady inserted his thumbs in his waistband and glared at Elaina. "See that you do. Until I hear from Dr. Conceito myself, I want to make sure this doesn't happen again. Understood?" He narrowed his eyes. "You wouldn't want to lose your job over this."

The woman looked terrified. "Yes, sir, I mean, no, sir. I mean, I understand, sir."

Addie returned to the classroom to retrieve the Dickens novel, which she'd left on her desk. She watched as Harry reached for an additional copy of the book and handed it to the woman from the cafeteria. She looked so grateful that for a moment

Addie thought she might actually kiss his hands. Holding the book against her breast, she spoke to him again in Spanish.

Seeing how much the other woman appreciated the book made Addie realize how fortunate she was. As she walked across campus toward the parking lot, she saw that the cafeteria remained open, although they'd finished serving for the day. Addie had eaten a light meal before heading to class and could use a latte. The wind whistled through the trees, and the moon was bright and full, casting shadows across the lawn.

Home only a few days and it felt as if she'd been back for years. It was a good feeling.

Thankfully, there wasn't a long line, so she ordered a skinny eggnog latte, which was the special for the month of December. As the barista with the name tag that identified her as Celeste made her drink, Addie slid onto the stool and removed her gloves. She reached for her phone and took it off silent, and noticed a text message from her mother.

Call me ASAP.

The last time she'd gotten a similar text from her mother it was to tell Addie her father had succumbed to a heart attack. Addie stared down at the phone, afraid of what this might mean.

The barista set the latte on the counter and looked at Addie. She must have gone pale, because Celeste asked, "Is everything all right?"

"I . . . I don't know." She didn't delay any longer but grabbed the phone and selected her mom's number from the contact list.

Her mother answered on the first ring, as if she'd been pacing the living room, awaiting Addie's call. "Addie," she said without greeting. "Is that you?"

"Yes, Mom, what's up?"

"Erich's been in a car accident."

"Erich Simmons? Is he all right? What happened?"

"I'm not exactly sure. Julie was too upset to explain it all."

"Is he going to be okay?"

"Yes, yes, apparently it could have been a lot worse. He's been injured, though. Both his wrists are broken."

Addie sighed. "That's awful." But it didn't explain why her mother appeared to have gone into panic mode.

"It's more than awful," her mother cried, sounding close to tears. "It's a catastrophe."

Addie wouldn't go so far as to say that. She sympathized with Erich, and while it would be awkward for him for a few weeks, he'd recover. This wasn't the end of the world.

"Don't you realize what this means?" her mother demanded.

Obviously, Addie didn't.

"It means," her mother said, her voice cracking, "that Julie and I have to cancel the cruise."

This wasn't making sense to Addie. "Why would you do that?"

"Why?" her mother asked, and then repeated herself. "Why? Because Julie can't leave Erich in this condition. Someone has to be there to help him. For the love of heaven, Addie, both his arms are in casts. He's going to be completely helpless."

"Oh." Addie hadn't stopped to think about that.

"Julie didn't tell me right away until she knew for certain the kind of help Erich is going to need. The accident happened the night he stopped by the house . . . when you put up the outside Christmas lights. He's out of the hospital, but he has to stay with Julie until he's able to return to work, and that will be up to six weeks. Can you imagine . . . that poor, dear boy."

Erich was no dear boy; Addie could testify to that. "I'm so sorry, Mom."

"Me, too." A soft sob escaped. "And so close to when we were set to leave, too. Julie and I have been planning this cruise for months. We both had our suitcases packed. I just knew something like this would happen. I just knew it."

Addie had rarely heard her mother sound more devastated. "That's dreadful, Mom."

"I guess it just wasn't meant to be."

Addie couldn't think of anything more to say.

She was disappointed for both her mother and her mom's friend.

"There will be other cruises," Addie said, and hoped she sounded encouraging. She felt bad, but really there was nothing she could do to change this unfortunate set of circumstances.

Chapter Three

Addie dropped her phone into her purse, feeling wretched.

She noticed that her classic literature teacher had stopped by the latte stand himself. Harry Mills was on the other side of the stand, opposite her. He sank onto the stool and braced his elbows on the counter and hung his head. He appeared to be having troubles of his own.

Celeste, the barista, ignored her latest customer and asked Addie a second time, "Is everything all right?"

Addie shrugged. Normally, she kept her problems to herself, but to her surprise she felt like talking. "The call was from my mother. She was set to take a two-week cruise over Christmas with her best friend. They're both widows and, well, there was an accident involving the other woman's son and now it looks like they're going to have to cancel the entire cruise."

"That stinks."

On the other side of the latte stand, Harry Mills straightened and looked sympathetic. "That's unfortunate."

"Is the son doing okay?" Celeste asked, looking genuinely concerned.

While Addie didn't particularly like Erich, she did feel bad for him. "He broke both his wrists."

"Wow . . . ouch."

The idea of Erich in pain had a curious effect on her. It made her stomach go queasy. She'd been looking forward to enjoying the Christmas-themed latte only minutes before, but now she felt as if she'd wasted her money.

Celeste looked toward Harry as if expecting him to say something. He stared back at her blankly as if to ask *"What?"* Addie had her money out, ready to pay for the latte, when Celeste turned back to her.

"You say your mother is disappointed?"

"That's putting it mildly." Addie's mother had sounded devastated. "My father died this summer, and the thought of spending this first Christmas without him was huge for her. The cruise was just the escape she needed."

Celeste tapped her index finger against her lips as if mulling something over. She glanced over at

Professor Mills again as though waiting for him to offer a suggestion. When it appeared he had nothing to say, Addie slid off the stool, and the barista said quickly, "Perhaps there's a way for your mother and her best friend to go on that cruise after all."

Automatically, Addie shook her head. "Julie can't leave Erich. With both his wrists in casts he won't be able to do much of anything without help." It was an unfortunate situation. An idea played briefly in her mind. "I'd offer to go with Mom, but I just started classes and . . ." She couldn't afford it and she definitely didn't want her mother to pay for the cruise, and basically that was what would happen. Her mother needed her friend, a woman who'd walked that same path of grief with the loss of a husband.

"What about you?" Celeste suggested, looking her straight in the eye. "Couldn't you be the one to help Erich?"

"Me?" Addie held up her hand, stopping the other woman before she said anything more. "That would never work. Unfortunately, Erich and I have been at odds nearly our entire lives. We've never gotten along, and I don't expect we ever could."

"Why not?"

Addie shrugged. "We're different people. He drives me crazy, always has. I can barely tolerate being in the same room with him."

"He might have changed." The English teacher

caught up to the conversation. "People do, you know."

"I don't think so," she said, remembering the conflicts of their youth. At one time she'd badly wanted to be friends with Erich and her brother, but they'd been set on excluding her. Then, because she felt she had to explain, she added, "Erich and I have a history that dates back to grade school, and none of it's pleasant." She remembered how, even as a kid, Erich had taken delight in teasing her mercilessly, and going out of his way to embarrass her in front of their classmates. Just thinking about how he'd treated her caused her to bristle. As much as Addie would like to help her mom out by looking after Erich so they could take the cruise, it'd never work. The mere idea was impossible.

"Didn't I hear you say you'd recently moved back into the area?" Harry asked.

Addie couldn't remember mentioning anything of the sort, but perhaps she had. "Yes."

"How long has it been since you've had anything to do with your neighbor's son?"

"A while," she admitted with some reluctance. "Six years, actually."

Harry smiled. "That's what I thought. Six years is a long time. You're not the same person you were when you left, are you?"

"No." Addie could already see the direction this conversation was taking, and she didn't like it.

"Erich isn't a teenager any longer, either."

"He hasn't changed," she argued. He might have been fairly decent helping her place the outside Christmas lights, but he was like that. Just when she felt she could trust him, he'd turn on her. One time, when she was about nine, Erich told her she could come into the fort Jerry and he had built if she ate a worm. As disgusting as that was, she would have done anything to get into that fort with them. She'd run inside the house for the can of whipped cream she knew was in the fridge. She almost gagged, but managed to let the worm glide down her throat along with the cream. And then he'd laughed and refused to let her in the fort.

It didn't get better when she entered junior high, either. Erich convinced her that one of the cutest boys in the class had a crush on her. The boy played along, making fun of her behind her back. Later, she'd learned Erich had asked for help because he wanted to distract her from following him around like a sad little puppy. All too soon the entire school was in on the joke and she'd been mortified. Oh no, Erich wasn't to be trusted.

"I guess it depends on how much you want to help your mother," Celeste added, on a sad note.

"Not really," Addie said, as she took her latte and headed off across campus. However, Celeste's last words followed her all the way to the parking lot, echoing in her head.

Caught up in her thoughts, she didn't hear anyone walking behind her until the dog barked.

Glancing over her shoulder, Addie saw that it was Andrew Fairfax from class. The dog trotted along at his side.

The Army veteran caught up with her and then slowed his gait to match hers. He wore a knitted cap over his head. When he spoke he kept his gaze downward and didn't look in her direction.

"Hi," she said.

"Hi," he returned, then hesitated. "I wanted to apologize about . . . you know."

"Hey, no problem," she said, quickening her steps. He didn't seem to know what else to say. An awkward silence stretched between them, but still he continued walking with her.

"I know I scared you. I don't like people touching me . . ."

"Like I said, it wasn't a big deal."

Andrew expelled a harsh breath.

Hoping to ease the tension, Addie looked down at the shepherd and asked, "What's the dog's name?"

"Tommy."

It wasn't a common name for a dog, but Addie didn't feel she should comment. "Hello, Tommy." They paused in front of a big parking lot. Addie bent down to pet his ears. She liked animals, especially dogs.

"Please don't," Andrew said, stopping her. "He's a service dog, and it's best that you don't touch him . . . either."

"Sorry, I didn't know. What is his job?"

"The Army gave him to me . . . as a companion, to help keep me calm. I wasn't interested at first, but I've changed my mind since he's come to live with me. My sister calls him my comfort dog, and you know what? She's right. He helps."

"Good!" Addie realized she wasn't the only one in this class who came with a load of emotional baggage; knowing that helped. She had more in common with this Army veteran than he realized.

Andrew quickly headed off in the opposite direction, almost as if he couldn't get away from her fast enough. Addie suspected it had taken a great deal of courage for him to find her and apologize. The military taught you to be tough, not to be vulnerable, and yet they were both opening themselves up by taking this class, taking a leap of faith.

When Addie arrived home, she found her mother sitting in front of the television, staring blankly at the screen. A wad of crumpled tissues rested on the side table.

"Hi, Mom," Addie said, and sat down on the ottoman and reached for her mother's hands, holding them in her own.

Her mother responded with a weak smile. "How was your class?"

"Not bad."

"What do you think of your teacher?"

Addie shrugged. "He's okay, a little awkward.

He seemed to know me from somewhere, but I swear I've never met the man in my life."

Her mother's knitting rested in her lap. It didn't look as if she'd had much enthusiasm for the project.

"I'm really sorry about the cruise," Addie felt obliged to say again.

A tear leaked from her mother's eyes. "Yes, me, too . . . Julie and I aren't even sure we can get a refund. We didn't pay for travel insurance . . . we were both so sure nothing would ever stop us from taking this trip."

"Oh Mom." Addie leaned forward and hugged her mother.

"The worst part is, we'll never be able to afford to do this again . . . especially without a refund."

Addie closed her eyes. She couldn't believe she would even consider making this offer, but . . . straightening, she expelled her breath and whispered, "Maybe there's something I could do to help."

"What was that look about?" Harry asked Celeste. He'd come to the Hub to reassure her all had gone well with the class and ask a few questions. When he'd arrived he'd found Celeste chatting with Addie Folsom. Before he fully understood their conversation, Celeste had sent him a look sharper than any dagger he'd ever seen. Clearly he'd missed something important having to do with his young charge. Frankly, he hadn't had a lot of time to think about Addie. He was upset about the way the security guard had talked with Elaina. Angels weren't supposed to get upset; problems bounced off them like tennis balls in a court. This feeling was foreign to him, and he needed to ask Celeste what was happening to him.

"Harry, you should have been the one to suggest Addie help her mother."

"Me?" He felt his eyes go wide.

"Addie is your first earthly assignment. You said helping her would be easy, remember? Apparently, it's *too* easy, because you have yet to become involved."

"I'm involved," he argued, taken aback by her reprimand. It wasn't like he didn't know what to do. "I suggested that if she'd changed in the last six years, then perhaps Erich had, too," he reminded his mentor.

"Yes, and that was good."

"Thank you."

"It wasn't enough."

Harry was beginning to think he'd already messed up his first earthly mission. He needed advice. Coming to Celeste had meant swallowing his pride and admitting he might actually have overestimated his abilities. This was something else he wanted to discuss. He needed to know where this pride thing originated. He'd been dealing with it from the moment he'd landed on Earth.

Leaning forward, he braced his hand against his forehead. "Unfortunately, I've gotten myself into a bit of a situation."

Celeste braced her hands against her hips. "Okay, tell me what's happened."

"First off . . . I flubbed up a couple of times with the students. No worries there—I was able to muddle through without a problem." Then, feeling he should explain a bit more, he added, "I called the students by their names before they had a chance to introduce themselves is all. No big deal, right?" He studied her and had the distinct feeling she already knew all this.

Celeste frowned. "There's more going on here than you're telling me, isn't there, Harry?"

He nodded, unsure exactly where to start.

"It involves Dr. Conceito, doesn't it?"

"Ah . . ."

"Harry, I warned you to stay away from the school president as much as possible, remember?"

"I remember."

"And what was one of the first things you did?"

Harry didn't need the reminder. That same feeling he'd experienced earlier—that she already knew—returned, and he cocked his head, unsure what it was.

"Harry?"

"I walked across the lawn." He pressed his hand

against his stomach in order to deal with the uneasy feeling that stole over him.

"What's the matter?"

Harry blinked several times. "I'm not sure."

She gave him a knowing smile. "You can tell me."

Lowering his voice, Harry said, "I was upset earlier. Angels don't get upset. Have I done wrong . . . is that why?"

"No," she reassured him. "You've forgotten something very important, Harry. You have a human body now, not a spiritual one; therefore, you will experience human emotions. They'll be foreign and uncomfortable in the beginning, but gradually you'll learn to recognize and deal with them."

"You mean like frustration, anger . . . that sort of thing?"

"Exactly. I tried to warn you earlier," she reminded him, "but you were convinced you knew it all. Now you see."

Harry couldn't very well comment. He'd brought this on himself, walked into this without realizing what it meant to be transformed from one body to another.

Celeste gently patted his hand.

Taking a sip of his latte, Harry lubricated his throat, which had gone dry and tight. "I met Elaina Gomez, who works in the cafeteria."

"I know Elaina," Celeste said, with a note of expectation. "She's a wonderful single mother with two little girls."

"She got caught standing outside the classroom listening in on the lecture. I sort of stepped in when the security guard was about to physically remove her from the building." Brady Whitall had been none too gentle, either. Harry suspected the guard had been waiting for an opportunity all night to get physical with someone. He was a man who seemed to be spoiling for a fight.

"That could only be Brady," Celeste said, frowning. "He's a piece of work. He tried out for the Tacoma Police Department six times and failed each time."

"I defended her and . . ." He paused as his mentor slowly started to shake her head.

"Harry, you can't do that. Your powers are limited to the students inside the class. Elaina isn't under your protection. Unfortunately, you can't help her."

"But . . ."

"No buts."

Harry wanted to argue, but he knew Celeste was right. He should never have gotten involved, especially on his first day of teaching. His downfall was he'd been touched by the gentle woman's desire to learn. She couldn't afford to take the classes, and apparently this wasn't the first time she'd been caught standing in the hallway, listening, in order to glean what knowledge she could. From their short conversation, Harry learned that Elaina was a voracious reader who liked to practice her English by reading novels. She had grabbed hold of the Dickens novel he'd given her as if he'd gifted her with a diamond.

"You realize Dr. Conceito will find out about this, don't you?"

Harry measured his response carefully. "I was thinking that maybe you could make that not happen?" His eyes were wide and hopeful.

"Sorry, Harry, I can't do that." To her credit, she did sound regretful.

Harry's throat tightened, but, wanting to downplay what had happened, he waved his hand. "I don't think there will be a problem. I can handle the school president."

"Might I remind you that unless it's a matter directly related to Addie Folsom or another one of your students, you're unable to use any spiritual powers to counteract Dr. Conceito? Didn't I warn you earlier that the man is a force to be reckoned with?" she reminded him.

Swallowing tightly, Harry nodded. "I'll do what I can to make matters right."

"Good. Don't hesitate to come to me with problems. I'll do what I can to help, but I, too, have limitations. And remember, your time here is probationary. I realize coming to Earth has been something you've been waiting a long time for, but you need to prove yourself if you're going to stay longer than the time it takes to teach this one class."

"Got it." This assignment wasn't nearly as easy as he'd assumed it would be. He'd viewed Earth from heaven and been intrigued. Now that he was here on the other side, he found it to be quite complicated.

"By the way," Celeste asked, lowering her voice, "what did you think of Andrew Fairfax's dog?"

Harry remembered how the shepherd had remained on the floor at the young veteran's side during the class. "He's well behaved," Harry said.

Then he noticed Celeste's quirky smile and recalled how the animal's gaze had briefly connected with his own. Harry was quick to make the connection. "He's one of us, isn't he?"

Celeste nodded. "Not all angels come in human form, you know."

"Andrew needs two angels?"

"Some humans require even more."

Harry had had no idea.

"Things will get better," she promised. "I feel bad that this first class caused you problems. Focus, Harry. Remember your assignment. You should have been the one to suggest Addie volunteer to help Erich, not me." She slapped his back in a comforting gesture. "Now, there's something more you need to tell me, isn't there?"

Harry's eyes widened. "You know about . . ."

"Oh yes, Harry, I do know. Now, let's talk."

He swallowed tightly and held in a sigh. He had the distinct feeling this next issue wouldn't be so easily resolved.

Chapter Four

Harry's stomach was in knots. This was a matter no one discussed in heaven. He understood that Earth had its limitations, and that he'd have emotions, but no one had mentioned . . . this. His gut felt like an alien creature had taken up residence. He planted his hand over his abdomen, hoping that would help. Nothing could have prepared him for . . .

"Harry?" Celeste said gingerly. "You've gone pale."

"Well . . . after class I had a visitor."

"Yes, I know. Tell me about it." Celeste's look was friendly, inviting him to speak openly.

"Do you know Michelle Heath? I had no idea humans could be so . . ."

"Attractive," Celeste supplied.

"Yes, and friendly, very friendly."

Celeste's face broke into a huge smile. "Ah, yes. Well, I'm sure it's not every day she meets an un-attached rather handsome man around her own age."

Harry straightened his shoulders. He hadn't thought of himself as handsome. The truth was, he hadn't given much thought to his looks; he'd been handed this body to use as a vehicle, nothing more. It had never occurred to him that how he looked mattered.

Celeste was about to say more when a student approached the coffee stand and ordered a peppermint skinny latte.

Skinny? Harry didn't have a clue what that meant, but apparently Celeste did, because she didn't hesitate. For the next few minutes the barista was busy brewing coffee and steaming milk.

While Celeste was preoccupied with the customer, Harry mentally reviewed the meeting with the French teacher. He'd been a bit shaken following the exchange between the young Hispanic woman and the security guard, which might be why his guard had been down. The classroom was empty and he had been sitting there, reflecting on what had happened and how he might have handled the situation differently.

Harry had been at his desk wondering what the ramifications would be if Dr. Conceito learned of his intervention in the incident between Elaina and the security guard. Because he was preoccupied and distracted, he didn't notice that someone was in the room—that was the only excuse he could think of that made sense. He had plenty to worry about, given the way Celeste had warned him to avoid the college president.

When Harry happened to glance up he found this lovely woman poised in the doorway. Her eyes were blue like Venetian glass, and her skin was creamy and soft like cotton. For the longest moment he hadn't been able to breathe or take his eyes off her. When she spoke, it was in this breathy sort of way that caused his skin to tingle. Right then he heard the tinkling of bells announcing danger; trouble was on the horizon.

All humans were said to struggle against weaknesses. It was all part of living in a fallen world, and Harry, while an angel, was in a human body and prone to all things human . . . like desire. This was definitely an uncomfortable sensation, unfamiliar and awkward. He'd swallowed tightly and realized he couldn't make his tongue work. His mouth didn't seem to want to cooperate, either.

Thankfully, she spoke first. "Welcome," she said, in a voice that made shivers run down his spine.

Unable to take his eyes off her, Harry managed to come to his feet and stretch out his arm in order to shake her hand and introduce himself. It demanded a monumental effort to remember his name. "Harry Mills."

She clasped his hand in her own. Hers was warm and soft. "Michelle Heath." She held on to his hand for a long moment, as if she was unwilling to let it go. "I teach the French class just down the hall," she told him.

He was so enraptured by her he forgot himself and responded in French. Being well versed in languages was a requirement for placement on Earth. Instantly, she brightened, her eyes nearly melting with appreciation.

The room felt warmer than it had been only moments earlier, substantially warmer. French was a beautiful language, and it flowed back from her lips like melted butter being gently poured over a culinary delight.

Caught in the magic of her spell, Harry found that he was incapable of responding further in either language. All he could manage was a weak grin.

Michelle sighed, as though he'd managed to completely charm her. "Your French is excellent."

"Ah . . . really? Thanks." He stuttered out a response. The tinkling bells he'd heard earlier had taken on the sound of an urgent fire alarm that insisted he evacuate the building as quickly as possible. To that effect, he reached for his briefcase and stuffed papers inside. He didn't have a clue what the papers were.

"Oh, are you getting ready to leave?" she asked.

He nodded. That was when he caught a whiff of her perfume. Closing his eyes, he breathed in the scent of roses and mist and something else so potent it sent his senses reeling.

"I won't keep you," she was saying.

Harry forced his eyes open.

"I just thought I'd stop by and introduce myself," she continued, stepping closer to Harry's desk.

My goodness, she smelled heavenly. *Heaven,* he repeated. *Think of heaven.* It didn't help. Heaven seemed a very long way away. Unable to stop himself, Harry leaned toward her and sniffed her neck.

Clearly, he'd surprised her, because Michelle released a soft gasp.

Instantly chagrined, Harry tried to explain. "I don't know what perfume you're wearing, but it's very nice."

She gifted him with one of her smiles. "It's called Divine."

"That explains it," he muttered, and reached for his coat.

Michelle sat on the corner of his desk, letting one leg dangle over the edge. "Harry . . . before you go."

"Yes."

Her eyes went wide and round. "Is there a Mrs. Mills?"

Harry paused, his hand clenching his briefcase handle in a death grip.

"Are you asking if I'm married?"

"Yes."

Harry didn't answer right away because he noticed that her eyelashes were especially long. When she blinked they seemed to brush against her cheekbones. "No . . . I'm unmarried." A wife, it was decided, would overly complicate his earthly visit. Other angels sometimes came as a couple, man and wife. Harry had been assigned to go solo.

"Surely you've been married?" she quizzed, blinking with the question, fluttering those exceptionally long lashes. It was akin to watching a butterfly take flight, and for a couple of uncomfortable seconds Harry was completely mesmerized and dumbstruck.

"Never." He was anxious to leave and get to Celeste. He needed to discuss the incident involving the security guard. And then . . . then there was this French teacher.

"You've really never been married?" Michelle followed him out of the classroom, sticking close to his side as their footsteps echoed in the hallway toward the exit. "I find that hard to believe."

Harry hadn't expected his words to be challenged. He'd assumed no one would question him about such matters. "I assure you it's the truth."

Her returning laugh was light and breezy, as if she'd been teasing him all along. "Oh Harry, I believe you. It's just that I find it hard to imagine that some lucky woman hasn't snatched you up long before now."

That was when it hit him, bull's-eye, square in the middle of his forehead. *This woman was flirting with him.* He'd heard of this when he was up in heaven.

The attraction he felt for her had been instantaneous. And now he realized it was mutual. The fire alarm became a tornado warning. Right away Harry remembered the first and most important rule. Angels don't get romantically involved with humans. That was strictly taboo.

Once he was outside, the cool evening air hit his face and seemed to free him from the spell he'd fallen under. What Harry hadn't expected when he'd arrived on Earth was that he'd be tempted. He shook himself in order to clear his head. It didn't matter how he felt about this highly attractive woman. Michelle Heath was dangerous to his mission. He couldn't allow her magnetism to distract him from what was most important.

"You heard about the Christmas concert, didn't you?" she asked, in that same soft voice that fell so sweetly from her lush lips.

"Concert?" Harry's mouth had gone dry. He'd read the notice but hadn't given it much thought.

"The college choral group is putting on a holiday performance. It's the highlight of the year. They have been practicing for weeks."

Harry hesitated, afraid of where this was leading. "I . . . I don't know."

"All teachers are required to attend," she reminded him. "Dr. Conceito is adamant about that."

Harry could feel a noose tightening around his neck. She was going to ask him to accompany her.

"We could meet in Massey Hall," she suggested ever so innocently.

Harry cleared his throat. "I'll have to check my schedule," he murmured.

"Oh please do." The entreaty in her voice couldn't be ignored.

Harry blinked, and could feel himself weakening. "Massey Hall?"

"The performance center, Thursday afternoon at four-thirty."

"Of course." His mind frantically searched for a way of extricating himself, and when he spoke, the words shot from his mouth in such a rush it was amazing anyone could understand him. "I'm teaching a class right before the concert. I doubt I could make it to the performance center on time. In fact, I'm sure I'm going to be late. I'd hate the thought of you missing part of the performance because of me."

"No worries," she assured him. "I'll save a seat for you, right next to me."

This was exactly what Harry didn't want to hear. "That'd be . . . wonderful," he said. They parted, and Harry rushed to seek Celeste's advice.

*   *   *

"Okay, where were we?" Celeste asked, joining him once again. "Oh yes, you were getting ready to tell me about your meeting with Michelle Heath."

"Before I do, tell me what you know about her," he said.

Celeste studied him closely. "She's been divorced for a long time, with two grown children. Be careful, Harry. Michelle's lonely and on the prowl."

Harry nodded hard enough to dislocate his neck. "I thought as much. She stopped by my classroom to introduce herself."

"You're attracted to her." Celeste's tone implied he might as well transfer straight back to the pearly gates after less than a week on Earth.

"It's more a case of her coming on to me," he assured his mentor. "She asked me to accompany her to the Christmas concert . . . I made an excuse, said I'd be late, but she insisted on saving a place for me. What do I do?" he pleaded, feeling almost desperate. His heart was pounding and his breathing had gone shallow. It was absolutely necessary that he find an excuse to get out of this concert.

"Well, Harry," Celeste said, slowly shaking her head. "It seems to me you've got yourself into a pickle."

That was the last thing he wanted to hear.

Chapter Five

Although she had twenty-four hours to think it over, Addie knew this situation with Erich was going to be a difficult one. They needed to talk, and frankly, Addie wasn't looking forward to the conversation. Her steps dragged, her feet heavy, as she crossed the matted winter lawn from her family home to the house in which Erich had been raised.

Julie Simmons opened the wreath-adorned front door even before Addie had the opportunity to ring the doorbell. Her eyes, the same shade of blue as her son's, expressed deep relief and gratitude.

"Erich's awake," she whispered. "He's home from the hospital, but he didn't have a good night. Because it's difficult for him to get up and down, he'll need to sleep in a chair for the next couple of days . . . maybe longer."

In other words, Erich wasn't in the best of moods. For that matter, neither was Addie. She hadn't slept well, either, tossing and turning in a futile pursuit of sleep. She glanced at him and saw that both his hands from midway up his fingers to his elbows were in casts, making any kind of movement difficult. Basically, he was helpless.

The instant she'd made the offer to take care of Erich, her mother and Julie had been filled with grateful relief. They'd gushed with appreciation, thanking her over and over again.

Addie had assumed she'd feel good about being able to do this for her mother. Quite the contrary. Already she was filled with dread, and her mother and neighbor hadn't even left for the airport. If Addie hadn't been able to get along with Erich for the first eighteen years of her life, it seemed crazy to think she would now. Being his caregiver would surely prove to be her worst nightmare.

And his, too.

"Come in, come in," Julie insisted, reaching out and grabbing Addie by the elbow and practically dragging her inside the house. The door slammed in her wake.

Her reluctance couldn't have been any more evident. Automatically, her gaze flew to Erich, who sat in the living room in a recliner, his feet raised. A hand-knit afghan covered his legs. Both wrists in their casts rested in his lap. He looked miserable and in pain. One side of his face was bruised, and his lips were swollen.

"I'll leave you two to chat," Julie said, and quickly left the room.

Addie moved into the living room and stood with her fingers tucked into the back pockets of her jeans.

"You can sit down if you want," Erich said. One eye had swollen completely shut, she noticed.

"Thanks, but no thanks." Addie preferred to stand. "If you don't mind, I'd rather stand."

"Have it your way."

"Your mother must have mentioned my offer."

"Yeah, she told me. Am I supposed to be happy about that?"

His mother was right—Erich was in a rare mood. She swallowed back a retort, doing her best to remember he was in pain and not to take it personally. She bit her tongue and managed to restrain herself from snapping back.

"I'd rather it be anyone but you," he said.

Oh, he liked adding salt to a wound.

"Trust me, the feeling is mutual."

He muttered, "I figured as much."

"Isn't there anyone else who could step in?" she asked. At first she was embarrassed to have been so blunt. Then she figured, what was the point of hiding her eagerness to escape this situation?

"Like who?"

"Don't you have someone who cares?" Because,

clearly, she didn't, and she wanted to be sure he knew it.

He rotated his head and looked away from her. "Not currently."

So much for that. "What about a friend?" She was beginning to sound desperate.

"Listen, Addie, you're not obligated to do this."

She was well aware of that.

Julie, who must have been listening in on their conversation, stepped around the corner from the kitchen. "The insurance company is providing a nurse to stop by once a day. She'll see to bathing him and so on. I asked about increasing the time she spent with Erich, you know, like a private nurse," she added, "but the cost was astronomical, far and away more than we could afford."

"My friends work during the day," Erich explained. "Even if they didn't, I wouldn't ask them to be my caregivers. Not this time of year . . . or any other time," he qualified.

All the solutions they'd tried were the ones Addie had hoped to suggest. She felt her heart sinking.

"Then I guess it's up to me." Her attitude was fatalistic at this point.

"Don't bother," Erich insisted, glaring at her. "I'll be just fine without you or anyone else."

"Sure you will," Addie murmured sarcastically. He couldn't do anything on his own. She'd literally have to spoon-feed him.

His mother dropped her voice as though that

would prevent him from hearing. "He hasn't been feeling well this morning, and that makes him a little cranky. I think it might be one of the side effects from the pain medication. I know you two had your differences when you were teenagers, but you're adults now, right?"

"Right," Addie admitted reluctantly.

"I'm sure it'll be fine." Her look was strained, but hopeful. "He won't always be this . . . unpleasant, I'm sure."

"Actually, I think his bad mood is related to the fact that he's about to be stuck with me," Addie returned, mustering a smile.

Erich smiled, too, for the first time since she'd arrived, letting her know she was spot-on.

"I'll leave you two alone to sort all this out," Julie said, rubbing her palms together as though to generate heat in a room that had gone decidedly cool. "I'm going to finish packing my carry-on."

Addie moved across the living room to stand in front of the fireplace. His mother had tacked up two Christmas stockings that looked crocheted. She focused her gaze on them.

"My grandmother made those for us when I was just a kid," Erich explained. "Mom still puts them up every year, but as far as I'm concerned, they're going down as soon as she walks out the door. I can't stand Christmas."

"Fine, if that's the way you feel. I'm not going to force you into a Santa suit." Nor was she interested in discussing how he felt about Christmas decorations. She had more important matters on her mind. Gathering her resolve, she faced him and asked the most important question, the one that had been on her mind most of the night. "Can we do this?" she asked.

From the intensity of his returning look, she knew she didn't need to explain the question. It went without saying that they didn't like each other. But were they capable of putting aside their differences long enough to survive the next two weeks? It wouldn't be easy on either of them. It would be more difficult for Erich than for her, being that he was the injured party and the one in need of help. He must hate the thought of being in her debt.

"Do we have a choice?" he returned, with a question of his own.

"I don't think we do," Addie murmured. She'd spent a good portion of the night seeking alternative solutions, all of which they had already considered and eliminated before she could even propose them.

"I don't like this any better than you do," Erich said, as if it was important that she understand his point of view.

"I know, and I don't blame you. I wouldn't like it, either. The question is whether we can set aside our dislike of each other long enough to see this through." Two weeks would feel like an eternity, and the worst part was that it fell over Christmas.

Once more, Erich centered his gaze away from her, focusing on the opposite wall. "I can manage, if you can."

"I'll do my best."

He nodded and then released what sounded like a pent-up sigh. "That's about all either of us can expect."

Addie sat down on the ottoman across from him and leaned slightly forward. "I have classes three days a week. It's important that I go to those." She was going to need to focus on her studies if she planned to make a go of schooling.

"No problem."

"I'll make sure you get food and have plenty of straws, but as for anything else . . ."

"Don't worry about it."

The picture of Erich stuck with her was a humorous one. Addie did her best to disguise her amusement.

"This isn't funny, Addie. I'm miserable and cranky, and I doubt I'll be a good patient. The fact is, other than when it's absolutely necessary, it might be best if you stayed away."

"Do you honestly think I'd want to spend more time with you than I need to?" Addie felt the heat fill her face. It seemed Erich thought she would go out of her way to be with him because she still had a thing for him. The man was living in a dream world.

"Don't go all Mother Teresa on me, got it?"

If he wasn't so serious, this would be downright comical. "Trust me, you don't have any worries there."

"Good," he said, and sighed as if their conversation had physically drained him. His eyes drifted closed and then flew open as if he'd caught himself in the nick of time.

"Did you hear our mothers decided to leave tonight?" she asked. Their flight was scheduled to leave early the following morning, and with the threat of snow, they'd decided to spend the night in an economy hotel next to the airport rather than risk missing the flight.

Erich's frown darkened his face. "Yeah, I know."

"We can do this, Erich," she said, hoping to sound positive and upbeat.

"We can try," Erich said, sounding none too confident.

Addie stood, eager to be on her way. "I'll stop by sometime this evening."

He nodded.

"I'll add my contact info to your phone—if you need anything before then, call me."

Again, he acknowledged the comment with a flippant nod. His phone was on the table next to the recliner. She reached for it and noticed several text messages.

"You have a text message here from someone named Ashley."

"I don't want to see anybody, especially Ashley."

"Do you want me to answer it for you?"

He looked up at her as if she'd suggested something weird. "No, delete them all."

"But—"

"Fine, don't. I'll do it myself later."

"Don't get snarky with me," she snapped. "I'm not your personal assistant. If you want those texts deleted, then fine. I was only trying to help."

"Just hand me my phone."

"Give me a minute," she mumbled, concentrating on adding her contact information to his device. When she'd finished and stored the number, she handed him his phone. It immediately fell out of his hand and onto the carpet. Addie reached down to get it and gave it to him a second time. He left it in his lap, leaned his head back, and closed his eyes.

"I'll be by again later."

He didn't comment one way or the other, which was just as well.

Later that afternoon, Erich and Addie's mothers loaded up the car. Addie was going to drop them at the airport hotel.

"I prepared Erich a meal," Julie was saying as she lifted the second of her two suitcases into the trunk of Addie's vehicle. In addition, she had a carry-on and a purse the size of an airplane seat. "But he didn't eat much. I think the pain meds have taken away his appetite."

"I'll check on him once I'm done dropping the two of you off," Addie promised.

"Unfortunately, when we're on the ship we won't be able to use our cell phones," his mother said, and sounded concerned.

"Don't worry, if I need to reach you, I'll find a way." Addie hoped that would reassure them both. "It should be fine, really. I'll take good care of Erich, I promise."

Once at the hotel, she helped them with their bags and check-in to make sure they had the proper arrangements to catch the shuttle first thing in the morning.

Julie gripped hold of Addie's shoulders and gave them a gentle squeeze. "I can't thank you enough for doing this. I don't know what we would have done without you."

As soon as she had her room key, Addie's mother hugged Addie close. "I hardly know what to say," she whispered, tears in her eyes. "You made this trip possible for us."

"Mom, you'd do it for me. Now go, and promise me you'll have the time of your lives."

"We will," Julie assured her.

"I'll buy you something wonderful from one of the islands," her mother said.

The two women chatted like monkeys as they headed off to their room. Her mother was as excited as Addie had ever seen her. You'd think they were schoolgirls from the way they giggled.

After dropping them off, Addie returned to the house and parked out front.

She stood outside for several minutes as the wind and winter cold whirled around her. She dreaded another confrontation with Erich, but it was unavoidable. From a few hints his mother had let drop, Erich was still in a bear of a mood. He hadn't exactly been Prince Charming earlier, and it sounded like his temper hadn't improved.

In other circumstances, she would simply walk away and let him suffer, but she had an obligation to see to his needs, whether he wanted her around or not. Perhaps she could reach out to Ashley. From Erich's response when he learned about the text messages, it was clear they'd had some kind of falling-out.

Addie hadn't read the full text, but it appeared Ashley was terribly, terribly sorry and wanted to make amends. Perhaps the ever-so-contrite Ashley might be willing to step into Addie's place as caregiver to the injured Erich. With that thought in mind, she headed toward his house.

The lights were off, and Addie feared he might be asleep. No matter, it was too early for bed. If Erich went to sleep this early in the evening, he'd be awake in the middle of the night and soon his entire schedule would be off balance.

After one polite knock, Addie let herself into the house. "I'm back." she said, coming into the living room.

He was still in the chair—she could make him out in the gloom. He ignored her.

"Can I get you anything?"

"No."

His mother was right. Erich was set on being difficult, if not downright impossible.

"You're sitting in the dark."

"So?"

"Would you like me to turn on the lights?"

"If I wanted the lights on, I'd do it myself."

She sighed. "You're getting snarky again."

Silence.

"If we're going to make this work, Erich, we're going to have to be civil to each other."

"Okay, whatever. As you might have guessed, I'm not in the best of moods."

"No kidding."

He ignored her comment. "The thing is, I'd rather be left alone."

"Feeling sorry for yourself isn't going to help, you know." Experience had taught her as much.

He didn't respond, so Addie reached for the lamp and turned the switch. Bright light instantly flooded the room. Erich squinted until his eyes had time to adjust to the change.

"Your mother mentioned that you hadn't eaten much. Can I get you anything?"

"No. Thanks anyway."

That was a slight improvement. "You'll feel better if you eat something."

"Thank you, Dr. Oz."

"It's the truth, especially when you're on pain meds. Most prescriptions are best taken with food."

"There you go again with the medical advice."

Ignoring him, Addie went into the kitchen and opened the refrigerator, looking for something Erich could eat without the need for utensils. She found an orange, which she peeled and laid out in sections on a paper towel.

"What's that?" he asked, when she returned.

"What does it look like?" she returned, and set it on his lap.

He ignored the question. "Addie, you still can't take a hint. What part of 'no thanks' do you not understand?"

That was a low blow, and completely unnecessary. If he wanted to be nasty, then fine, she'd let him. Addie sighed expressively, and then before he could stop her, she grabbed his phone off the side table. Walking to the other side of the room, she tapped the screen of his phone a couple times.

"Addie?" he shouted after her. "What are you doing?" This was followed by a few choice words she was sure would shock his mother.

Addie walked around the corner where Erich couldn't see her.

"Hello, is this Ashley?" she said, loud enough to be sure Erich could hear her. "I'm a friend of Erich's. He's been badly hurt. It's a matter of life and death, and he's begging to see you one last time."

Chapter Six

"Addie?" Erich's growly voice was low and angry. "What have you done?"

Addie stuck her head back around the corner and, holding the phone in her hand, smiled sweetly back at him. "What have I done? Why, Erich, I've shown you proof positive that two can play at that game. Oh, by the way, Ashley sounds terribly, terribly upset. She wanted me to reassure you she'll be here as soon as she can. Is there anything else you'd like me to tell her?"

"Give . . . me . . . the . . . phone," he demanded, speaking each word slowly and distinctly. "Give me the phone, otherwise I swear . . ." He started to get out of the recliner but was struggling to stand up without being able to use his arms. He looked like he was about to hurt himself.

"Oh, for the love of heaven," Addie said, returning to the living room. She handed Erich his phone.

He tried to grab it, but with limited use of his fingers, it fell to the carpet.

Addie retrieved it for him. "Stop freaking out. I didn't call her; there's no one on the other end of the line."

His relief was instantaneous.

"But I should have called her. It was what you deserve for being so difficult."

He continued to glare at her with a look that would have made other women run for cover. Not Addie.

"Listen," she said calmly, "this won't work if you're going to continue being so immature. It's only for two weeks. You can manage to be agreeable for that short amount of time, can't you?"

He exhaled slowly. "Me? You're just as immature as I am."

"That's a matter of opinion. I'm not the one behaving like a five-year-old."

Erich took a moment to consider her words and then shrugged. "Okay, you're right, I was acting a bit childish. Can we start over?"

Addie hadn't expected a concession on his part and did her best to hide her surprise. Sitting down in the recliner next to his, she reached for the remote control. "Do you ever watch *Jeopardy!*?"

"Some."

She flicked a look in his direction. "I suppose you get all the answers right."

"Not all."

She snickered. "Modesty doesn't become you."

He chuckled again. "I'm not that smart, although it does my ego good that you seem to think so."

She rolled her eyes. "Don't let it go to your head."

"No problem there, considering the source."

Addie decided to ignore the comment and changed channels until she found the right station. They sat in silence, except for calling out answers when they knew them. Not surprisingly, Erich got far more than she did. If they'd been keeping score, by the end of the game show his total would have been well ahead of hers.

When the show finished, Addie stood. "Can I get you anything before I leave?" She had homework yet and was determined to read the assigned pages, no matter how long it took.

His face revealed regret, as if he would have liked her to stay, although it went without saying he'd never admit it. "I'm fine, but thanks for asking."

"See, that wasn't so hard, now, was it?"

"What?"

"Being civil."

He frowned. "I can be civil if you're civil."

She held up her hand. "No problem. Now, before I leave, do you have your phone close at hand so you can call if you need anything?"

"Right here." He patted it, indicating it was well within reach.

"Okay." She got all the way to the front door and then hesitated. This probably wasn't the time or place, but curiosity took hold and got the better of her. "Can I ask you something?"

He seemed surprised by the question, and shrugged. "I guess."

"What's the story with Ashley?"

He groaned. "I should have guessed you weren't going to go quietly into the night."

Addie was curious, but not at the expense of this fragile peace. "Forget I asked," she said, and held up her palm in an effort to keep him from explaining. "It's none of my business."

"Thank you." He seemed genuinely grateful to find she was willing to drop the subject. It was plain that whoever Ashley was or had been at one time remained a sore spot with him.

Addie reached for the door handle. "I'll see you in the morning."

"Sleep tight," he called out after her.

"You, too."

"Not much chance of that. I much prefer a bed over this chair."

Addie didn't blame him. Not only was he in pain, but sleeping in a chair was bound to be uncomfortable. No wonder Julie had mentioned Erich hadn't slept well the night before. Addie wished there was something more she could do to help, only there wasn't. Erich had basically told her he didn't want her going all Mother Teresa on him. He'd hate it if she started hovering.

Once Addie was in her own home, she brewed a cup of tea and settled in the chair that had once been her father's favorite. It still carried a faint scent of him, and she found comfort in that. How she wished she'd made a stronger effort to reconcile with him. For a long time she simply sat with the Dickens novel in her hand, thinking about her father.

From childhood, Addie had been described as different. She'd struggled the first few years in school until she was tested and learned she was dyslexic. She still remembered when they gave her parents the diagnosis; Addie was in second grade, and in her mind, if she was going to be told she wasn't the same as everyone else, then she would be as different as different could be. In order to stand out and find her own identity, she'd purposely chosen to wear mismatched clothing and cut her own hair. Her mother defended her and claimed Addie liked to march to the beat of a different drum, although she was never entirely sure what that meant.

Her grandmother called her eccentric. Once she

figured out how to spell it, Addie looked the word up in the dictionary. She discovered it came from a geometry term and one definition was "not having the same center."

The way she figured it, she was always a little off-kilter. Her grades improved, but school had never been her thing. While in elementary school she felt like she was being suffocated, and after a while, young as she was, she decided she could only be herself. She would never fit in with the norm. Pretty deep thoughts, she realized, for a girl barely eight.

Perhaps it was egotistical of her, but Addie liked to think of herself as uniquely shaped. Gifted, but not in the traditional way. As a result, she often clashed with authority figures, but no one more than her headstrong father.

She missed him. She missed him terribly. For years she'd avoided talking to him. Now it came as a shock to realize the one she'd hurt, the one she'd been so intent on punishing, hadn't been her father, but herself.

Addie ran her hand down the chair arm as if giving a silent apology to the father she had never fully appreciated.

Sighing now, and feeling a bit maudlin, she looked around the house at all that was familiar. Although it was only a week away, it didn't seem like Christmas, although there were signs of it throughout the neighborhood. Several of the houses down the street had decorated with a dazzling display of lights. The single string around each of the two small arborvitae in the front of the house seemed like a meager effort. In past years, the whole house would have been decorated, top to bottom, inside and out. The Christmas tree would be up, with an array of cheerfully wrapped gifts stored at its base.

Not this year.

Her mother had escaped to a tropical paradise and Addie was alone . . . well, other than Erich, who wanted nothing to do with Christmas.

Her tea had cooled considerably before Addie tackled her reading assignment. She had fifty pages of *A Christmas Carol* to read before her next class. Even then, the text lay open in her lap as she considered her teacher and fellow classmates.

Mr. Mills was knowledgeable enough despite being a bit odd. He certainly wasn't like any teacher she'd ever known. She liked his style, though. He brought Dickens alive, giving them the details of the author's life, giving him a story of his own.

It was a tall order keeping the students engaged. Addie suspected that, like her, a number of the other students had signed up for the class because they needed the credits in order to receive their high school diplomas.

For sure, Danny, who'd served time in prison. She couldn't help wondering about his story. He was a kick, chiming in with an opinion for nearly everything discussed. It was a bit much, but still he was a likable guy.

Andrew, the Army vet with the shepherd, was another interesting character. Addie wondered what had brought him there. She doubted he was in need of a high school diploma. He seemed to be in need of something above and beyond what was taught inside a classroom.

The security guard . . . it took her a moment to remember his name. Brady something . . . was almost a caricature of a mall cop. Just thinking about him caused her to frown. He'd been so rude to the woman from the cafeteria when it wasn't necessary.

Her thoughts continued to wander from one subject to the next until Addie realized this day-dreaming was all a delaying tactic to avoid reading the Dickens novel. It was sure to be wordy and boring, but then on the bright side, she already knew the story.

"What's wrong with me?" she said aloud. She'd been excited by this class. Perhaps *excited* was overstating her enthusiasm, but it had been years since she'd dropped out of high school and she'd been hopeful she could make it work this time.

It came to her then.

Addie was afraid.

The thought amused her. Gutsy girl Addie was afraid of failing, afraid that six years out of high school she not only would have the same problems getting through a lit class, she'd also flounder yet again, struggle with reading and comprehension.

Maybe she wouldn't have to read the entire book. Just the beginning to get the hang of the story, which she pretty much knew anyway. If necessary, she could watch the movie. There'd been several adaptations produced over the years. And surely there was a study guide available she could purchase through the bookstore. For that matter, there might well be online help. With all these resources, she should be able to muddle through. It was time to face those fears head-on and quit flirting with thoughts of failure.

With that mind-set, Addie turned the page and started the book. It wasn't exactly easy reading, she decided, but it wasn't all that difficult, either. If Dickens was alive, she wondered how his ego would handle her opinion of his much-loved classic. Truth was, she found the author far more fascinating than his writing.

At some point, she must have fallen asleep, because she woke with a start and then realized that irritating noise was her phone.

"Hello," she muttered, and rubbed her free hand over her eyes.

"Did I wake you?"

"Who is this?" she asked, and then realized it was Erich on the other end of the line. Instantly alarmed, she sat up so straight that she nearly slid off the edge of the cushion. "Are you okay?"

He ignored the question. "You doing anything?"

The question was innocent enough, but Addie read between the lines and they said plenty. He was in trouble. "No. Now answer me. What's wrong?"

He hesitated.

"Erich, I mean it; what's wrong?" She didn't know what had happened, but clearly something had. It had probably killed him to have to call her.

"Okay, okay, if you must know. I've fallen and I can't get up."

Chapter Seven

Addie made it across the yard to the Simmons family home in record time. Thankfully, the front door remained unlocked. She made a mental note to lock it behind her next time. Right away she noticed the interior was completely dark.

Just inside the house, she paused and called his name. "Erich."

"Leave the lights off," he shouted from somewhere distant. It sounded as if it'd come from the hallway or the kitchen.

Leave the lights off? "Why would I do that?" she demanded, blindly searching the wall for a light switch. She hadn't been inside his home often enough to remember where it was situated.

"Just do what I ask." Erich sounded none too happy.

"No way. I'm not stumbling around in the dark." She found the switch by the door and flipped it on. The small entry was quickly ablaze in light.

"You had to do it, didn't you?" he grumbled.

Addie searched the living room, where Erich had been sitting when she left. The footrest on the recliner was down and the blanket he'd had over his legs was puddled on the floor.

"Where are you?" she called out, coming farther into the house.

"The hallway. Leave the hall light off," he demanded, and then, in a voice so soft she barely heard, he added, "Please."

He must have hit his head to request anything so nonsensical, but in an effort to keep the peace she did as he asked. "Any particular reason I won't need to see where I'm headed?"

"Several," he muttered. "Mainly because this is humiliating enough without you seeing me sprawled across the floor in my underwear."

"O-k-a-y." Now she understood. He appeared to be sitting on the hardwood surface at the far end of the hallway by the entrance to the bathroom. The dim light from the entry illuminated his outline.

"What happened?" she asked, stepping closer. She wondered if the pain medication had made him a bit unsteady.

"You don't want to know." His robe was open

and spread out around him on the floor like a skirt around a Christmas tree.

"Of course I want to know," she said, moving to the side and leaning against the wall, being careful not to trip on him or the robe.

"Well, I don't want to tell you. Can you kindly leave it at that?"

She walked all the way around him in an effort to evaluate the situation. While unsure exactly how he'd gotten into this position, she could understand his predicament. Without the use of his hands, it would be nearly impossible for him to get to his feet unaided.

"If you could just help me raise myself enough to use my legs, I should be fine," he said, frustration evident in his voice.

Addie suspected he'd called her as a last resort once he'd exhausted his own strength and resources. "How long have you been like this?"

"A while." He was back to growling responses. "Can you please get me to my feet before I answer your questions?"

As Addie assessed things, she decided the best way to manipulate him to a standing position was from behind. She moved around to his back side and slipped her arms under his. "You ready?"

"I was ready an hour ago," he muttered.

Using every bit of strength she possessed, Addie strained to lift him enough to give him leverage to get to his feet. Despite her best efforts, he didn't budge.

"Good heavens, just how much do you weigh?" she asked, breathing hard.

He grumbled a reply. From what she could make of it, he wasn't discussing his weight.

"Temper, temper," she chided.

"It isn't you who's as helpless as an infant," he reminded her.

He was right. This situation must be mortifying for Erich. There'd been a time when she would have gotten a great deal of pleasure seeing him down and helpless. She didn't feel that way any longer. It was far too easy to see herself in a similar situation.

"Let's try again," she suggested. "This time I'll put a little more oomph into it."

Erich snorted sarcastically. "You mean to say the first attempt was just for practice?"

"Quit complaining. I'm doing the best I can." If the initial try was any indication, she could see getting Erich to his feet wasn't going to be easy.

She tried again, straining her muscles for all she was worth. Clenching her teeth, she tilted her head back, grunted hard, and gave it her all.

Nothing.

She couldn't lift him so much as an inch off the floor. He was a huge guy—easily six-three. He'd clearly continued to work out after high school and was as broad and muscular as ever. Given that she was slight, lifting him was sure to be a challenge.

Exhausted now, she slumped down on the hardwood surface, her legs stretched out in a wide V.

"Are you hurt?" he asked, glancing over his shoulder.

"No, but this isn't working."

"No kidding, Sherlock."

After Addie caught her breath she crawled on her hands and knees around Erich so that they could talk face-to-face. Her eyes had adjusted to the dark and she noticed he'd modestly tucked his robe around his front.

"You have any other ideas?" she asked. Maybe, with his engineering background, he might offer a couple of other suggestions.

He leaned his head back and expelled a grating breath. "Unfortunately, not a one."

Although she couldn't see his face that clearly, from the way he spoke, she could tell he was exhausted.

This was a last resort, but Addie felt she had to suggest it. It went without saying, Erich would object. "If worse comes to worst, I could always call for help."

"Who?"

That was a legitimate question. Knocking on the neighbors' doors would most likely mean rousing them from bed. Then Addie had an idea.

"Nine-one-one would be my first option. Firefighters are trained for situations just like this." The more she thought about it, the more sense it made.

"No way." Erich's response was sharp and automatic. He wasn't even willing to listen.

"Come on, Erich, you're in an impossible situation here."

"I am not going to have a bunch of firefighters see me in my underwear." Just the way he said it left no room for argument.

"Okay, okay." Addie held up both her hands as if surrendering. "A man and his pride."

He sat pouting for several seconds before he muttered, "Pride's all I've got left, and I'd rather keep it, if you don't mind."

Despite their differences through the years, Addie felt bad for him. "Then we'll think of some other way." She tried to sound confident although it was more bluff than any real sense they could successfully pull this off.

They waited a few minutes in order for them both to catch their breath. Thirty minutes passed along with several attempts, all of which ended without success. They'd been nearly successful with a chair, but it was plain that putting too much pressure on his arms was not an option. When she saw the considerable pain on his face, Addie put a stop to it.

"You're hurting yourself."

"I don't care."

"I do," she argued, and pushed the kitchen chair aside, refusing to let him do any further damage to his broken wrists.

Addie slumped down on the floor, knees bent. She was too tired to stand up. "Any other bright ideas?" she asked.

"One." He chewed on his lower lip as though giving this some additional thought.

"Don't keep me in suspense," Addie chastised. "Tell me."

"If I can get to my knees."

"We tried that with the chair," she said, cutting him off.

He waved her objection aside. "The chair didn't work, but if you gave me your arm, I might be able to lift myself up enough to kneel."

"Not with your hands!" She was aghast he'd even make such a suggestion.

"Not with my hands," he agreed. "Just hold out your arm."

Addie wasn't sure what he meant until he showed her. He wanted her to hold her forearm out like a trapeze bar. She did, using all her strength to hold it stiff as a support for his own forearms to wrap around her one, and with that he was able to shift his weight enough to get to one knee. Then, gradually, the other. Soon he was upright.

After a long series of failed attempts, Addie wasn't sure why they hadn't thought of this earlier.

It'd worked. It hadn't been easy, nor was it pretty, but it did the trick.

For the longest moment, they stood facing each other, too stunned to speak. Both their shoulders heaved with exertion.

"We did it," Addie whispered. "We actually did it."

"We did," Erich agreed, and then he started to sway.

In half a heartbeat, Addie was at his side with her arm wrapped around his waist. He felt warm and muscular, and she kept him close to her side, offering him her strength, which admittedly was pretty shaky. "Let me help you back into the recliner."

"Give me a minute," he said, and sounded pitifully weak.

"Sure."

He dragged in several deep breaths. "I never thought I'd have the opportunity to say this, but thanks, Addie. I'd never have managed getting off that floor without you."

"No problem."

He chuckled softly. "I beg to differ; it was a major problem."

Because he was exhausted, she kept her arm tucked around his waist, and walked with him back into the living room. Once there, he eased himself into the recliner. Without asking, she left him long enough to go into the kitchen and bring him a glass of water. She found a straw and brought it out with her.

"Here," she said. "This should help."

He had the blanket over his legs. "Thanks."

She set the water down on the tray where he could lean forward and sip without the necessity of using his hands. She waited long enough to make sure the water was close enough. Even then she was reluctant to leave, but she didn't have a good excuse to linger.

"Would you like anything else?" she asked, easing her way toward the front door.

"Nothing, thanks."

She rubbed her palms together. "Then I should probably get back."

He nodded. "Would you mind turning off the light on your way out?"

"Sure." She headed into the foyer and flipped the switch she'd turned on when she'd first entered the house. The area went dark. Addie's hand was on the doorknob when Erich spoke.

"I met Ashley in college."

She froze, uncertain if she should comment, ask questions, or simply pretend that she hadn't heard him. Curiosity won out, and she decided to learn what she could. "Ashley seems to have been important to you at one time though."

"At one time," he agreed.

"You broke it off?"

"No, she did. I had never been in love . . . well,

not like this, and I took it hard. It didn't take me long to realize she'd been using me. Later she made an effort to patch up the relationship, but by then I knew being with her wasn't worth the heartache. Frankly, I don't care if I ever see her again."

"When was the last time you saw her?"

"About six weeks ago. She has a hard time taking no for an answer."

In other words, this was an on-again/off-again relationship that had dragged on for several years. Apparently, they were in the off-again cycle.

"Do you love her?" she asked, then realized that was far too personal a question. "I'm sorry," she added quickly. "You don't need to answer that."

"I did love her," he said, his voice dipping slightly, "at one time." It seemed talking in the dark evoked confidences. "But not anymore," he added.

"You don't sound that sure of yourself."

His responding laugh was wry. "Let me put it like this: I had to learn my lesson about Ashley more than once. I got the message loud and clear the last time."

Addie moved all the way back into the living room. "I guess we all go through that kind of rejection at some point or another."

"You, too?" he asked, keeping his voice soft and low.

"Big-time." Funny, a few months earlier she would never have admitted this, least of all to him.

"I moved to Montana and met the love of my life. Some love. Some life. The relationship didn't last six months. If I'd been smart I would have packed my bags and headed home right then, but oh no, I wasn't about to put on my big-girl pants and admit I'd been wrong. I refused to give my dad the satisfaction, and so I stuck it out, freezing in the winter in a leaky trailer."

How foolish she'd been. How stubborn.

"We all make mistakes," Erich said sympathetically. "The key is learning from those mistakes and not repeating them."

Addie hadn't expected him to show this much self-awareness. "What mistake did you make with Ashley?"

He took his time answering. "It wasn't just one; it was several. I fell for a pretty face, but unfortunately she didn't have the heart to go with it. She was the sun of her own universe. It took far longer than it should have for me to recognize how shallow and vain she is."

Actually, now that she thought about it, Addie was fairly sure she had seen the beautiful Ashley one Thanksgiving when she'd flown home to be with family. As she recalled, Erich had paraded her into the house as if she were on a fashion runway. She'd been dressed all in bright, flashy colors that made her stand out wherever she might be.

In an effort to be generous, Addie suggested, "She might have changed."

"Doubtful." He dismissed that out of hand.

Addie had a small confession to make. "I didn't read the text she sent, but I did see the word *sorry.*"

He sighed. "Ashley can't stand the thought of not having the last word. I was the one who got away, and she will say or do anything to get me back just so she can dump me again. I've seen her do it with other men and I refuse to play that game. Apparently, there was a report of my accident in the newspaper and she read it."

"Oh."

"You asked about her. A few hours ago you would have had to torture the information out of me."

"And now?"

"Now . . . I guess you earned the right to know. I appreciate your help tonight. I mean it. Thanking you hardly seems adequate. Telling you about Ash is my way of . . . I'm not sure . . . letting you know I trust you, I suppose."

Addie sat in the recliner next to Erich. She didn't know what to say. Twenty-four hours ago she would have said this transformation in her relationship with Erich would have been impossible. After years of ill will, it came as a shock to realize she might not actually dislike him. She might even be able to look past the fact that he'd broken her tender heart all those years ago.

"Are you going to say anything?" he asked, after an awkward silence.

"Wow."

"Wow?" he repeated.

She waved her hands. "In case you hadn't noticed, something has happened between us."

"Excuse me?"

"We're talking."

"Yeah, and your point is?"

"We're talking, like two normal people. We aren't arguing or sniping at each other. I . . . might even discover that it's possible to get along with you."

He laughed as if that was one of the funniest things he'd ever heard. "Don't let this go to your head. You make it sound as if the next thing you know we'll be kissing."

"That ain't gonna happen," she assured him.

His amusement faded. "Frankly, I don't know that I'm willing to rule it out."

Chapter Eight

Thursday evening was the dreaded Christmas concert. Harry had been uneasy about it from the moment Michelle Heath, the French teacher, had mentioned she would save him a seat next to her. But now he had other, bigger worries.

In fact, the concert and his fellow instructor were the least of his troubles. Dr. Conceito, the college president, had asked to meet with Harry. They needed to have a little chat, or so he'd been told.

By comparison, the concert was sure to be like a stroll in a winter wonderland. Harry enjoyed music, although Earth couldn't compare to the thunderous choir of angels who sang praises in heaven. Now, that was some kind of performance. The music was simply "out of this world" and completely unlike anything heard on Earth.

For the last twenty-four hours Harry had managed to avoid talking to Michelle. They'd passed each other in the hallway now and again, but either he or she had been caught up in a gaggle of students each time.

As Harry passed, she raised her hand and called out, "See you later."

A sense of dread settled over Harry. If his attendance wasn't mandatory, he would have skipped the performance and made excuses later. However, Dr. Conceito had made it abundantly clear that Harry's presence was more than expected; it was demanded.

Dr. Conceito.

Although he'd been on the job only a few days, Harry had come to appreciate Celeste's warning regarding the college president. The man was more than a stickler for the rules, he was a tyrant. Even while on his best behavior, Harry had already had two run-ins with the school's dictator.

It seemed Dr. Conceito walked the halls looking for infractions with the same enthusiasm with which an anteater seeks out insects. He had a nose for it and a cohort in the security guard who took delight in reporting any behavior that appeared the least bit suspicious.

No doubt Dr. Conceito had heard from Brady Whitall, the security guard, about the cafeteria worker Harry had championed. Really, what harm did it do if the dear woman stood in the hallway and listened in on a literature class?

Angels weren't accustomed to being nervous. Heaven was serene and calm. No worries, be happy. He'd made the assumption that it would be similar on Earth. Not the same, of course, but he'd expected that being in the very center of God's will equated smooth sailing. He'd been wrong. And then there was the whole issue of dealing with human emotions . . . like attraction. Harry had yet to figure out how he was going to avoid sitting next to the French teacher at the concert.

With his heart pumping hard against his ribs, Harry entered the administration building and headed toward the president's office, hoping to get this meeting over as quickly as possible. Dr. Conceito's assistant looked up when he entered the room.

"Harry Mills," he said, as a means of introducing himself. "I believe Dr. Conceito is expecting me."

The assistant, a middle-aged woman whose thick, dark hair was streaked with gray, continued to stare at her computer screen. The name plate at her desk identified her as Patricia Ziglar. "Ah yes, here you are. If you'd kindly take a seat, Mr. Mills. Dr. Conceito shouldn't be long."

"Thank you." Harry claimed a chair and, hoping to look casual and relaxed, crossed his legs. In his nervousness, his calf slipped against the fabric of his pants and his foot thumped against the floor.

The assistant's eyes caught his, and Harry grinned nervously.

"Not to worry," the woman assured him kindly. "Dr. Conceito's bark is worse than his bite."

The college president was going to bark at him? Knowing this did nothing to settle his nerves. Earlier in the day, Harry had tried to find Celeste but couldn't. The limitations of Earth could be downright frustrating. In heaven there was no such thing as distance or, for that matter, time. Everything flowed together. Nothing was ever lost, nor did he need to look for someone. All he had to do was think and they were there. So easy. So convenient.

Earth was at a grave disadvantage, and sadly, humans had yet to realize it.

A buzzer went off on Patricia's desk. She looked back at Harry. "Dr. Conceito will see you now."

Harry leaped to his feet as if the chair came equipped with a huge spring that propelled him upward.

"It'll be fine," Patricia whispered, as she escorted him to the door with the frosted-glass window.

Harry stepped inside and the assistant closed the door behind him. He glanced over his shoulder at the clicking sound, then turned his attention to the college president. "You asked to see me?"

"Yes," Dr. Conceito said, and motioned toward the chair in front of his desk. "Take a seat."

Obediently, Harry sat. Perhaps it was better that
Celeste not know about this meeting. He'd already
gotten on the negative side of the man by walking
on the grass, getting caught red-handed. The president's reaction had made it seem that Harry had
taken a machete to bushes and desecrated the landscape of the entire campus.

Dr. Conceito leaned forward in his high-backed
desk chair, pinning Harry with his gaze. "I got a
report about you from Officer Brady Whitall."

Officer?

"I have to assume this is in regards to Elaina
Gomez?" Harry asked, presuming innocence.

"Yes," the college president confirmed. "In case
you weren't aware, it's strictly against school policy for an employee to leave their position while
the kitchen is still open."

"I understand," Harry said. Elaina had explained that she'd managed to finish cleaning up
early and her supervisor had dismissed her for the
night. Because she had extra time before the bus
arrived, she'd come to listen to the lecture in Harry's
class. "But—"

"There are no *buts* at this school," Dr. Conceito
said, interrupting Harry. "The rules are the rules,
and bending them even the slightest amount is unacceptable."

"I understand, however—"

"Furthermore, I am told this woman was listening in on your lecture."

If the school president was looking for evidence to take away Elaina's job, Harry was determined not to give it to him. "That I wouldn't know."

"Did you or did you not see her outside the classroom?" he pressed.

"I did, but only after the class was dismissed."

"Not before?"

"No." Harry could say that in all honesty.

Dr. Conceito thumped his fingers against the desktop as if weighing his options. He sighed and then said, "I was also informed that you gave Ms. Gomez a copy of the Dickens novel *A Christmas Carol,* which I understand the class is currently reading."

"Yes—"

"You do realize the book is school property." This was more statement than question.

"Yes, but—"

"Mr. Mills," Dr. Conceito said, impatiently interrupting him a second time. "What did I just tell you about *buts*?"

Harry looked down in an effort to avoid eye contact. "There are no buts at this school."

"Correct. Now, would you like to rephrase what you were about to say?"

Harry took a couple moments to collect his thoughts. "I wanted you to know that I stopped off at the bookstore to personally pay for the copy I gave Ms. Gomez."

"That's unnecessary," Dr. Conceito insisted, his face tightening.

Harry was undeterred. "It's my feeling we should encourage reading at all ages and economic levels."

"I agree," the school president said. "Tell me, did the bookstore accept payment?"

"No."

The grin on Dr. Conceito's face revealed no real amusement. "Did they give you a reason they wouldn't take your money?"

Harry didn't know where this conversation was going. "No, they didn't."

The smile disappeared. "Then let me keep you abreast of the results of your actions."

Harry leaned back and tried to appear to be relaxed. "Yes, please do."

Dr. Conceito exhaled sharply. "First off, you should know that I was required to visit Ms. Gomez and ask for the return of the novel."

Harry's shoulders sank, picturing the disappointment the young mother must have felt, having to return the book she'd accepted with such appreciation and excitement.

"I was willing to pay for the book," Harry reminded the president.

"That is unacceptable," Dr. Conceito argued. He stood and leaned toward Harry, planting both hands on the desk. "In case you are unaware, the Dickens novel was part of a government grant. To freely hand it out indiscriminately would be in violation of the terms and conditions of the grant."

"Ah . . ." Harry was fairly certain the government that had generously supplied the grant would be more than happy to see Elaina Gomez receive the novel. Arguing, however, would do him no good.

"I hope you understand that by bending the rules, you have, within a few short days, put our entire community college in serious jeopardy of receiving future funding."

Harry clenched his teeth to keep from arguing. How ridiculous; Dr. Conceito was overreacting. What a small-minded man. Celeste had warned him, and without even trying, Harry had already waded waist-deep in trouble.

"I deeply regret causing any problems," Harry said, as contritely as he could manage. The pompous so-and-so. How he wished he could give this man what he so richly deserved. It took every shred of control Harry possessed to sit and do nothing. It hit him then: So this was what anger felt like. He was experiencing anger for the first time. Anger and frustration. The emotions were so powerful they nearly overwhelmed him.

Dr. Conceito continued. "I want to be sure nothing like this will ever happen again."

"It won't," Harry managed to assure him.

"Good." He dismissed Harry with a wave of his hand. That smile that was no smile was back in place. "And you'll be at the choral performance this evening."

"I'll be there," Harry murmured, more than eager to leave the president's office before he said or did something to get himself dismissed entirely.

He was halfway to the door when Dr. Conceito stopped him. "I have my eye on you, Mills. You're a troublemaker, and if this sort of behavior continues, you won't last long on this campus."

Harry clenched his fists. "I understand."

Dr. Conceito's assistant sent him a sympathetic look as he left the office. He didn't have a destination in mind, other than to escape. Passing the Hub, he headed toward his classroom and was stopped by a familiar voice.

"Harry."

Celeste stood outside the cafeteria area, sipping a hot drink from one of the coffee bar's cups. She wore a bright turquoise scarf, which was wrapped multiple times around her neck over a red coat.

Harry paused.

"What did I tell you?" she asked softly, then took a sip. Steam rose from her cup as she met his gaze above the rim.

"Stay away from Dr. Conceito. But I blew it, and now Dr. Conceito claims he's got his eye on me."

"He does," Celeste agreed, "but that's inevitable."

"It is?"

"The man has his demons, Harry, and your light clashes with his darkness."

What she said made sense. "He wants to get rid of me."

"Don't worry, we've got you covered."

"We?"

Celeste grinned. "You don't honestly believe God would send you on your first earthly assignment without backup, do you?"

Harry grinned. He should have realized he was being looked after. "I was angry." The power of the emotion surprised him.

"Eventually you'll learn to deal with these human feelings. It takes time," Celeste told him. "Emotions are what makes becoming friends with Michelle Heath so dangerous."

"How's that?"

The barista's gaze showed sympathy. "You can't become romantically involved with her, Harry. She's a beautiful woman and she's taken a liking to you."

He understood far too well; he'd taken a liking to the French teacher, too. "I fully intend to avoid her."

"What about the concert?" Celeste asked.

"When the time comes, I'll find a way to sit elsewhere." Harry wasn't worried. It shouldn't be difficult.

"How are matters with Addie Folsom progressing?" Celeste asked next.

Ah yes, his assignment. "She was in class on Wednesday but seemed distracted."

"Do you know why?"

"Not completely," he was forced to admit. "Erich fell, you know, and needed her help."

"And?"

"Addie willingly came to his aid." The young woman had made several strides in the right direction, and Harry was proud of her. "I'm still not sure what she is meant to learn from him, but she is evolving, conducting herself more maturely—and with more generosity—and that can't be bad."

"What happened after she helped him?"

This was the best part. "They started talking and realized their differences, despite everything, weren't all that great. It's a start. I think Erich is seeing her in an entirely different light."

"And Addie? Has her opinion of Erich changed, too?"

Harry grinned and nodded. "I believe it has."

Celeste looked pleased. "This is excellent news. Humans tend to build walls when they should be opening doors."

Harry regarded his mentor in a fresh light. "That sounded almost poetic."

"Thank you." She sipped her drink and then looked him square in the eye. "Now for the big question. Is Addie ready?"

Harry's thoughts felt as though they were caught

up in a tornado, whirling around inside his head. *Ready for what?* He decided to wing it, no pun intended. "I think so."

"Good, because it won't be long now before Ashley arrives."

Chapter Nine

It was a couple days after her late-night summons for help, and Addie woke with her mind full of Erich. She pushed thoughts of him from her head and reminded herself that she hadn't finished reading the next fifty pages of *A Christmas Carol*.

Since helping Erich off the floor, their relationship had made a dramatic shift. Whereas before she was constantly on guard and tense around him, since his fall they'd found reasons to work together and even joke with each other. Never in all her life had Addie expected to laugh with Erich Simmons instead of at him or vice versa. This was completely unfamiliar territory. Even now she wasn't entirely sure she could or should trust him. He was everything she'd spent the last six years trying not to be.

But then, look where that had gotten her. Nowhere, to be precise.

For breakfast, Addie blended fruit and protein powder along with milk and ice cubes into a frothy mixture that would be easy for Erich to drink without the use of his hands. This was the second morning she had mixed up the drink. She hoped the extra protein would give him badly needed strength. He'd seemed to enjoy it the day before, weakened as he was from all his efforts to get up off the floor.

Inhaling a calming breath, she put on her coat and carried the glass over to his house, letting herself in after a polite knock.

"Come in," he called, just as she came through the door.

As she expected, he'd spent the night in the recliner and was awake.

"Morning," she said, with a bit of uncertainty, holding on to the glass with both hands. Her heartbeat felt like a pogo stick pounding against her chest.

The evening before, they'd watched *Jeopardy!* together and then a movie. It'd been almost midnight before she'd gone to bed, and here she was again first thing in the morning. Given how incapacitated he was and that it was her job to care for him, that seemed appropriate. But she was unsure he would welcome her company so soon, so she waited a few seconds before moving into the living room.

"Morning," he said, and avoided eye contact.

That said a great deal. He, too, was at odds over all the time they'd spent together in the last couple days. She was fairly certain he was as uncomfortable about this shift in their relationship as she was.

"I made your breakfast," she said, stating the obvious, with the glass in her hand.

"I appreciate it."

She brought it over and set it down on the side table with a straw, and then stepped back awkwardly.

She waited, unsure what to do or say next, if anything.

The silence felt both heavy and bleak.

"Did you sleep well?" she asked, hoping to make polite conversation.

He glanced up and nodded. "Better than the night before. How about you?"

"Okay." Actually, she'd had a difficult time falling asleep, and when she did, her dreams had been filled with nightmares. She'd even dreamed of that time from her childhood when Erich handed her a dead worm and insisted she eat it if she wanted access to the fort he'd built with Jerry and Karl.

Silence again.

"Can I get you anything more?" she asked, eager now to be on her way.

"No. I'll be fine."

"Okay." There didn't seem to be anything else to

say. Clearly, they were both uncomfortable with each other now, uncertain and hesitant. Although they'd lived next door to each other nearly all their lives, she realized that basically they were still little more than strangers.

His phone buzzed, indicating he had received a text. He read it and then glanced up at Addie. "Do you remember Carrie Hoffert?"

"Of course." They'd attended high school together. Carrie had been a homecoming princess and the leader of cheer squad.

"She's Carrie Welsh now. She heard about the car crash and wants to stop by."

Earlier, Erich had made it clear he wasn't in the mood for visitors. "How do you feel about that?"

He shrugged. "Okay, I guess. Carrie and I attended the University of Washington at the same time. Her husband and I work together at Boeing."

In other words, Carrie probably knew Ashley. That might prove interesting.

After chatting a few minutes more, Addie returned to the house and settled down to finish her reading assignment. To her surprise, the pages of Dickens's Christmas tale went rather quickly. It wasn't as if Addie didn't know what to expect in the story line; it was probably the most well known and loved of Dickens's novels. But even knowing the plot, she still found herself caught up in the characters and turning pages as eagerly as she would have if she hadn't known what would happen next. She looked forward to the classroom discussion and to hearing the reactions of her fellow classmates, especially Danny. He seemed to have a unique view of life in general.

The sound of a car door closing alerted Addie to a visitor. This was about the time the visiting nurse usually arrived, but it could be Carrie, too. Standing, Addie looked out the dining room window, which offered her the best view of the Simmonses' house.

Only it wasn't the visiting nurse, and it wasn't Carrie, either. The tall, thin, fashionably dressed woman in skinny jeans could only be the beautiful Ashley. She walked up the path to the front door as if she owned the street. She paused only long enough to flip her long, blond, perfectly styled hair off one shoulder before she rang the doorbell.

Unable to look away, Addie watched as Ashley let herself into the house. Addie wasn't sure how long she remained at the window. Her chest started to hurt, and after a moment she realized she'd been holding her breath.

Apparently, Erich and Ashley were enjoying a lengthy conversation, because Ashley stayed inside the house for a good long while. Addie checked her watch and could have sworn far more than only ten minutes had passed. It felt more like an hour. This was crazy. What did she care if Erich reunited with his ex?

Forcing herself away from the window, she returned to the kitchen and placed dirty dishes in the dishwasher. When she finished, she hurried back to the dining room window. Ashley's car was still there.

For reasons Addie didn't want to examine, she was angry, pacing the house, walking aimlessly from room to room. By the sheer force of her will she refused to look out the window again.

Thirty minutes passed, and when she could stand it no longer, Addie looked again. The other woman's car was gone. While she stood at the window, another vehicle pulled in to the same space so recently vacated.

It wasn't the nurse then, either, unless Carrie Hoffert Welsh had taken up a medical profession. She didn't look like any nurse Addie had ever seen, dressed in a red hooded coat. It seemed Erich had an entire parade of women at his beck and call.

Addie watched as Carrie stood on the front porch with a basket draped over her arm. She suspected Little Red Riding Hood had lovingly prepared chicken soup for poor, disabled Erich.

Addie pulled herself up short. Oh crap, she sounded as though she was jealous. Of Ashley and Carrie? Unbelievable! She refused to even consider such a thing.

Determined to push aside her less-than-kind thoughts, Addie returned to her book, although her thoughts wandered away from the page. More than once she had to force herself to refocus.

About fifteen minutes later her doorbell rang. She was surprised to find Carrie on the other side of the door.

"Carrie," she said, as though it was a complete shock to see the girl from her high school class. Well, actually, it was a surprise to see her at the door. "Come in, please." She invited her into the house.

"Addie, hello. It's been way too long; you look great." Carrie's smile was warm and sincere.

"You, too," she managed, and genuinely meant it. She remembered Carrie being a good, caring person, and it wouldn't surprise her if Erich had maintained their friendship through high school and college.

"Dave told me about Erich's accident, and so I brought him some Christmas cookies. He told me you're looking after him, and I thought I'd just pop over to say hi—it's been a long time. I hear you are helping so your two mothers can go on a cruise. That's really thoughtful of you, Addie. How's he holding up?"

Before Addie could answer, Carrie continued, "He put on a brave front, but I could see this is difficult for him."

It'd be difficult for anyone, but Addie refrained from saying so. "Erich is doing about as well as can be expected," she said.

"It's really kind of you to help him and give your mother and his the opportunity to travel."

"It's the least I can do." It wasn't necessary to explain that it'd taken a gentle shove from a barista and a classic literature instructor to convince her to take on the task. Needless to say, the only reason she'd agreed was for her mother's sake. She hadn't exactly gone into this with a pristine attitude.

"If I'd been thinking, I could have brought Erich chicken soup instead of cookies," Carrie continued.

"You're the thoughtful one," Addie said. "I'm sure he'll enjoy the cookies."

"I hope so. It's good to see you, Addie. Erich tells me you're in school. That's great. I better get to work or I'll be late. Merry Christmas," she said, and started for the door.

"Merry Christmas," Addie returned.

Addie's spirits lifted as she walked Carrie to the front door and watched her drive away.

She waited until the visiting nurse had come and gone before she stopped by Erich's again. It was close enough to noon to think about preparing his lunch. She heated up tomato soup out of a can and brought it over to him, along with a grilled cheese sandwich.

She knocked once and then let herself into the house. Erich had changed clothes and shaved, or rather been shaved. He looked good, better than she could remember seeing him since the car accident. The swelling had gone down in his eye and the bruises were fading. The color was back in his face and there was a spark in his eyes. No doubt the beautiful Ashley was responsible for that.

"I see you've had a busy morning," she said, putting on her best candy-striper smile. She didn't intend to bring up Ashley, but hoped he'd volunteer the information.

"Yeah." He didn't elaborate.

"I brought your lunch."

"So I see."

She set the cup and plate down and made a conscious effort not to leap back the way she had earlier. If he noticed, he didn't say anything. She stared at him intently, waiting. Nothing.

He frowned slightly. "What did you do this morning?"

She couldn't very well admit she'd been glued to the window, watching his house. "I read."

He seemed in a much better mood than earlier. And why not? Most likely his romance with Ashley had shifted to the on-again stage. It was on the tip of her tongue to ask him about his visitors, but she refused to do it. No way did she want Erich knowing she'd been watching the house.

"I'm going out this afternoon," she told him.

"Oh?"

If he wanted to keep secrets, then she could as well. There was no need to tell him she planned to attend the Christmas concert at the community college. Leave him guessing. "I'm meeting a couple guys from my class." A slight exaggeration. She was bound to run into Danny, who'd mentioned he'd be at the concert. And there was sure to be one or two others attending.

Some of the sparkle left his eyes. "Will you stop by later, then?"

She shrugged as if it was no big deal. "If you'd like."

"Sure, why not? It gets boring just sitting here for hours on end."

He seemed to be making sure she knew he wanted her company only out of sheer desperation. He wasn't interested in her, which was perfectly fine by Addie, seeing that she had no romantic interest in him, either.

"See you later," she said, eager to be on her way.

"See you," he called after her.

Addie couldn't get away from him fast enough. Once back at her own home, the same restlessness that had plagued her earlier returned. She showered, did a bit more housework, and then drove over to the college. She was an hour early for the concert. With time to kill, she stopped in at the Hub and ordered a latte before she remembered that she'd forgotten to eat lunch. No wonder she was hungry. The barista was the same one she'd spoken to earlier.

"I was hoping you'd be back," Celeste said, as Addie slid onto the stool. "What did you decide to do about your neighbor?"

Addie was reluctant to talk about Erich, but at

the same time she needed a sounding board. "I took your advice."

"So how's it going?" The other woman busied herself with brewing the latte while she spoke.

Addie hesitated and then shrugged. "All right, I guess."

"Problems?" she asked, as she set the drink on the counter in front of Addie.

Taking the cash out of her purse, she considered her answer. She wanted to talk, but wasn't sure what to say, finally settling on "Not really."

Celeste braced her hands against the counter. "Then why do you look like you've lost your best friend?"

"Do I?" She had no clue she was this readable.

"Is he as disagreeable as you remember?"

Addie shook her head. "Not really . . . we actually seem to be getting along. I guess I was more comfortable when I couldn't stand the sight of him."

"Really?" Celeste looked surprised.

These questions unnerved Addie. "I . . . don't know. I'm sort of waiting for him to say something that will bring us back to the way things used to be. I'm more comfortable with that, and I think he is, too."

"Change is hard," the barista commented, as another student approached the stand and placed an order.

Celeste made a second latte and continued to

chat with Addie as she worked. "Isn't that what Dickens's story is about?" she asked.

Addie hadn't thought of it in that way, but she had to agree. *A Christmas Carol* was indeed about change. Like her, Scrooge acknowledged the mistakes he'd made and realized he'd been given a second chance. The same way she'd been handed this gift of a second chance with education . . . and with Erich. She wasn't the only one, she realized. Danny, who'd served time, had been given a second chance as well, and Andrew Fairfax, the veteran who'd come to class with the service dog named Tommy.

Addie's thoughts were full of her short conversation with Celeste as she headed toward the concert hall. She saw Danny going into the building where their classroom was. Out of curiosity, she followed him inside, but once she was through the doors, she didn't see him. She headed down the hall toward their classroom.

The janitor was inside, but he didn't see her as he picked up the garbage can. Instead of emptying it, he rifled through the can and took out a couple of wadded-up pieces of paper and read them.

Addie scooted back from the doorway, not wanting him to know what she'd seen. She had to wonder what he thought he'd find.

Addie was standing outside the classroom when Danny exited the men's room. He saw her and looked surprised.

"Hi, there! You going to the concert?" she asked.

"I thought I might. You?"

"Yeah. Mind if I walk over with you?"

"Sure thing." Danny was more than accommodating. "Did you finish the reading assignment yet?" he asked.

She nodded. "You?"

"Yeah. You kind of have to hate Scrooge. He was a greedy, mean SOB. Making Bob Cratchit work on Christmas." A thoughtful frown came over him and he lowered his voice and said, "I had a job once."

Once being the operative word, Addie realized.

"I would have worked on Christmas, but they closed the restaurant for the holiday."

"What was the job?"

He shrugged as if to tell her it was no big deal. Although from his body language, she felt it might have been.

"It was a barbecue place. I bused tables. My crew dissed me when they saw me wearin' an apron, so I bailed. Big mistake."

"We all make mistakes, Danny. Big and small. But you don't have to let them define you forever. And isn't that what this book is about?"

"I thought it was about ghosts. Freaky!"

"Well, it is about ghosts and a whole lot more, don't you think?"

"She's right," Harry Mills said, walking up and joining them, heading toward Massey Hall.

Because she'd been involved in conversation, Addie hadn't realized anyone was behind them.

"I'm anxious to hear what you both think in class tomorrow," Harry said. "It seems like you're reading the story very thoughtfully."

When Addie had signed up for this course she'd been determined to do whatever it took to get through with a passing grade. She hadn't expected to enjoy it or even learn from it. Yet the novel they were studying was filled with life lessons that seemed to apply directly to her.

Chapter Ten

Harry waited until the very last minute to enter Massey Hall, where the choral group was about to make its Christmas presentation. It'd been his intention to arrive late. The later, the better.

He hadn't needed to make up an excuse. After speaking with Addie and Danny, he'd returned briefly to his classroom and been waylaid by the custodian.

"Mr. Mills," the janitor whispered, motioning him over. He leaned against the mop handle, which rested inside a large metal bucket.

Harry knew the man's name was Jonas from something Celeste had mentioned earlier, although he couldn't remember exactly what it was she'd told him. Human frailties could be downright frustrating. Memory being one of those.

"Yes," Harry said, as he approached the other man. "How can I help you?"

"You're new here, right?"

"I am," he said, and thrust out his hand. "Harry Mills."

The other man clasped his hand. "Jonas Spelling." He looked directly at Harry in an unsettling way as if measuring his words. "I heard you came from a teaching position at Oregon State Community College."

This was a gray area Celeste had told him was best to avoid. "I did."

The other man looked him over from head to foot as though Harry was in a police lineup and he was about to make a positive identification. "I have a brother who works at the same college where you taught. He knows everyone and he claims he's never heard of you."

Red lights started flashing right before Harry's eyes. He was not used to having to lie. "I'm sure if your brother checks the records, he'll find my name."

"Yes, yes, of course," Jonas said. "Anyway, that isn't the reason I wanted to talk to you." He lowered his voice as though afraid someone might be listening in on their conversation.

Harry made a point of glancing at his wrist, letting the other man know he had commitments. Then, in a flash, Harry remembered what Celeste had told him. Jonas Spelling was a known snoop.

Harry had to wonder how it was that he attracted all the oddballs.

"I won't keep you long," the janitor promised.

"I appreciate that. I have a concert to attend." He did his best to sound as official as Dr. Conceito.

"Yes, yes." The other man hesitated and looked down. "I have a couple concerns I thought you should know about."

"Concerns?"

"Yes." Again he lowered his voice and glanced over his shoulder. "It's about that war vet in your class. The one with the dog."

"Andrew?" Harry had done his best to draw the reticent student into the class discussion, without success. Andrew sat in the very last seat in the back of the room and kept his head lowered, avoiding eye contact.

"Didn't know his name," Jonas continued, whispering now.

"Is there a problem?"

"A potential one. I think the man might be mentally unstable."

Harry feigned surprise.

"Furthermore, the dog sheds hair. It isn't a good idea to be bringing a dog into a classroom."

"I disagree," Harry said. "I think this class is exactly where Andrew needs to be, and as for the dog, federal law allows service animals into classrooms. Even if I did have a problem with Tommy, and I don't, I couldn't do anything about it." *And wouldn't,* he added silently.

Jonas nodded as if he understood. "You're a kindhearted person, I can see that. Still, I thought you should be aware of the potential danger you and the class might be in. You never know about these returning veterans. They can go ballistic without warning."

"Thank you for your concern," Harry said pointedly, tamping down his irritation, "but I have everything under control."

The janitor leaned closer, causing the mop handle to sway toward Harry. "You don't need to worry. I've spoken to Brady Whitall, and he's keeping close tabs on the vet and the dog."

"The security guard?" This didn't bode well.

"Yes. Brady will keep a close eye on Andrew and on that felon."

"Felon? What felon?"

"The one on parole. Watch him closely; he's not to be trusted. He could rob you blind before you know what he's doing. He's a troublemaker if ever there was one."

Rather than argue, Harry made his excuses and hurried toward the performance center. As he walked, he tried to digest the conversation. This was a shock. Harry hadn't expected Earth to be filled with such mean-spirited people.

Once inside the performance center, it didn't take Harry long to spot Michelle. She sat near the front of the auditorium, close to the aisle. She'd placed her winter coat over the back of the seat next to her, the one she'd purposely saved for him, Harry realized. She glanced over her shoulder a couple times while he stood out of view. He was determined to follow Celeste's advice and stay away. Michelle was dangerous. Human, beautiful, single, and looking . . .

Harry waited until Michelle turned back around before he ducked into the first available seat and hunkered down. To his dismay, she stood as though to come in search of him. A trapped feeling settled over him. Harry had to do something, and quickly. He closed his eyes and did what was necessary. This was an emergency situation: Under normal circumstances, he wouldn't use his heavenly powers, but he had no other choice.

After a thorough search of the area, Michelle reluctantly returned to her seat. Harry released a sigh of relief.

Then Michelle hesitated and her head came slightly back as she realized the chair she'd saved for him had vanished. The person who had been two seats over was now sitting directly next to her. She glanced down the row but seemed to realize that something was strange. It wasn't as if her neighbor had moved, because there were no other empty seats. And no one else had come into the row. The chair had simply disappeared. She asked the person sitting directly behind her, apparently a friend, who shook her head and shrugged. With even more reluctance, she removed her jacket and reclaimed her seat.

Everything would be fine as long as Celeste didn't catch wind of what he'd done. He knew this was not really within parameters.

It wasn't until Harry relaxed that he realized he'd sat down next to Addie Folsom.

She smiled over at him and he smiled back. Actually, this had worked out amazingly well. He'd hoped to have a friendly chat with her and catch up on the progress she'd made with her neighbor. He had recently had a major insight. He'd become convinced that whatever Addie and Erich had to learn from each other might involve them falling in love. And he even thought the seeds were already there and taking root. Addie had had a crush on Erich in her early teens, and he suspected her feelings had never really changed.

"Hello, Addie," he said. "When I heard you and Danny talking earlier, I was impressed—you have a keen grasp of Dickens and this novel."

A smile flickered in and out of her eyes as though she was pleased by the compliment but unwilling to show it. "Thank you."

"Your progress has been excellent; I'm eager to read the written assignment when you turn it in."

It surprised him that his compliments caused her to blush. She didn't seem like a woman who blushed easily. As an angel, he wasn't really familiar firsthand with the feelings that caused blushing, but he was starting to pride himself on his insight into human nature. He changed the subject to help her out. "I understand you decided to look after your neighbor."

She frowned and looked away. "Yes."

He wanted to ask what had happened, but clearly he couldn't. He wondered if Ashley had made an appearance, just as Celeste had said she would. It didn't seem like matters had smoothed themselves out, either, whatever had happened. He felt the need to reassure her without making mention of anything specific. Weighing his words carefully, he leaned over and whispered in a conspiratorial manner, "You don't need to worry. I realize you harbor deep feelings for your neighbor."

Addie jerked away as if he'd struck her. "You've got to be kidding! Erich and me? No way. I can't imagine what ever gave you that idea."

"Ah . . . ah sorry, I thought . . ."

"You thought wrong," she snapped, and crossed her arms tightly across her chest.

"Clearly I made a mistake." Harry backpedaled as if in training for the Tour de France.

"You sure did." She glared at him as if to state she had nothing more to say on the subject.

Another blunder. Harry didn't understand. He knew in his heart that what he said was true; Addie did have feelings for Erich at one time, and he was fairly certain she still did. This is what made humans so difficult to understand. Addie did care for Erich, and yet she wasn't willing to admit it. He shouldn't have gotten ahead of himself.

Nothing could compare to the music he'd heard in heaven, but the concert had been lovely, the music quite good. When the presentation ended, there was a large round of applause.

Before Michelle could find him, Harry quickly left the performance center. He sought Celeste at the Hub. She was just getting off work and left with him so they could talk privately.

"So how'd your day go?" she asked, as they walked side by side.

Harry held his hands behind his back as he matched his steps with hers. He knew this was a rhetorical question, as she knew very well his day had been a challenge from the moment he'd set foot on campus. He was walking on eggshells after his meeting with President Conceito.

"Better, I hope." No need to try to fool Celeste. "I'm doing everything within my power to avoid making another mistake."

"You're learning." The words were devoid of censure. "The adjustment from heaven to Earth takes time. You're bound to make errors in judgment until you find your footing."

"I am? I mean . . ." He bit off the rest of what

he'd intended to say, for fear anything he said would be digging himself deeper into a hole from which he couldn't escape.

"I understand you sat next to Addie at the concert and the two of you were able to talk."

She would bring that up. "We had a short conversation." Short because Addie had been quick to cut him off. She'd buried her face in the program flyer, letting him know she had nothing more to say.

"She's upset that Ashley stopped by." It was a statement of fact rather than a question.

"Apparently so." The less he said, the better.

"Did Addie mention what happened?"

Harry felt bad for Addie, who didn't seem to recognize her own feelings for Erich. "She didn't say, but she was unwilling to discuss it with me."

Celeste considered his words, then suggested, "Why don't we check out the situation for ourselves?"

"You mean now?"

His mentor smiled at him. "Don't look so worried. This won't be an inquisition. We'll take a nice stroll in their neighborhood just as we have before and check out the two houses."

"Ah, sure. Good idea."

Addie's home was several miles from campus, but they had walked only a few minutes when they turned the corner to Addie and Erich's street.

They stood across the street, again hidden against

the backdrop of fir trees. The neighborhood was bright, with colored lights strung across rooflines and tree trunks, and with the chill in the air it was beginning to feel very festive. It was a beautiful clear night, and the stars sparkled above the lights sparkling below.

"Both houses are lit up inside, so both Addie and Erich seem to be home," Celeste said, as she motioned toward the two houses.

"I see Addie," Harry said, a bit excited. His young charge stood in the dining room, holding back the drape and looking out the window at Erich's home.

"Yes, I see her. She's wondering if she should check on him before she turns in for the night."

Harry didn't ask how Celeste knew what the other woman was thinking.

"She brought him dinner right after the concert, but she barely said a word to him."

"I was afraid something like that might happen," Harry said. He had a feeling that matters had taken a turn south in their relationship and that he might have inadvertently contributed to that.

Celeste sent him a meaningful look. "Apparently, your remarks shook her up a bit, not to mention Ashley's visit earlier. Addie was in and out of the house within minutes. Conversation was kept at a minimum."

"I was only trying to speed matters along," Harry murmured. He wanted Addie to recognize her feelings for Erich, but now he realized his comments had done more harm than good.

"Addie's miserable," Celeste said, sighing.

"What's Erich thinking?" Harry asked. If she was privy to Addie's thoughts, she could probably read Erich's as well.

Celeste moved slightly and looked up at the full moon that shed golden light across the lush green landscape. "He's confused. While Addie was at the concert, he painstakingly changed clothes and anxiously awaited her return. He was going to suggest she stay and watch television with him."

This was going from bad to worse. Harry felt guilty. "Any way to fix this?" he asked.

"Addie likes hot cocoa."

Harry wasn't sure what that had to do with anything.

"Erich does, too."

"And?" He needed a bit of direction. More than a hint, because he didn't have a clue what a hot drink had to do with the situation.

"You might plant the idea of Addie taking Erich a mug of hot cocoa."

"I can do that?" he asked, and then realized that he could. "I can do that!" he repeated emphatically. He shouldn't have forgotten. He had special powers he could use to help those in his classic literature class.

Closing his eyes, Harry concentrated on placing the thought in Addie's mind.

When he opened his eyes, he saw that Addie remained standing in the dining room, looking out the window at Erich's house. "It didn't work," he said, feeling defeated.

"Don't be so sure."

"She hasn't moved."

Celeste smiled. "She's weighing her options. We can only suggest, Harry. Humans have the gift of free will. They have to make the decision themselves once we prayerfully urge them in one direction or another."

This wasn't new information. Yet Harry needed the reminder. He tried again and watched as Addie released the drape she'd held to one side and moved away.

"Where's she going?" Harry asked, anxious now.

Celeste glanced in his direction and smiled. "She's headed toward the kitchen."

Chapter Eleven

Addie released the drape and moved away from the dining room window that looked over the Simmonses' property. Her nerves were on edge. When delivering Erich's evening meal she'd been abrupt and short-tempered, eager to get in and out of the house with the least amount of fuss. It was on the tip of her tongue to make some derogatory comment about seeing Ashley, but she kept her nastiness to herself.

When she'd first arrived with his dinner, Erich had tried to engage her in conversation. She'd snapped at him about being extra-busy and hurried home.

Erich looked completely baffled by her behavior, and, frankly, she didn't blame him. To this point, well, other than the first couple of meetings, they'd managed to be decent to each other. This evening she couldn't get away from him fast enough.

As soon as she was home, Addie regretted the way she'd acted. For the last two hours she'd paced the house, angry with herself. Finally, she'd settled in front of the dining room window, wondering what she should do now, if anything. It might well be that her gruff behavior had destroyed the fragile peace between them.

Because she was upset, Addie hadn't eaten dinner. She had no appetite, but felt she needed something in her stomach to stop the growling. Searching the kitchen cupboard, she found a tin of cocoa mix. For an elongated moment all she did was stare at it. Erich and her brother used to love drinking hot cocoa after one of their epic snowball fights whenever there was a rare Seattle snowstorm. It stung briefly to remember how the boys wouldn't let her join in their fun. Cocoa would make a nice peace offering, she decided.

Before she could talk herself out of it, Addie made them each a cup, carefully heating the milk and stirring in the cocoa. Then she carried two steaming mugs across the yard. Precariously holding the mugs in one hand, she knocked on the front door with the other and then nervously let herself into the house.

Erich was up and about. Surprise showed in his eyes when he realized it was her. The instant he saw her, he scowled.

"What's that? Poisoned cocoa?" he asked.

Despite herself, Addie smiled. "No, it's a peace offering."

His head came slightly back as if he wasn't sure he should believe her. "Oh?" The question carried more than a hint of sarcasm.

"I'm here to apologize," she clarified.

His gaze narrowed suspiciously. "What's your problem? One minute you're warm and the next minute I get the Arctic freeze."

"I'll be honest. I happened to look out the dining room window earlier today and saw you had . . . company, and I'm not talking about Carrie. That was Ashley, wasn't it?"

He didn't answer right away, and when he did his voice dropped several decibels. "Yeah, that was Ashley."

"I can understand why you're attracted to her. She's . . . beautiful."

"She's heartless."

Addie didn't know what to make of that. "She seemed to stay quite a long time, and it seemed, you know, that the two of you might have decided to have another go at the relationship." Now that she'd started talking, she couldn't seem to stop. "Which is wonderful, if that's what you wanted. I mean, she's stunning and the two of you make quite a couple."

The air went still and flat between them. Addie

continued to hold both mugs of hot chocolate and was beginning to feel foolish.

After a minute, Erich said, "My guess is, you didn't see Ashley leave."

"No." Mortified at her morbid curiosity, Addie had forced herself to move away from the window. When she'd looked again, Ashley's vehicle was gone.

"If you'd been watching, you would've noticed that we didn't exactly part on the best of terms. I told her before and I meant it: We're finished. She's out of my life."

"Oh." She wasn't sure what to say beyond that.

A huge grin appeared, dominating his face. "I'm beginning to think you were jealous."

Her denial was swift and adamant. "No, I wasn't."

"Au contraire."

"No," she insisted a second time. "I figured if the two of you were together again, Ashley wouldn't want me around, so I decided to stay away."

Grinning like the cat who'd found a bowl of cream, Erich slowly shook his head. "You were jealous."

"Fine, think what you like. Now do you want the cocoa or not?"

He cocked his head to one side, narrowing his gaze. "If you'd decided to make yourself scarce, then why are you here now?"

She gestured with the mug. "Do you want this?"

· "I want it."

His smile relaxed the lines in his forehead. "Thank you, Addie. I'm glad you're here."

"I am, too." She probably shouldn't be so willing to admit it.

"Would you like to hang for a while?" he asked.

She shrugged, struggling to hide her delight at his invitation. "I guess, sure."

"Watching *Jeopardy!* wasn't nearly as much fun without you."

"That's because your fancy degree guarantees you'll win."

"Nope," he countered. "Truth is, you're the only person my age who likes it as much as I do."

Setting the mugs down on the side table, Addie made herself comfortable in the recliner next to Erich. A classic Christmas movie, *The Bishop's Wife,* was playing.

"I remember seeing this as a kid and loving it," Addie admitted, as she reached for her drink and took a sip, keeping her gaze focused on the television screen. She immediately recognized the ice-skating scene. What she didn't tell Erich was that she used to close her eyes and try to imagine it was Erich who held her in his arms, guiding her across the ice. What fanciful dreams for a thirteen-year-old with her head in the clouds.

"It's one of my favorite movies, too," Erich said. "In fact, I've seen it two or three times. I certainly wouldn't mind seeing it again."

"You like *The Bishop's Wife?*"

He looked a bit embarrassed. "Don't tell anyone, but I'm sort of an old-movie buff. I'm especially fond of the movies from the late 1930s and 1940s. Weird, huh?"

"No, not at all. I am, too."

That opened the conversation to other classic movies they enjoyed, and Addie was surprised by how in tune their likes and dislikes were. It surprised and pleased her. She never would have guessed that their tastes in movies or anything else would be the same.

When the last scene played, Erich turned off the television. Addie couldn't think of a reason to linger; they'd both finished the hot cocoa and it was getting late. She started to get up.

"How's the reading for your class coming?" he asked, stopping her.

"Really good. I find it particularly interesting to hear the perspective of others in the class."

"What's your take on the novel?" he asked, and seemed genuinely interested.

"It's about change." Addie had gleaned that from the text from the first, but now she was more sure than ever. "It could be my thoughts are leaning that way because of where I am in my own life. I'm making a big change, and that's the message I want and need to hear. Still, I think that's what Dickens was writing about."

"How so?"

"Look at Scrooge," she said, becoming more animated as she spoke. "Isn't he a great character? We haven't gotten to the part near the end of the book where he purchases a Christmas goose and delivers the gifts to Bob Cratchit and his family, but everyone already knows that's how the book ends. Scrooge went from that greedy, self-absorbed individual to a man who was giving and kind; it was an overnight transformation." She realized that kind of dramatic change didn't generally happen as quickly, but this was fiction and that was the way the story needed to be told.

Erich appeared to be weighing her comments carefully. "Do you believe this turnaround in Scrooge's personality lasted more than a few days or weeks?"

Addie had the feeling Erich was really asking about her and the steps she'd taken to change her own life. "I'd like to think it did. Scrooge recognized that he was wasting his life. He had nothing but his gold. It took three ghosts to show him that all the stuff in the world was incapable of bringing him happiness."

"Giving his money away did?"

"Scrooge didn't give away his gold," she corrected kindly, speaking off the cuff. "He gave of himself . . . and in doing so, he found what he'd wanted and needed all along."

"And what was that?"

"His heart. Until then, Scrooge had completely

ignored his need for others, for relationships, and because he did, he became bitter and mean."

Erich's look became thoughtful. "It sounds to me like you have a good grasp of the story and the symbolism."

She relaxed back in the chair, more pleased than she wanted to admit by his compliment. "The thing is, I wonder if Dickens was thinking about symbolism when he wrote the story."

She went on, "This is pure conjecture on my part, but it seems to me that Dickens's purpose more than anything was to engage the reader in the tale. The symbolism was all part of the story, a natural by-product of a good storyteller." In sharing her insights, Addie voiced her thoughts aloud for the first time.

"I can't say what Dickens was thinking," Erich said.

"I can't, either," she was quick to tell him. "Like I said, my thoughts are speculation."

"Still," Erich continued, "you make a good point."

"Thanks." She hadn't meant to prattle on as if she were an expert on the subject, because heaven knew she wasn't. If anything, reading was her weak spot. But it would be interesting to hear what others in her class had to say about Scrooge.

They sat in companionable silence for a few moments, at ease with each other.

Erich glanced out the window. "Did you hear

the weather reporter is forecasting snow over the next couple days?"

"Snow?" Addie hadn't paid much attention to the television since she'd gotten back from class. The prospect of snow thrilled her. "No, I didn't hear. I love it when it snows!"

"Don't look so happy. You know what it's like around Tacoma; everyone goes a little crazy."

While snow in the Pacific Northwest wasn't unusual, it wasn't the norm, either.

"But it's perfect for Christmas."

"Bah, humbug," Erich said, scowling again. "I may have just watched a classic holiday movie, but that doesn't mean I'm going to get all celebratory."

Oh yes, she'd forgotten, Erich wasn't a fan of the holidays. "I can't forget about Christmas, and I don't know how you can, either." Earlier Erich had said something negative, but she honestly couldn't believe it was possible to hate Christmas. "I hope you didn't actually mean you don't like celebrating Christmas. That was all a joke, right?"

"I meant every word. People go way overboard, spending money on things they can't afford, buying gifts for relatives they don't like who will either re-gift or return them."

Addie was aghast. "It seems to me you need a visit from three spirits yourself, Erich Simmons. Where's your goodwill-toward-men attitude? Your Christmas spirit?"

He snorted. "I must have left it behind in the car after the crash."

"That's what I was thinking." She got up from the chair. "It's clear to me you're going to need a bit of help getting into the true spirit of Christmas."

He rolled his eyes. "Spare me, please."

"I most certainly will not. You and I are stuck together for Christmas, and I refuse to let you put a damper on it."

"Stuck together?" he asked, adding inflection to his voice. "Is that supposed to be a compliment?"

"I didn't mean it like that."

"Then tell me, how did you mean it?"

"What I intended to say was . . ." She hesitated, unsure how best to explain herself. "Seeing that we're going to be spending the holiday together, I'd like to make it a happy occasion."

"Are you planning on cooking me a Christmas goose?" he asked, sarcastically.

"If that's what you want."

"Can you cook?"

She arched her brows and slowly shook her head. "It seems to me, you aren't aware that I spent the last several years working in a diner. A couple times I had to step in when the cook got sick and prepare the orders myself. So, yes, in a word, I'll be able to manage Christmas dinner, only . . ."

"Only what?" he asked, revealing how skeptical he was.

"Only I'm not sure I can cook for two. Every

recipe I know is for twenty servings or more," she teased.

He grinned, and it was all Addie could do to tear her eyes away from him. It amazed her how good-looking he'd become . . . Well, he'd always been cute, but he was no longer a boy now, and it was different.

"I've never cooked a goose, but I'm willing to give it a try," she said, in an effort to distract herself, tearing her gaze away from Erich.

"I don't want anything special. As far as I'm concerned, Christmas is the same as any other day of the week. It's certainly nothing special to me."

Addie ignored him. "I think a small turkey, stuffing, cranberries, and a couple of side dishes will be perfect."

His look hardened, and when he spoke he raised his voice slightly. "Apparently, you didn't hear me."

"I did," she returned nonchalantly, "but I prefer to ignore what you had to say." She stood, and, placing her hands on her hips, she surveyed the room, doing a slow turn. "What we need is something tangible to put you in the spirit of the holidays."

Erich stood, too. "You aren't listening."

"A Christmas tree will put you in the holiday mood."

"I don't want a Christmas tree."

Addie ignored him again. "No worries. I don't

need your help setting it up. I'm happy to do it my-self."

"Not at my house you won't."

"I'm thinking a five-foot tree would be the per-fect size." She studied the room, filling her mind with the vision of a fully decorated tree. That was a sure way to help the Grinch's heart grow three sizes. He might object now, but a decorated tree was just the ticket. He wouldn't be able to resist the holiday when every time he walked into the room he was confronted with the bright, twinkling lights of a Christmas tree.

"Addie, I'm serious. If you want to go through all the trouble of putting up a silly Christmas tree, do it at your own house and not here."

"I'm serious, too," she countered.

He grumbled under his breath. "Don't you have someplace else you need to be? Homework that needs to be read?"

"Are you saying you're sick of me?"

"As a matter of fact . . . I'm not, which sort of shocks me. Heaven knows I should be, with all this talk about Christmas."

Staring at him, she was struck anew at the deep shade of blue his eyes were. How was it she'd never noticed that before?

"I find it unsettling how much I like hanging out with you," she said. "You're not half as bad as I remember."

"I was thinking the same thing," he said, joking

back. "With the exception of you insisting on decorating a tree." He smiled then, and the mood lightened.

They stood there goofily, smiling at each other. Suddenly it seemed like the most natural thing in the world for him to kiss her. Addie wasn't sure who leaned toward whom first. It might well have been her.

Erich placed his wrists on top of her shoulders, the weight of his twin casts catching her by surprise. She tilted her head back to look up at him and closed her eyes as his mouth settled, warm and gentle, over hers. His lips were soft and his kiss stole her breath.

He released her quickly. As if they were two children who'd been caught doing something wrong, they stepped away from each other.

Erich spoke first. "Wow," he whispered. "That was wild!"

Addie smiled. "I know, right?"

He stepped closer and rested his forehead against her own. "Do you remember when we were eight?"

"Vaguely."

"You offered to pay me your allowance if I'd kiss you."

"I did?" Addie didn't remember any such thing. "Tell me you're making that up."

"Nope. I swear it's true."

"You didn't take me up on my offer, though, did you?"

Erich did a poor job of hiding his amusement. "Actually, as I remember it, I kicked you in the shins."

Addie's smile grew bigger. "That sounds like something you'd do."

"I was just thinking . . ."

"Yes?"

"I was just thinking," he repeated, "that I wouldn't be so willing to turn you down if you were to make that same offer again."

Chapter Twelve

The next morning Addie hardly knew what to think. Erich had kissed her. Actually, she might have kissed him! She couldn't remember who had done what. What did stick in her mind as she tossed and turned the night away was the absolute shock of it.

Erich?

Her?

Even as she sat on the edge of her bed, fighting off the last dregs of sleep, she didn't know how it'd happened. Nor could she figure out when things had changed or even what had changed. Clearly something drastic had.

Was it her?

Was it Erich?

She decided she'd blame Christmas. Perhaps this

was his way of telling her his relationship with Ashley was completely over. That sort of made sense. It could be that they'd gotten caught up in the moment. Addie had always considered the holidays an extra-special time of year. Magic hung in the air, and people were gentler, kinder to one another. Differences were set aside, friendships deepened, and people in general were more charitable and happier.

That explained it, she decided. She would chalk the kiss up to Christmas.

Once she'd showered and dressed, Addie glanced out the dining room window toward Erich's house. Despite the early hour, she saw that his lights were on. Apparently he'd had trouble sleeping, too. She couldn't help speculating if he'd spent the night wondering about their kiss the way she had.

Maybe. Maybe not.

He'd probably brushed the incident aside and had completely forgotten it'd happened.

Seeing that he was awake and she was awake, Addie cooked him a breakfast of scrambled eggs plus toast and carried the meal from her house to his.

As was her habit, she knocked once and let herself in. Erich wasn't in the living room the way she'd expected. Standing just inside the entry, she called out for him.

"Erich?"

"In the kitchen." His voice came from the far end of the house.

He moved about considerably better now, she noticed. After several days sitting and sleeping in the recliner, she suspected he was thoroughly sick of remaining in the same position for hours on end, which gave her an idea.

"I brought you breakfast."

"Another protein drink?" he asked.

"No, eggs this morning."

She found him sitting at the kitchen table with the morning newspaper spread out across the surface. He was able to use his fingers more and more.

"Eggs." His eyes lit up.

"With cheese and chives."

He looked impressed. "Wow, you can actually cook."

Amused, she tossed him a dirty look, then set the plate down in front of him. "Do you want coffee?"

"Please."

Addie brewed him a cup and then made one for herself. When she finished she carried both mugs to the table and sat down across from him.

To this point, Addie had served him finger food or thin soups that he could drink through a straw. It pleased her to note that he was able to manage a fork. It wasn't easy or pretty, but he'd become adept enough to get the food to his mouth. It was evident that the effort taxed his patience, though.

"I have a question," she said, leaning slightly

forward as she placed her elbows on the table. She could be opening a hornet's nest, but curiosity had won out and she couldn't stop herself.

He looked up. "Okay."

"Did we . . . you and I actually kiss last night?"

He paused and considered the question. "I seem to remember that we did."

"Didn't you find that just a little bit odd? You and me . . . kissing?"

Once more he mulled over her question, letting the fork dangle above his plate, holding it between his fingers. "I'd say it was more surprising than it was odd."

Addie didn't see it that way. "I found it shocking."

He held her gaze and studied her as though curious. "Do you always analyze a kiss this way?"

"Not before now."

"So I'm the first?"

"Yes."

He frowned slightly. "Should I take that as a compliment or insult?"

The question gave her pause. "I don't know. How do you feel about it?"

"Kissing you or how I felt afterward?" he asked.

She wasn't sure. "Both, I guess. You didn't plan it, did you?"

"Hardly. At the time it seemed the thing to do. I don't regret it, if you're looking for an apology."

He set the fork down and pierced her with a single look. "What are you thinking?"

"I don't know yet. I think I probably should regret it, but I don't."

He grinned then, as if he found this discussion highly amusing.

"I'd like for the two of us to go out today," she said, speaking impulsively.

"And do what?"

"Just walk. You need the fresh air."

"Really?"

"Yes. It will do you good. You've been cooped up in this house far too long. You're up and about now and looking more like yourself every day. We don't need to go far."

"Not interested."

"Erich, don't be difficult. It'll be good for you."

He exhaled and leaned back in his chair. "I have the distinct feeling you're going to badger me until you get what you want."

"I won't badger you."

"No, you'll probably torture me into submission."

If he expected her to pout and demand her own way, she was sure to disappoint him. "You make me sound heartless, and I assure you I'm not."

"It won't be easy getting me ready for this."

"I know."

"You'll need to help me with my shoes and my

coat." He said this as if it would be enough to cause her to change her mind.

"I'll be happy to do that."

No more than a half hour later, Addie opened the front door and they stepped into the cold December air. The morning was crisp, and the frost crunched beneath her feet as she stepped onto the lawn. The sky had clouded up to a shade of battleship gray.

Erich's gaze followed hers as he carefully moved down the three short steps leading off the porch. "If I could, I'd hold your hand."

"Ah, that's sweet," she said, and slipped an arm around his elbow, wanting to be sure he was steady on his feet. "How are you feeling?"

"Not bad."

The park where they'd so often played as children was two blocks away. Addie thought they could walk there, rest a bit, and then return to the house. That would be an outing enough for one day.

Erich looked toward the low-lying clouds a second time. "It smells like snow."

She appreciatively sniffed the air and agreed. "It does."

"No class today? No Mr. Mills?"

"No, it's been canceled due to the threat of snow, although I wish there were classes. I'm surprised how much I like this class and the people I'm meeting, especially Danny and Andrew."

"Hey, have I got competition?" he joked. "Have you been kissing them, too?"

"No," she said, laughing. "Andrew's the war vet I mentioned earlier. The one with the service dog named Tommy."

"What about the other guy? Danny, was it?"

"Yes, Danny. He's this big, tough-looking guy who's like a huge puppy. It seems he's got a comment for just about everything Mr. Mills says. He's got a great attitude, although his personality is a bit quirky."

"Quirky?"

"You'll know what I mean when you meet him."

Erich slowed his steps to a crawl. "And just when am I going to meet this felon friend of yours?"

"At the Christmas party Mr. Mills mentioned in our last class. It's a potluck. Everyone is bringing something."

"And you want to bring me?"

"Yes."

"I think," Erich said pointedly, "when Mr. Mills suggested you bring something, he was referring to a dish to be shared with others, not a person."

"I know what he meant, and I am bringing food. In fact, I'm baking cookies."

"Can you explain why you want to drag me to your class party?"

Addie had hoped that by mentioning the invitation casually, Erich wouldn't make a big deal of it. "I want to include you. It'll be fun and you'll enjoy the outing."

He automatically shook his head. "Thanks anyway."

Addie couldn't hide her disappointment.

Using his index finger, he lifted her chin so their eyes could meet. The last time he'd looked at her with the same intensity had been right before they'd kissed. "I don't think you were listening when I mentioned how I feel about Christmas."

"I heard you, but I didn't like what you had to say." He didn't know it yet, but she fully intended on purchasing that Christmas tree and decorating it. Furthermore, she planned to set it up inside his house. Erich could ignore the holidays if he wished, but she was going to make it as hard as possible.

"Are you saying," he asked, skeptically, as they continued on their walk, "you were so overwhelmed by the emotional magnitude of our kiss that you completely lost track of our conversation?"

"If that's what you'd like to believe, then sure, why not?" She flashed him a brilliant smile, hoping to dazzle him with her charm and wit. All too soon she realized it hadn't worked.

"Addie, I hate to disappoint you, especially when we're getting along so well. I'm not interested in this friendly little class get-together. I don't want to think about Christmas. My goal is to get through the next few weeks as best I can while I'm in these casts and ignore everything else."

"It's just that I'd hoped you'd come."

"Why would you even want me there?" he probed.

"Because I think you'd enjoy it. Is it me you're looking to avoid or everything else?" she challenged.

"Listen," he said, stopping in the middle of the sidewalk and turning to face her. "I don't want to put a damper on your festive mood. Both my wrists are in casts. Even the simplest movements that everyone takes for granted are beyond me. I'm not up to celebrating much of anything. Can you leave it at that?"

As much as she would have liked him to attend the class potluck, she understood what he was saying. "Okay, got it."

His shoulders sagged. "Darn. I was sort of hoping you'd want to argue."

"You were?"

"Yes." He looked down and smiled at her. "Then we could kiss and make up."

"Are you looking for excuses to kiss me again?" she teased.

He lifted his thick eyebrows with the question. "You interested?"

"Could be."

They reached the park just about the time it started to snow. The flakes were heavy and thick.

"Stick out your tongue," Addie urged excitedly.

"What?"

"Don't you remember when we were kids, we used to catch snowflakes on our tongues?"

"The key phrase here is: *We were kids*. That's something kids do. Not adults."

"Erich. What's happened to you? When I knew you before, you were up for just about anything."

"The point is, I have two broken wrists," he returned in quick order. "This past week hasn't been fun, you know."

"I realize that, but it isn't enough of an excuse to be mad at the world."

"The person I'm mad at is the driver who slammed into my car at fifty miles an hour. I'm mad because I'm as helpless as a baby. And I'm mad because I'm being forced to use my vacation time and accumulated sick leave to sit around my mother's house and be treated like an infant. And I hate Christmas. Let's leave it at that."

That left her wondering if he was talking about something other than the accident that'd happened in his own life. His father hadn't died in December. Addie remembered getting word about his dad around Saint Patrick's Day, so it must have been in March.

The silence seemed to throb between them.

"Okay," she whispered. "Message received."

By unspoken agreement, they started walking back toward the house.

It was Erich who broke the silence. "Frankly, I think Scrooge got a bum rap."

"You do?"

"As far as I'm concerned, he had the right idea when it came to Christmas."

Chapter Thirteen

Humming a Christmas carol, Harry headed toward his class. His spirits were high. He'd managed to avoid Dr. Conceito for the last couple of days, and he found himself adjusting to the ways of Earth. Dealing with emotions continued to be a bit tricky, but he was getting there.

Two inches of snow had accumulated the day before, with more forecast for later in the afternoon. Harry loved snow. For several generations, youngsters had been making snow angels without ever suspecting where the original idea had come from. He smiled to himself as he crossed the campus. He was scheduled to meet with Celeste later and give his mentor an update on Addie Folsom.

The idea of his young charge taking Erich cocoa had worked famously. Harry knew the two had kissed and that Addie had managed to get Erich out of the house for a short walk the day before. Oh yes, matters were progressing nicely. Addie had shown vast improvement when it came to attitude. She truly had matured in the years she'd been away from her family. As for her relationship with Erich, it was too soon to tell. Still, Harry could see significant progress had been made. He couldn't take all the credit, he realized, but Celeste would be pleased.

In fact, Harry could hardly wait to tell Celeste about the kiss. She'd be thrilled. Two people who had never been able to tolerate the sight of each other were now . . . friends, with the potential for a whole lot more.

Harry was caught up in his thoughts and didn't notice until he reached his classroom that his room was the only one down the long hallway with the lights on.

He opened the door to his classroom and stopped cold.

Michelle Heath, the French teacher, was inside his room. She'd spread a red-and-white-checkered tablecloth on the floor, with one corner anchored by a wicker picnic basket. Two champagne glasses rested on top of the basket.

"Welcome, Harry," she whispered seductively.

His tongue felt like it was glued to the roof of his mouth. "Hi," he finally managed.

"I missed seeing you in Massey Hall at the performance." Her lips formed a soft pout. She sat on the tablecloth with her legs bent behind her and looked up at him with the most enticing smile he'd ever seen. His heart was doing jumping jacks inside his chest.

"I . . . know. All the seats were taken by the time I arrived." He remained frozen, standing in the doorway.

"Come in," she beckoned, motioning him by wiggling her fingers.

Harry felt his Adam's apple bob up and down in his throat. "What . . . about class?" His students would arrive any minute. He could only imagine what Dr. Conceito would think if he were to make a surprise visit to the room and find Harry sipping champagne with the French instructor when he was scheduled to be teaching class.

"Didn't you hear?" Michelle asked, her eyes rounding with surprise.

"Hear?"

"Classes have been canceled due to the snow."

"Ah . . . no one told me."

"It was announced earlier." She removed the champagne flutes from the top of the basket and opened it. She set aside the lid and reached inside to take out a cutting board, a long loaf of crusty French bread, a block of cheddar cheese, and a bottle of champagne. When Harry didn't immediately join her, she glanced up.

"No need to be shy, Harry. Come sit with me."
She patted the space on the floor next to her.

His knees had turned to the consistency of
gelatin.

"I'm going to need you to open the champagne
bottle for me," she said, looking at him with wide
blue eyes that seemed to say he was the strongest,
most capable man she'd ever known.

"Um . . . okay." He came all the way into the
classroom and took the bottle from her hand.

"Sit," she urged.

Harry sank to the ground. His hands trembled
slightly as he removed the wire mesh from the top
of the bottle and discarded it in the wastepaper
basket that was close at hand. Then he remembered how Jonas, the custodian, often rummaged
through the trash, and quickly retrieved it. He
thrust it into his jacket pocket along with the foil.
He was determined there would be no incriminat-
ing evidence left behind.

"My first husband was French," Michelle explained.

"Your first husband?"

Her eyes were round and sad. "I've been married
twice."

"Oh."

"You know what they say," she said, looking up
at him with a hopeful expression. "The third time
is the charm."

Harry's Adam's apple did a complete lap. "Third time?"

"Yes, I don't want to be alone any longer."

He was in trouble here. Big, big trouble.

"But that isn't what I wanted to tell you," Michelle continued. "This is about the champagne. Pierre said there was a trick to opening bubbly. Instead of twisting the cork, one must gently turn the bottle."

She made it sound easy, but when he attempted to do it, Harry discovered it was anything but. He gripped the cork and, following her instructions, gently rotated the bottle.

"If you open it slowly and carefully, it shouldn't make a popping sound. In fact, Pierre said when properly opened, champagne should have the sigh of a contented woman."

It was only by sheer good fortune that Harry managed to save the bottle before it went crashing to the floor. *The sigh of a contented woman.*

Heaven hadn't prepared him for this!

Harry didn't have a clue what a woman's satisfied sigh meant, but whatever it was sounded dangerous.

All at once the cork shot from the bottle with a popping sound loud enough to send fire engines racing toward the building. Harry nearly fell backward with the shock of it.

Michelle, however, barely seemed to notice.

"Shall I pour?" she asked, when Harry remained frozen, clinging to the bottle with both hands.

Unable to respond any other way, Harry nodded.

Celeste had warned him about Michelle, and here he was like a fly trapped in a spider's sticky web, hardly able to move and struggling valiantly. But not nearly valiantly enough. At this point, Harry found breathing difficult. His head was wandering into territory no angel should explore.

Harry needed help. And he needed it fast.

Then, when he least expected it, the classroom door flew open with such force it bounced against the wall. Brady Whitall leaped into the classroom in a crouched position with his weapon drawn. Both hands held on to the Taser gun, which was pointed directly at Michelle and Harry.

Michelle screamed.

So did Harry, who toppled the champagne bottle.

Brady stared at them long and hard before he blinked and lowered his weapon. "What's going on in here?"

With her hand pressed against her front, Michelle looked as if she was about to faint. Harry was feeling light-headed himself.

"A . . . picnic," Harry managed, although it was difficult to speak with his mouth so dry.

Michelle started to mop up the champagne. "Let

me explain, Officer," she said. "Would you care to join us?"

By the time Harry was due to meet Celeste an hour later, he was an emotional mess. Once more he'd failed, and she was sure to reprimand him. With good reason. He had made a terrible error in judgment.

With his hands over his face, Harry sat in the vacant cafeteria at one of the tables. The kitchen staff was just finishing the cleanup when Elaina, the young single mother he'd met earlier, saw him. Right away she came over.

"Hello, Mr. Mills," she said in perfect English, smiling. "I'm happy to see you again."

"Hello," he whispered back.

She frowned. "You okay?"

He nodded. It would be too difficult to explain that he'd just looked down the barrel of a police weapon. Because they were both badly shaken, they'd drank the entire bottle of champagne. Michelle insisted it was exactly what they needed. Now Harry wasn't so sure.

"You don't look so good." The frown had turned into worry lines that creased her brow.

"I don't?" This didn't bode well. Celeste would know right away that he'd messed up. It would be a miracle if he was allowed to finish teaching the course. He wouldn't be surprised if she banished him from Earth, and he wouldn't blame her.

Elaina pressed her hand against his forehead. "No fever."

He smiled weakly and hiccupped.

Next she reached for his hand, and, looking at her watch, she checked his pulse. After a moment, her eyes widened with alarm. "Your heart is beating very fast."

No doubt. Hers would be, too, if she'd come face-to-face with RoboCop.

"I'm fine," he insisted, although he didn't feel the least bit well.

Celeste was finishing counting out her register and would be joining him in a matter of minutes.

"I'll bring you something to calm you," she said.

"No . . . no."

"Please. You have been so nice to me."

Harry couldn't very well refuse and so he smiled, agreeing. "You're very kind."

"I hurry back."

"No rush."

Elaina left him and trotted back into the kitchen. She wasn't gone more than a couple minutes. When she returned, she carried a mug of steaming water, which she set down on the table in front of Harry.

"Sip this," she instructed. "Don't swallow fast. You understand?"

Harry nodded. Tea leaves, or what he assumed must be tea leaves, covered the bottom of the mug.

"Sip," she said again.

"I'll sip," Harry promised.

"Medicine from my country," she whispered. "It will relax you."

Harry watched as she returned to the kitchen. From the look, this was some herbal concoction she kept on hand for emergencies. Some home remedy. He took his first sip and noticed that Elaina must have added a tablespoon of honey, because the tea had a sweet taste.

Celeste approached and Harry yawned. He didn't know what it was that Elaina had put in the tea, but whatever it was had a powerful calming effect on him. Maybe it was the champagne, because now he seemed to be having trouble holding up his head. He was tempted to fold his arms and rest his head on the tabletop.

He gave Celeste a huge smile and then yawned.

She frowned. "Harry? What are you drinking now?"

"Tea. Elaina gave it to me to calm my nerves after Brady Whitall threatened me with a gun."

Celeste slowly shook her head. "I was afraid something like this would happen."

"Not only me, but that beautiful French woman, too."

"Michelle Heath," Celeste supplied.

"Right. She isn't French . . . she just speaks it."

"She's a French teacher."

Harry nodded and held up his index finger. "It

was all my fault. I accept full responsibility. No one told me what the sigh of a contented woman sounds like."

Celeste grabbed the back of the chair. "I think I better sit down."

"Good idea," Harry whispered. "Can you tell me about that? Because I can assure you there was no such lesson in heaven. No one explained about French teachers with champagne, either. Were you aware," he said, waving his finger, "there's a very particular way to open champagne? It's dangerous, I tell you. Dangerous."

"Yup," Celeste whispered, pulling out the chair, "I think it might be best if I sit down."

"You shouldn't hurry home," Harry pointed out. "It's snowing."

"Yes, I know."

"Classes were canceled."

"So I understand."

"Someone should have told me. It would have saved me from all this." He waved his hand in front of his face. "Is it hot in here or is it just me?"

"It's just you," she said kindly, and patted his hand. "I need you to tell me what transpired from your point of view. Start at the beginning."

"In the beginning, God created . . ."

"Not that beginning," she said, stopping him. "Start with the French teacher and the gun."

Harry's shoulders sagged and he covered his face

with both hands. "I don't think you're going to like this."

"Probably not," she agreed. "Go back to Michelle and the champagne. And you drank the entire bottle. Oh Harry, you should know better."

"You're right, I should have resisted." He dropped his hands and then placed one against his forehead. He'd failed when he was convinced he wouldn't have any problems. But then, he hadn't known Earth had women as lovely as Michelle Heath and drinks that tasted as wonderful as French champagne.

He'd been sent to Earth to help humans. Now he was badly in need of heaven's help.

Chapter Fourteen

"Just what are you doing?" Erich demanded when Addie breathlessly opened the front door. "I thought you were supposed to be studying for class."

"What does it look like I'm doing?" she returned, shoulders heaving with the effort of carting the five-foot-long fir tree from her car up the sidewalk and into the Simmonses' house. "I'm planting a tree in your living room." Actually, Addie was pleased with herself. It'd taken some doing getting the Christmas tree home.

"I already told you: no tree."

Addie had barely managed to get the Christmas tree through the front door, and already Erich was making noises. "Did you?" she asked, playing dumb.

"Take that ridiculous monstrosity to your house," he insisted, none too gently.

She ignored his protests and dragged the tree all the way inside his living room. Who knew a tree could be so heavy? She'd found one at the lot when she stopped off at the grocery store. It was snowing, and she simply couldn't resist. Erich had made his point, but Addie refused to accept it. It wouldn't be Christmas without one of the most important traditions.

When she happened to look his way, Addie noticed that Erich's face was tight with agitation. "It's perfectly fine if you want to put up a Christmas tree, but do it at your house and not mine."

"I would, except for one thing." She stood in the middle of the room with her hands on her hips. The tree lay on the floor in all its natural glory.

"I can hardly wait to hear this," he muttered, his words thick with sarcasm.

"You're the one in need of Christmas spirit, not me. I can't think of a better way to put you in the mood for the holidays." She hesitated. "Oh, and you might want to reconsider attending the holiday potluck with my class."

"No to both," he said, scowling.

She released a low sigh. Clearly her plan wasn't working, but she was too committed to change course now. "Okay, fine. Whatever. I'll give you an out on the potluck, but not the tree."

"I always knew you were stubborn, but this is

over the top. Would it be too much to ask you to listen to reason? This is my home, and I don't want anything to do with Christmas. Can I make it any clearer than that?"

"Message received."

"But you're not listening."

"No." He was being a Scrooge, and she wasn't going to let it happen. "Be careful or those three spirits might just pay you an uncomfortable visit," she warned.

"I'd rather deal with them than one stubborn female."

Erich looked away. With effort, she stood the tree against the wall and paused to look around to decide where best to set it up. "I bought something else while I was shopping."

"Whatever it is, it's a waste," Erich grumbled.

"You'll have to decide that for yourself," she said, as she continued to survey the room for the perfect spot for the tree. Her choices were few, but if she moved some furniture around a bit . . .

He mumbled something else, but Addie was only half listening. She reached for a small sack and brought out a sprig of mistletoe. "A waste, you say?"

"Yes, I already told you . . ." He stopped mid-sentence. The look on his face was priceless, as if he was debating how to react. "Mistletoe?"

Addie tossed him a saucy smile. "Aha, just as I

thought. You have no objection to certain aspects of Christmas."

Scowling, he refused to meet her gaze. "In the interest of compromise, keep the mistletoe, take back the tree."

"Sorry, no can do."

He mumbled something unpleasant under his breath.

"Complain all you want, Erich Simmons, but I refuse to allow you to ignore Christmas. It's not happening on my watch."

Erich tilted back his head and closed his eyes. "Why me, God? First I break both wrists and then you send me this stubborn woman who refuses to leave me be. Why? Why? Why?"

"God sent you exactly what you need," she said. Inwardly, she was pleased God had sent her, not that she'd admit it to Erich, especially when he was in this sour mood.

"Get rid of it," he returned.

"The mistletoe?"

He grumbled again and shrugged as if he didn't really care one way or the other. "You can keep that."

Addie was exhausted. This Christmas-tree business was hard labor. "My dad used to say I was stubborn. I would have thought you'd know that by now."

"Now, that's an understatement if ever there was one."

"Ah, come on, Erich, lighten up. A Christmas tree is exactly what we both need. Okay, maybe you don't, but I do," she countered. This was as much for her as for Erich.

"Okay, fine; have it your way."

"Your enthusiasm overwhelms me," she joked.

"If you're looking for enthusiasm, you'll need to search elsewhere." His face was tight and dark.

"What is it with you?" she demanded. He should at least appreciate the effort she'd made to bring a bit of cheer into his life. As a kid, she recalled that Erich had been as excited about Christmas as Jerry and she were. He might pin his bad attitude on the car accident, but there was more to it than that.

"My attitude is not changing," he said, "so you'd better get used to it."

She reached for her coat and headed toward the front door.

"Hey," he said, stopping her, "where are you going now?"

She paused in the entryway. "To my garage for the tree decorations."

"You're coming back?" The question sounded as if he wasn't sure he'd welcome her company.

"Would you rather I stay away?" She was only half-serious.

"It's tempting to say yes."

Addie grinned because she knew he didn't mean it.

For the next half hour, Addie hauled plastic containers from her garage to Erich's house. It was demanding work. Erich watched, his gaze following her movements, but he remained stubbornly silent. When she'd finished stacking the containers in the living room, she went directly into the kitchen.

"Now what are you doing?" he said, following her into the other room.

She opened and closed cupboard doors. "I'm looking for a pan to pop popcorn."

"You're hungry?"

She shouldn't need to explain. "In case you're unaware, it's impossible to decorate a Christmas tree properly without eating popcorn and listening to the appropriate music."

"What's wrong with microwave popcorn?"

It shocked her that he was unaware of the most basic Christmas traditions. "It's not the same. Real popcorn is popped on the stove."

"This is a joke, right?"

She glared at him with a look that would have melted kryptonite.

"Okay, okay, you're serious," he said and backed away. "I'm sorry I asked."

He returned to the other room and Addie was just as glad. While he was out of sight, she set her phone on the kitchen counter and went into her playlist for her favorite Christmas songs, everything from Bing Crosby to Bruno Mars.

The popcorn smelled heavenly, and the scent of it soon swirled through the house. Addie filled a

large bowl, brought it into the living room, and set
it on the end table next to Erich.

He glanced at her, then the popcorn, and announced, "I'm going to my room."

"Have it your way." This disappointed Addie,
but she refused to let him know it. The music
played as she cheerfully strung the lights around
the tree, stopping now and again to nibble on popcorn. It really tasted so much better popped the
old-fashioned way.

She finished the lights and had started hanging
the ornaments when Erich returned. He slumped
down into his chair as if he expected her to make
a derogatory comment. Instead she came over to
the chair, leaned over, and kissed him, letting her
mouth linger playfully over his for several breathtaking seconds. Then, without a word, she returned
to the task at hand, placing the ornaments on the
tree.

"You need a few more toward the left-hand side
of the tree," Erich instructed, sounding breathless
following their kiss.

Stepping back, Addie tilted her head to one side
and then the other. "You're right."

"Everyone's a critic," he said, almost regretfully.

The last decoration was the angel for the top of
the tree. Addie brought it out of the protective box
and studied it. The angel's white dress had faded
over the years and her wings weren't what they'd

once been; still, she was beautiful to Addie because of all the memories associated with her.

"Dad bought this for Mom the first year they were married," she said, carefully cradling the figurine in her hands. "He always waited until Christmas Eve before he placed her on the tree. We'd attend church services and come home around nine or ten. Then Dad, with a great deal of ceremony, would put the angel on top of the tree."

"Traditions are important," Erich surprised her by commenting.

"They are. It's those memories that stay with us, that bond us as family. It's one of the reasons I made sure I was home nearly every Christmas. I couldn't imagine not baking cookies with Mom, or decorating the tree with my father. We might have argued a good portion of the time, but it would be unthinkable to give up that special time together because of our differences."

She'd finished with everything except the angel, which she tucked back into the box. Pushing the empty containers out of the way, she stepped back and then slowly smiled. "I don't care what you say, this is one truly beautiful Christmas tree."

He shrugged.

"Oh come on, Erich, admit it, this tree is gorgeous."

"I'll admit nothing of the sort."

"Twit." That was a name he'd called her as a kid, when she'd get upset with his teasing.

He grinned as if he, too, remembered the name-calling of their youth. "When do you intend to put up that mistletoe?"

"Soon. But I seem to remember kissing you only a few minutes ago."

He smiled for the first time that afternoon. "And to think you didn't even need to pay me," he said, referring to her childhood attempt to buy a kiss.

"Very funny. Consider that kiss a reward."

"What'd I do?"

"You left your room and joined me."

"I did that because I was bored and the smell of the popcorn was too hard to ignore."

"I don't care what brought you back; I'm simply glad you decided to be with me."

"I could leave and come back again," he said, his eyes sparkling.

Addie held on to his gaze before glancing about the room. "I'm going to need a bit of help deciding where to place the mistletoe. I've heard certain areas of the house offer advantages over others."

"I'm at your service." He urged her toward the archway that led from the entry to the living room. "How about here?"

"Yes, this location looks promising."

Erich brought her into his embrace. "Don't be hasty. We should try it out first. This is an important decision, after all." Before she could comment, he leaned down and kissed her. The kiss they'd exchanged earlier was a prelude to the potency of this one. His arms were heavy on her shoulders, but Addie barely noticed as she tilted back her head and opened to him. The kiss went on until they were both breathless. Erich broke away, his shoulders heaving. He kept his eyes closed.

"Well?" she asked, her voice unsteady. "Should we place it here?"

"It's definitely in the running, but let's not be too quick to make this all-important decision. What about the hallway?"

Addie laughed softly and tightened her grip around his middle.

"You don't agree?"

"Of course. Location is of great significance."

Erich kissed the tip of her nose. "I feel we should test several rooms. Give each area ample consideration."

Addie gazed up at him, marveling that this thing between them was real. "Can you believe this is happening, Erich?"

"What?"

"Us kissing. I never would have believed it."

"Me neither. I never liked you, you know?"

She didn't need the reminder, especially since the feeling was mutual. "And how do you feel now?"

"And now," he repeated in a whisper. "The truth is, Addie, I can't stop thinking about you. You've changed, I've changed. You're wise and funny, caring, nonjudgmental, and fun. When you're away I wish you were with me, and I wonder how long it

will be before I can see you again. I told myself it
was the circumstances, my situation, and then I
realized I don't care what it is. I like you. I can't
help myself. I enjoy your company."

"Really?" Addie was far too tongue-tied to say
anything more.

"It's crazy, isn't it?"

"Crazy and wonderful," she agreed. "Now tell
me you're happy about the Christmas tree."

The warmth in his gaze faded ever so slightly.
"Can't do it, sorry, but I am extremely happy that
you're here. The last thing I intend to do when I'm
holding you is argue. Now let's test out that mistletoe in another room."

Addie pressed her finger against his lips. "Before
we do, I need to ask you something."

He frowned. "Okay, ask, just as long as it doesn't
have anything to do with Christmas."

"No, my literature class."

"Ask me later," he murmured, and lowered his
head to claim another kiss. All too soon any
thoughts or questions were gone from her mind.

Chapter Fifteen

Harry was nervous and uncomfortable. This was an unfamiliar emotion for angels. He wanted to talk to Celeste and share his concerns, but once he did, he was afraid she'd deem it necessary to send him scooting back to heaven. Heaven was wonderful. He wouldn't want to give anyone the wrong impression. It was just that he'd worked so long and hard to earn this position on Earth.

Thankfully, class had gone well, even with the summons to Dr. Conceito's office resting on his desktop. The entire period, Harry had done his best to ignore the request.

Meet me in my office following your class.
President Conceito
Southshore Community College

Harry didn't need to speculate as to the reason he'd been asked to visit the college president's office. He assumed Brady Whitall, the security guard, had gone directly to Dr. Conceito following the disaster the afternoon it'd snowed.

Harry dismissed class. The papers his students had written on the Dickens novel were scattered about his desktop. He lifted a handful and straightened the pile while he mulled over the confrontation awaiting him.

Danny Wade stood in front of the desk. Harry liked the young man. Danny tended to speak his mind and had no qualms about sharing the fact that he'd served time in prison. He seemed to believe his public record earned him a certain amount of respect with his peers.

"Hey, Mr. Mills."

"Yes, Danny?"

Danny was a big guy, tall, with broad shoulders. The tattoo ran halfway down one side of his thick neck. As large as he was, Danny would have excelled if he had turned out for football in high school. Being in sports—part of a team—would have helped him avoid trouble.

"Are you going to take points off for spelling on those papers you had us write? 'Cause I don't spell so good."

"No worries, Danny. Content is more important to me than spelling," he assured him.

"Content? What's content?"

"What you wrote. The meaning behind the words."

Danny rubbed his hand across the back of his neck. "Then why didn't you just say so in the first place? I like this book. It's nothing I would normally read, though."

"So you enjoy reading?"

Danny shrugged. "We got books when I was in prison. I read a few and they were okay, but this Dickens guy . . . he's deep, man. Real deep. He made me think about the stuff I've done and how it's affected others, and it makes me wonder, you know?"

"That's good, Danny."

"I went to see my mama. She's messed up, but I told her I was taking a college class and I could see she was impressed. She didn't ever think one of her kids would go to college. I told her I was gonna make something of myself, and I will."

"I know you will," Harry said, as he collected the remaining papers. "You're doing just fine in this class."

"I never did good in school before, but when Mr. Anderson, he's my parole officer, suggested I take a class, I came to the college. This was the only class that had space available, and I wasn't going to take a class that made me read, but then Mr. Anderson said that it would help me get a job. I'm going to need a job to stay out of trouble, so that was when I decided I was going to do it, so now I'm here."

"That was a good decision. Just keep doing the next right thing, Danny, and you'll be fine."

"I'm doing okay in this class?" His look was almost childlike, his eyes wide and hopeful.

"I'd say you're doing better than okay."

Danny's wide smile was immediate, showing his teeth. "Some in class say I talk too much. You think that, too, Mr. Mills?"

"Not too much," Harry said, carefully choosing his words, unwilling to squelch Danny's enthusiasm. The young man wasn't the least bit shy about sharing his opinions, that was a given. "But it might be a good idea to give others a chance to share once in a while," Harry added.

Danny was completely readable, and some of the excitement left his eyes.

"But I wouldn't want you to stop contributing in class. Your thoughts are impressive and add another layer to our discussion."

The spark returned in Danny's eyes, and Harry was relieved.

"Mr. Mills, being in your class makes me want to open up. It's weird, no teacher's ever done that before." Harry could barely hide his surprise and delight at this comment.

"I was thinking I would bring my mama to the potluck we're having," Danny continued. "She isn't much of a cook, though."

"You bring her, Danny. I'd be happy to meet her, and don't you worry about contributing anything. There's going to be lots of food."

Harry didn't have time to dally long. Keeping Dr. Conceito waiting wasn't a good idea. "Looking forward to meeting her," Harry said, as he reached for his briefcase.

Danny's grin was huge. "Good talking to you, Mr. Mills." Danny tucked the Dickens novel into his coat pocket and headed out the door.

"Good talking to you, too," Harry whispered, as the young man disappeared down the hallway. Danny showed a great deal of promise, and Harry sincerely hoped that God would choose him to guide Danny Wade when the time was right.

Harry draped his coat over his forearm and was ready to leave when he was stopped yet again.

Michelle Heath stood framed in the doorway, holding on to a slip of paper identical to the one Harry had received earlier in the day.

"Oh Harry," she whispered, her face a mask of concern. "This is all my fault. I am so sorry."

"Dr. Conceito wanted to see you, too?" This was bad news. Harry was certain he'd been the only one targeted, no thanks to Brady Whitall. It went without saying that the security guard had taken delight in informing the college president of their infraction against school policy. The janitor might have ratted on her as well.

"I should never have brought the champagne

here," Michelle continued. "Dr. Conceito has a real thing against any form of alcoholic beverage on campus grounds. I assumed that since classes were dismissed, we'd be alone and . . ."

"We'll explain what happened," Harry said, doing his best to disguise his own concern.

"I would have invited you to my house . . . I should have, but I didn't think you'd come and so I planned this little surprise, not realizing. Oh dear, I feel dreadful, just dreadful."

"We aren't children being called to task," Harry said, and pushed his eyeglasses farther up his nose. Although that was exactly the way he felt—like a child sent to the principal's office for misbehavior.

"We should go together, don't you think?" Michelle asked. "And explain."

"Good idea."

Michelle wrapped her arm around his elbow and briefly leaned her head against his shoulder. "I feel better already, just talking to you."

"Me, too."

She looked up at him with the roundest, most beautiful eyes he'd ever seen. Her gaze was filled with hope and something else he couldn't read. Admiration? Infatuation? Harry couldn't tell, but whatever it was stirred his blood and the desire to protect her.

"You forgive me, don't you, Harry?"

"There's nothing to forgive." When he first met Michelle, Harry found himself flummoxed by her attention. After that first meeting he recognized that this woman could easily distract him from his mission. On Celeste's advice, he'd avoided Michelle as best he could. The problem was, they saw each other nearly every day, passing in the hallway. Lately it'd become his habit to stop and chat with her a few minutes here and there between classes. In the process, he'd become comfortable with her. Way too comfortable.

Celeste had warned him to avoid anything hinting at romance with a human. It would complicate his mission, possibly compromise it. Harry couldn't allow that to happen, and he wouldn't. Still, he found he'd grown fond of Michelle. He liked the way she tucked her arm around his and leaned her head against his shoulder. It was those human emotions again, warring with his earthly mission.

When Harry and Michelle arrived, Dr. Conceito was waiting inside his office. They were ushered in and thoroughly lectured. They remained for thirty or more minutes and explained the circumstances. Thankfully, the meeting didn't go as badly as Harry feared. They were reprimanded and then sent on their merry way. Harry realized he would need to tread carefully from this point forward or he might find himself without a job. Then Celeste would have no option but to send him back.

Michelle and Harry parted outside the office. She had things she needed to do, and for that matter, so did he.

Now that the meeting was over, Harry felt he should talk to Celeste. He found her at the coffee stand in the Hub. She wasn't busy when he sidled up to the counter, and while he avoided making eye contact, she focused her attention squarely on him.

Right away, Celeste asked, "How'd the meeting go with Dr. Conceito?"

Harry shrugged. "All right, I guess."

"The news of the two of you is circulating the campus."

"What are people saying?"

"What do you think, Harry?" she asked, sounding concerned. "Word has it that you have a thing for the French teacher and that both of you've been called out. And you already know who started that rumor."

Harry didn't need two guesses. "Brady?"

"Most likely," Celeste concurred. "I wish you'd talked to me before the meeting with Dr. Conceito."

Harry felt her disappointment.

"You don't ever need to be afraid to tell me something," his mentor continued. "I'm here to help with your adjustment in the same way that you're helping your students."

Celeste was right. He should rely on her more.

"So tell me," Celeste said, as she set an Americano on the counter for Harry, "how do you feel after dealing with Dr. Conceito?"

"Better."

Celeste pinned him with a look that had the potential to cut him in half. "Because Michelle went with you?" she asked.

He probably shouldn't admit the truth, but that was unavoidable. "Yes."

"You seem to be falling for her. Are you?" Celeste was nothing if not direct.

Again, lying wasn't an option. "Is that bad?"

"Not really. We are blessed with feelings and emotions. It's all part of being human, even if only for a short time when we're on Earth. The key is learning to adjust. We have to remember that while we might live as humans, we aren't actually human." She paused and studied him for a few moments. "I hope that makes sense."

More and more it did.

"But for Michelle's sake and yours, do not become romantically involved," Celeste warned.

"Duly noted." Harry was more determined than ever to keep his distance from the French teacher, lest he succumb to her charms.

"Now tell me about the potluck," Celeste said.

Harry brightened. It'd been a spur-of-the-moment decision. Classes would be dismissed over Christmas and New Year's but would start up again after the first of the year. The students were just beginning to know one another and become friends. Harry wanted to encourage that. He'd suggested a Christmas potluck and invited the class to bring a favorite dish and a friend to the last session before the break. The response had been enthusiastic.

"Can you come?" he asked.

"If I'm not working."

"I hope you will."

"I'd like that," Celeste said. "It is a good idea. By the way, how is the war veteran in your class working out thus far?"

"Andrew Fairfax?" Harry was concerned about the young man, who had remained silent throughout each session. A number of times Harry had tried to engage him in the discussion. To this point, he'd had little success.

"Andrew is a complicated case," he said, assessing his student. Harry was anxious to read Andrew's file, which would tell him a lot about where the man was mentally.

"I agree," Celeste said, echoing his thoughts.

"Will I be assigned to help him along with Tommy?" Harry asked. He smiled at the prospect of working alongside an angel who'd taken the form of a dog.

"Not right away. Tommy is his constant companion, but the time is coming when Tommy will leave him. When that happens, it's going to be a rough road for Andrew. I want to be sure you're available then."

"I will be," Harry promised.

"Now give me an update on Addie," Celeste

said, and hopped onto a stool on the other side of the counter.

This was by far a more comfortable subject for Harry. Celeste very well knew everything Harry did. What she wanted, he suspected, was his perspective on the situation.

Harry couldn't hold back a grin. "She brought him a Christmas tree, and despite his protests, set it up in his house. Oh, and she tacked up mistletoe. Say, can you explain what it is with mistletoe?" he asked. He'd been meaning to find out but had gotten sidetracked. "Addie and Erich took it from room to room and kissed. I couldn't figure it out. Seems to be potent stuff. Funny, I've never heard of anything like this before now."

The smile on Celeste's face was huge. "I'll explain it later."

"Erich is being stubborn about Christmas," Harry said, continuing the update on the two. "Addie is doing her best to ignore it."

"Addie has come a long way," Celeste said, and sounded pleased.

Harry wished he could take more credit for the changes in his young charge. The truth was, he'd done very little.

"Her father is proud of the changes he sees in her."

"You've talked to her father?" Harry asked, unable to hide his surprise.

"Well, yes. Why else do you think you're here?

He was the one who asked for angelic intervention, and God granted his request. It's because of him that you received this assignment."

Harry had had no idea. "Should I do anything about Erich?" he asked.

Celeste sadly shook her head. "Erich isn't your concern. He isn't one of your students. Your ability to influence and guide is available to only those in your class. I'm surprised you need the reminder."

"I didn't . . . I was hoping is all."

"It is a bit of a disappointment. I understand Addie wants him to come to the Christmas pot-luck, but he refuses. That's unfortunate."

"She's disappointed, but that isn't going to stop her from attending." Harry was fairly certain she wouldn't allow Erich or his attitude to keep her away.

"It's gratifying to see how well you've worked with Addie," Celeste said, complimenting him. She got very serious then. "Now let's go back to your meeting with Dr. Conceito."

Harry looked down at the hot coffee and pondered his time with the college president. "As you can imagine, he was upset about Michelle and me indulging in a bottle of champagne on school property."

"That's to be expected."

Harry had gotten good news, though. "He said he was willing to make an exception this one time because classes had been dismissed due to the snow."

Needless to say, Harry and Michelle had been deeply relieved to have gotten a reprieve.

"But one more instance and . . ."

"One more instance and I am in danger of losing my job," Harry reluctantly admitted.

Celeste sat back and heaved a heavy sigh. "Dr. Conceito is an interesting man," she said, almost as if she was speaking to herself. "He keeps a bottle of bourbon in his bottom desk drawer."

Harry was unable to hide his shock. Dr. Conceito had a drinking problem? "He needs angelic intervention," he said, wondering if the day would come when he would personally receive the assignment.

"He does need help," Celeste agreed, "but right now his heart is too hard for him to be open to the kind of help we can provide. But hopefully that will change."

Chapter Sixteen

Addie was just about to get ready for bed when the lights flickered. She hesitated when it happened again. This time, the lights went out and stayed out. After waiting a couple minutes to see if they came back on, she reached for her phone, turning on the flashlight app, and found her way into the kitchen, where her father always kept the regular flashlight. Thankfully, it was still there.

For most of her growing-up years, Addie had thought of her father as a stuffed shirt, which was probably a term few people used any longer. She'd overheard it once and thought it suited her father perfectly. Now that he was gone she didn't feel nearly as judgmental. In fact, she was grateful he was the kind of person who took care to be so prepared and organized. Finding the flashlight was quick and easy, thanks to his pragmatic nature.

She checked at the window and saw that it wasn't just her house. The entire street was without electricity. Then she wondered about Erich. She'd left him after only a quick visit following class and dinner. He'd been grumpy ever since she'd set up the Christmas tree, which he continued to complain about every visit. As a result, she'd spent less time with him for the last few days. Still, he was her responsibility, and she couldn't ignore him, especially if the power was off.

Addie selected him from her contact list and hoped he had his phone close at hand.

"Hello," he grumbled.

"Hi. You okay?" she asked.

"Is there a reason I shouldn't be?"

She could see his mood hadn't improved. "Are you in bed?"

He hesitated. "No, but I can be if that's what you'd like."

"Very funny."

"Hey, I was serious."

"I'm not playing around," she said. "In case you hadn't noticed, the power's out."

"Yeah, I know."

"Then you're okay?"

Her question was followed by a short pause. "Do you want to come over and hang out?"

"Is that what you'd like?"

He didn't hesitate. "Yes. Do you have your pajamas on?"

"No," she drawled, "but I can put them on if you want me to."

He chuckled. "Come on over."

By all that was right she should ignore him and go back to bed, just the way she'd planned. However, she found his invitation too irresistible to refuse.

"Okay, I'll be there in a few minutes."

The street was coal dark. Thick clouds obliterated any chance of moonlight reflecting off the remaining snow. Without the flashlight, Addie didn't know if she could have walked the short distance between the two homes without incident.

As was her custom, she knocked once and let herself into the house. "Erich?" she called from the entryway.

"In here."

She flashed the light into the living room to find him sitting in the recliner.

"Any idea what happened to cause the power to go out?" he asked.

"It isn't the weather, as far as I can see." The wind or snowfall was often a cause of electrical failures, but the storm had come and gone before they lost power.

"No doubt demand is bigger than supply," he complained. "All these lights. It's ridiculous. Half the street is lit up with decorations. It's a waste of energy."

"Oh, honestly. What is it with you? You weren't like this when we were kids. I'm totally confused by your attitude."

"Don't worry about it."

"What changed, Erich?"

"I grew up. Now sit and hang awhile, okay?"

"First you have to promise no more complaining."

"If it means you'll stay."

"Deal." She hesitated. "Would you like me to build a fire in the fireplace?" That would create a romantic atmosphere and perhaps put Erich in a better mood.

"No thanks."

So much for that. She sat in the chair next to his and gradually relaxed. Addie had missed spending time with him. Refusing to allow him to dominate her time and, more important, her head, had taken some doing. She'd needed time away to put order to her thoughts. This thing with him and Christmas was rooted in something deeper than he was saying. Whatever had happened, he clearly had no intention of sharing with her, and she found that upsetting. They'd come a long way in the last ten days.

They sat in the dark in companionable silence for several minutes. Not being able to see him offered a unique sense of freedom. In a strange way it lowered Addie's walls and allowed her to feel she could be more open, honest, and direct with him.

After a while, Erich said, "I've missed seeing you the last couple days."

So the darkness freed him to share his own feelings with her, too.

"I've been here," she said.

"True, but you were in and out as if you had places to go and people to see. You didn't seem to have much time for me."

It did her heart good to see that Erich had noticed her absence. "Guilty as charged."

"Is it about Christmas?"

"I was tired of hearing you whine. But, yes, the truth is, I also had things to do."

"Like?"

"I went shopping."

"At the mall?" he asked incredulously. "Are you crazy? This time of year it's a madhouse—"

"Grocery shopping," she said, cutting him off, "for the class potluck."

"Ah yes, I forgot about that. Thanks for not bugging me about it."

"I believe you made your decision perfectly clear." It rankled that he'd refused her invitation and hurt her feelings. "As it happened, I asked someone else."

Right away, she could tell he was suspicious. "Who?"

"You don't want to go with me, so it's none of your business."

"Male or female?"

"Does it matter?"

"Yes," he countered sharply. "It matters to me."

"Why?" she asked.

Silence. "Why?" he repeated. "Because I've got a thing for you."

"A thing? Translate, please."

Again he hesitated. "I like you . . . a lot. No one is more surprised over this than I am. For a long time I had trouble believing it, but then you kissed me—"

"Hold on a minute," she said, stopping him. "I kissed you? I sort of thought you were the one who kissed me."

"Getting back to my point."

"Yes," she said, displaying the utmost patience.

"I will if you stop interrupting me."

Addie grinned.

"The point is, I'm falling for you, Addie. I didn't much like it at first."

"Well, thank you ever so much." The man needed a bit of tutoring when it came to giving compliments.

"That didn't come out right. I mean, think about it: We have history, and most of it is negative. And then I had to rely on you for practically everything, which didn't do much for my ego. I wasn't sure what to expect, but frankly, it's been great. Better than great, and it all started about the time we first kissed."

Addie had to agree, it hadn't been easy in the beginning. They'd been tentative with each other, hesitant and unsure. That hadn't lasted long, though, and she was grateful. The only thing that stood between them now was whatever had led to his attitude toward Christmas.

"Do you remember the last time we were in the dark?" Addie asked. She remembered that night all too well. "That was when you told me about Ashley."

The room went silent for the longest time.

"Ah yes, Ashley."

Addie strained harder, fearing she heard longing in his voice as he said the other woman's name. It came to her then what should have been obvious all along—something she'd chosen to ignore. "You're still in love with her, aren't you?"

It took him a minute to admit the truth. "I was at one time, not anymore."

"I don't believe you. You still love her." Addie's stomach felt as though someone had given her a swift, hard kick.

"No," he insisted. "I was honest with you before; for a time I was crazy about her, and if you must know, I was devastated when she broke up with me. I'd never experienced pain like that." He laughed softly. "Girls had broken up with me more than once, so it was hard to understand why it hit me so much harder this time around. Then I realized it was the way she did it. She waited until she knew I was in really deep and it would cut me to the core."

The thought of Erich loving another woman completely unsettled Addie. She had no right to feel that way—she had no claim on him. But that didn't change how it affected her to hear it. Addie took a moment to absorb this mixed bag of emotions that assailed her.

"No comment?" he asked, after several taut seconds in which neither spoke.

"What would you like me to say?"

He chuckled, his amusement drifting into the darkness like smoke dissipating in the wind. "I'd hoped you'd be insanely jealous."

"That can be arranged."

He laughed again. "Were you this witty when we were kids?"

It hit her then, and she sat up straight as a stick pin. "Hold on a minute," Addie murmured, and placed her hands on top of her head. Everything was starting to add up.

"What?" he asked, sounding concerned.

"Erich, when did Ashley break up with you?"

"Why do you want to know?"

"Just answer the question." She wasn't about to let him get away without answering.

He hesitated and then answered on the tail end of a sigh. "On Christmas Day. We were with family and I got down on one knee to propose and . . . well, you can imagine the rest."

"I knew it. I knew it."

"What did you know?"

"It isn't just *this* Christmas that's got you down. You're still dying for the beautiful Ashley . . . the love of your life. That's the reason you're so negative about the holidays. That's the reason you didn't want me to put up the Christmas tree, or cook a special dinner. You're living in the past, holding on to the memory of a broken heart, hanging on to the pain."

Addie leaped out of the chair. All at once it was much too difficult to sit in one place. For reasons she had yet to digest, she was red-hot angry. "How long do you intend to stay hidden while your heart heals?"

"Ashley and I are finished. When I saw her the other day it was hard for me to believe I could ever have loved her."

"Right, and that was great for your pride, too, wasn't it?"

"Yes, but it was necessary. What I don't understand is why you're so mad."

"You," she cried. "You make me furious. You know what? I don't think I can do this any longer."

"Do what?"

She didn't want to be rash and say something she would later regret. "I think it might be best if I left now. You don't need me."

"You're wrong, Addie. I need you more than ever. I don't understand why you're offended. What did I say? All I know is that I don't want you to leave until we settle this. I did love Ashley, I'll admit it, but it's over. I swear to you it's over."

Addie sucked in a deep breath and exhaled it, torn about what she should do. Before she could decide, the lights on the Christmas tree went on, and flashes of red, blue, and green filled the room, warming it with color.

"The electricity is back," she whispered.

"No, it's not. The lamp and the television are still off. The only lights are the ones on the tree, which I didn't have on to begin with. What's going on?"

Addie glanced out the window, and he was right. The streetlights were still off, and so were the other lights in the neighborhood. Not a one shone in the darkness. The only lights that she could see were those on the Christmas tree.

"That's really strange," she whispered.

"It's more than strange. This isn't possible," he said.

"Maybe it's a sign," Addie suggested.

"Who from?"

"One of the three spirits from the Dickens novel," Addie said, teasing. "I warned you this negative attitude of yours was going to get you in trouble. Well, here you are."

Whatever it was, she would leave him to it. "All I can say is, you're on your own."

He followed her to the front door. "Addie," he whispered, touching her shoulder.

She turned around.

His gaze held her captive. "I don't want you to be angry with me."

"I'm not angry. It just bothers me that you're choosing to hang on to your pain, because it means you're not over Ashley as much as you think."

"Don't be so sure," he murmured, as he reached for her and brought her close. "Kiss me and show me you aren't upset."

"I shouldn't."

"Yes, you should," he insisted, and lowered his mouth to capture hers.

The kiss left her weak in the knees, a kiss that she felt all the way to the soles of her feet. It was as if he had to prove to her in a single kiss that he was completely over the other woman.

"Addie?" he whispered, dragging his mouth reluctantly from hers.

"Hmmm?" she asked, unwilling to open her eyes.

"Will I see you in the morning?"

She nodded. Despite everything she already knew, it would be much too hard for her to stay away.

Chapter Seventeen

With Christmas music playing in the background, Addie slid the last sheet of cookies inside the oven and turned on the timer. She set the oven mitt aside when her phone rang.

As soon as she saw it was Erich, a sense of happiness filled her. She'd taken him breakfast an hour ago, lingering a few minutes while he ate. It'd been a good visit. He'd talked to her a bit more about his relationship with Ashley, opening up to her.

Their talk the night before seemed to have given him a lot to think about.

"I did love Ashley," he'd admitted. "But there's something more I didn't tell you because my pride wouldn't let me. Ashley didn't love me at all. She didn't know what it meant to love one person. She's the kind of woman who will always seek attention from other men, without ever caring for them. The word *faithful* isn't part of her vocabulary."

She hadn't wanted to test his newfound openness, so she'd left before wearing out her welcome.

"Hi," she now greeted him, as she answered the phone.

"What are you doing?" he asked.

"Baking cookies," she reminded him. She'd told him her plans for that morning before she left.

This recipe was one her mother had always baked for the holidays. Peanut butter was one of the main ingredients, and then just before the cookies were completely cooked, she added a chocolate kiss to the top and set them back inside the oven. The chocolate didn't melt completely, but just got gooey and creamy. They'd been her favorite as a kid, and it didn't seem like Christmas without them.

"Don't tell me you miss me already."

"I've had lots of family and friends stop by ever since my accident, but the only person I ever really want to see is you."

"Anyone ever tell you you're a smooth talker?"

"Will my sweet talk earn me any of those cookies you're baking?"

"It might." Addie enjoyed the banter between them. It seemed good that they could have had such a serious discussion only an hour earlier and then could laugh and tease each other now.

"You still plan on attending that potluck?"

"Yes, what makes you ask?"

He paused. "You never said who you'd asked to join you."

"You're right, I didn't." Mainly because she hadn't actually invited anyone else. Pride insisted she not admit this fact to Erich. Pride could be a demanding master, she'd come to learn.

Then again, Erich had opened up to her that morning. "If you must know . . . I didn't invite anyone else. You're the only person I wanted to bring with me."

The line went still and silent. "I called because I was wondering if it was too late to accept your invitation."

"Because you were jealous?"

"No, because I really do want to come with you . . . okay, and maybe I was a little jealous, but that's not my primary reason."

Addie didn't care what his excuse was. "Oh Erich, I'm so glad. I'd love to have you with me."

"You know what? I think I'm actually going to enjoy this. And you're right. It's time I put this thing I have about Christmas behind me."

"That's great."

He chuckled. "Do I sound anything like Scrooge on Christmas morning?"

"Not quite, but you're getting there."

*   *   *

Several hours later, Addie parked in the school parking lot and hurried around to open the passenger door and help Erich out of her car. He held the plate of cookies in his lap, and she reached for those.

"You didn't bring the entire batch, did you?" he asked.

"No worries, I set aside a dozen for you," she promised.

Right there in the middle of the school parking lot, he rewarded her with a lingering kiss. It took every bit of control Addie possessed not to drop the cookies to the ground and wrap her arms around him.

"Hey, hey," a familiar voice shouted from behind her.

Addie reluctantly broke away from Erich to see Danny walking toward her. At his side was a stylishly dressed woman with a wide-brimmed hat fit for royalty. "Merry Christmas, Danny," she said, feeling a bit sheepish that she'd been caught kissing Erich.

"Yo, Addie. Meet my mother, Tamika. Mom, this is the girl I was telling you about."

Addie looked at the woman, amazed that someone so young could be Danny's mother. "I'm pleased to meet you. Danny's been doing great. He adds a lot to the class."

Danny's eyes beamed with pride. "I told you, Mom. I'm at the head of the class."

Tamika Jackson nodded shyly and stayed close to her son's side.

"Erich Simmons," Erich said, introducing himself. "I'd shake hands, but as you can see it's difficult at the moment."

"I heard about you," Danny said, flashing him a big smile.

"Have you, now?" Erich's gaze shot to Addie.

"Yeah, Addie told me she'd asked you to our party and you turned her down. Glad you decided to come after all."

"I am, too. I've heard lots about you, too."

Danny looked happy. He turned his attention to Addie. "What'd you bring?" he said, eyeing the foil-covered plate.

"Cookies. What about you?"

"Mama don't cook much, and I sure don't, so we stopped off at the store and I got Twinkies."

"Well, it looks like we're going to have plenty of desserts."

"No worries," Danny told her. "Andrew's bringing a pot of chili. His sister made it for him."

"This should be one interesting potluck," Erich mumbled, close to Addie's ear.

"It isn't about the food," Addie whispered back.

The four walked into the building together. Several classmates had already arrived and a table had been set up along one wall, with a paper tablecloth printed with holly and red berries. Addie set down the plate of cookies next to a Crock-Pot full of simmering meatballs. They were covered in what smelled like a hickory-flavored barbecue sauce. Danny proudly opened the box of Twinkies.

The room was soon full. Apparently, Mr. Mills had wanted to make sure he included everyone. Even Elaina, the woman who worked in the cafeteria, was there.

"I have an invitation," she explained, as she set a large plate of tamales in the center of the table. "Mr. Mills invited me and I asked my supervisor and she said I could come as long as my shift was over. I'm not working." She spoke directly to the janitor, Jonas Spelling.

"I'm glad you're here, Elaina," Mr. Mills said, coming up behind the cafeteria worker and placing his hands on her shoulders.

The tamales were piping hot. "I made them fresh."

"Wonderful."

Michelle Heath, who taught the French class down the hall, stopped by with macarons, though they weren't anything like the coconut ones Addie knew. These looked as if they were made from two meringue cookies pressed together, with filling in the middle.

Just as Danny had said, Andrew arrived with Tommy, with a large pot of chili.

Another woman who wasn't a student was one of the last to arrive. It took Addie a moment to place her. It was Celeste from the Hub, the woman who worked at the latte stand. She brought scones, adding to the assortment of desserts.

The desks had been shifted about until they formed a circle. Mr. Mills stood in the center of the room and asked for their attention. "Before we fill our plates, I'd like everyone to go around the room and introduce themselves and their guests."

They started with Danny, who was generally the first to speak up. "Everyone knows I'm Danny and this is my mama," he said with pride, as he placed his arm around his mother's shoulders. "She won't say much."

"She won't need to, with you doing all the talking for her," someone called out, and the rest of the class laughed.

The two young high school students went next. Addie had barely spoken to either one and made a mental note to get to know them better after the first of the year.

When it was her turn, she introduced Erich. "Erich and I grew up next door to each other."

"We weren't always friendly," Erich went on to explain. "It's only been in the last couple weeks that we've learned to get along." He smiled at Addie.

"Now they're really getting *friendly*," Danny announced. "I ran into them making out in the parking lot."

Everyone laughed and clapped.

When it was the janitor's turn, he stepped forward. "Jonas Spelling. Most of you won't recognize me without me holding my broom. I'm here at Mr. Mills's invitation. I wasn't sure about him when he first arrived, but he keeps a clean classroom. I take my job as custodian seriously. I have custody of this building. It's my responsibility."

Elaina blushed when it was her turn, and she spoke in Spanish until she looked at the confused faces of those around her. "I'm sorry," she said in English. "I forget to speak English when I'm nervous. I work in the cafeteria, and Mr. Mills invited me, too."

"I invited the security guard, too, but he was unable to attend," added Mr. Mills.

"He's probably cleaning his gun," muttered Michelle Heath, under her breath. Addie was fairly certain she wasn't supposed to hear.

"Before we help ourselves to this fine meal," Mr. Mills said, "I'd like to say what a pleasure it is to have each one of you in the class. You've welcomed and encouraged me. Merry Christmas and God bless."

"Merry Christmas," the group echoed back.

As they formed a line at the table, Addie thought she caught sight of someone outside the window, attempting to look inside. But when she went to gaze outside, she couldn't see anyone.

Erich joined her. "What are you looking for?"

"Nothing," she assured him. "I thought I saw someone." It was probably her imagination. Anyone who wanted to come into the building was welcome. The doors weren't locked.

"I understand now why you've enjoyed this class so much. They're cool."

Addie's gaze drifted around the room. They'd started out as strangers and had become her friends. "They're great. I love Danny's enthusiasm, and I've got a soft spot for Andrew."

"Do you have a soft spot for me?" Erich asked, holding her look.

She offered him an affectionate smile. "Not in the same way. Do you remember what you told me the other day?" she asked, and then elaborated. "What you said about thinking about me all the time and missing me when I wasn't there?"

"I meant every word."

"The thing is, I feel the same way about you, Erich. It bothered me that you refused to enjoy Christmas because of an old girlfriend."

"I think I'm finally getting over it. Remember last night when the power went out?"

Addie wasn't likely to forget. "Of course."

"When the tree lights came on and nothing else did, I realized how stupid I've been. The thing is . . ." He hesitated and looked around the room, then lowered his voice. "The thing I realized," he said, starting again, "is that if Ashley was in my life I would never have had this time with you. I wouldn't have ever known what an amazing woman you are."

"Does this mean you're going to stop complaining and start enjoying the holiday?" she asked.

"Bring on the holiday cheer. This Scrooge has had a change of heart."

Addie laughed and leaned her head against his shoulder. "What will our mothers think once they're back from the cruise, I wonder?" she asked.

"I can't speak for yours . . . mine is going to be excited."

"Mine, too," Addie assured him. "I realize that in a few weeks everything will be different. The casts will be off and you obviously won't be dependent on me or anyone else anymore."

"My feelings for you aren't going to change."

"You can't be sure of that," she said. "I understand, I mean . . ."

"Addie." He turned her around and held her look prisoner. "The only thing that's going to change is that I'll return to my own condo. I assumed after Ashley that I'd never be able to feel this deeply about another woman again. You proved me wrong. In case you haven't figured it out yet, I'm really crazy about you."

Addie swore her heart swelled to twice its normal size just hearing those words. "I've fallen pretty hard for you, too."

A slow, easy smile slid into place. "Where's the mistletoe when you need it?" Erich complained.

"I don't think we need mistletoe," she whispered.

His gaze held hers for the longest moment, and it felt as if she could melt into a puddle. Falling for Erich was the biggest surprise of her life. She wasn't sure where it would lead or if it would last. One thing she did know: This was bound to be one of the best Christmases of her life.

Epilogue

"That was a lovely party," Celeste said, after everyone had cleared the classroom and only the two of them remained.

Harry agreed. "I think Addie and Erich have had a breakthrough."

"I do as well," Celeste agreed. "You helped quite a bit, with her and with Erich."

Harry murmured noncommittally.

"I know about the Christmas tree lights, Harry."

"You do?" He knew he was skirting the edge of what was acceptable, since they'd really been designed to help Erich over his hurdle. But they'd been for Addie, too, and therefore could be justified. He waited for Celeste to reprimand him, but she didn't.

"I believe Addie has started down the right path

now. She's happier than she's been in a good long while. It took courage for her to pack up her life and return home. It meant admitting she was wrong and doing an abrupt about-face. Before she could grow as a person, she needed to learn to temper her stubbornness, and she has."

"Yes, she really did it. She has plans to continue with classes, and she wants to get into the medical field."

"Like her father," Harry murmured. "That's fitting, isn't it?"

"She will shine when it comes to dealing with patients."

"Again, like her father, right?" Harry asked.

"Yes. Only recently has she come to recognize how alike they are."

Harry agreed as he started to straighten the desks, using that as a distraction so he wouldn't have to look at Celeste as he said, "I hope you didn't mind that I invited Michelle." Celeste had certainly given him enough warnings when it came to a relationship with the French teacher, and he assumed his mentor would be annoyed that he'd invited her.

"Not at all," she surprised him by answering. "You need friends on the faculty, Harry."

"I'll be careful not to allow matters to progress beyond friendship."

Celeste nodded. "That would be wise." She walked over to the far side of the room near the windows. "I don't suppose you noticed Dr. Conceito."

Harry stiffened with alarm. "He stopped by?"

"Not exactly."

Frowning, Harry asked, "What does that mean?"

"He was outside, peeking in the window."

"Dr. Conceito?"

"No worries. I can promise you that all he saw was you teaching class just as you would any other day."

"But—"

"Brady Whitall told him about the potluck. You probably aren't aware that holding functions such as this potluck is strictly against school policy."

"The handbook doesn't say anything about—"

"It's in the small print. It's one of Dr. Conceito's little tricks," Celeste informed him.

"Why peek in the window when he could have walked right into the classroom?"

"He didn't want to do that."

"Why not?"

"Dr. Conceito wanted to see who was attending the party before he raised a fuss. He didn't want to offend an ally."

"You mean someone like Jonas?" It'd surprised and gladdened Harry's heart that the custodian had shown up.

"Exactly."

"But regardless, when Dr. Conceito looked . . ."

"There was no party," Celeste assured him.

Harry's shoulders sagged with relief.

"I wonder if you picked up on something else going on at the party."

Plenty of sharing and laughter had taken place, but Harry wasn't sure what Celeste meant. "What?"

His mentor looked rather pleased with herself. "Jonas and Elaina."

"What about them?" Harry had done his best to spend time with each of his students and exchange greetings with their guests. Preoccupied as he was, he didn't get a chance to notice anything else.

"Jonas helped himself to a second tamale and complimented Elaina. You should have seen her blush. Then they got to talking. I think you might find him more of an ally than an adversary in the upcoming weeks."

"Really?" This was an interesting development.

"What are your feelings about Danny?" Celeste asked.

Harry had given plenty of thought to the young parolee. "Danny's got a good heart. All we need to do is keep him on track. He has tremendous potential."

"I agree," Celeste concurred. "You've done well, Harry. You've adjusted to human emotions and have come to love these humans just as God intended."

His heart raced as he asked, "Does this mean I'll be able to continue with my work here on Earth?"

"I believe there's a very good possibility that you will."

This was the best news Harry could have gotten. Oh yes, just as Addie had thought. This was going to be the best Christmas ever.

If you love Debbie Macomber's
special holiday magic,
Christina Skye's novella
will keep the spirit bright.

THE BRIDE WORE MISTLETOE

Continue on to read the full novella,
exclusive to this edition!

Chapter One

It all started with the white cat.

But it ended with handcuffs and the most gorgeous man that Summer O'Neal had ever seen.

It was unseasonably warm for a December in England, and everyone was on edge. Her cat, Churchill, had been whining at her back door, restless and filled with unpredictable energy. Summer O'Neal knew just how he felt. Lately she felt caged and restless, too.

But she was too busy for a vacation. She had recently snapped up the bridal commission of the decade. Her small-but-elite custom bridal design shop was still finding its feet, and she knew this commission could make or break her.

She scowled at the bolts of Alençon lace on her worktable, stacked next to vintage satin ribbons and pink pearls. Fighting back a cascade of wild auburn hair, she glared at the elegant gown she'd spent nearly three months planning and creating.

Hours of precision beadwork and hand-sew lace had made a dress fit for a princess—or the wife of the heir to a Greek shipping dynasty, which is what the famous Hollywood bride would become after the ceremony.

Lace and Dreams, her exclusive shop, was tucked beneath a six-hundred-year-old slate-tile roof on a cobblestone street on England's quiet Sussex coast. History hovered in the narrow alleyways and lovingly preserved houses. When the fog swept up from the bay, Summer could almost hear the cry of smugglers leaning to their oars and the oaths of hard-eyed government agents bent on their capture.

For two busy years the spoiled daughters of new and old European money had jammed Summer's shop in search of sheer kimonos of antique satin, handmade evening slippers, and tiny jeweled evening bags.

As her new business grew, Summer had less and less time for a life of her own. She certainly had no desire for the demands of marriage. She liked choosing what she did and where she went, with no conditions on her time. The way she had grown up had left her gun-shy. And the truth was, Summer had never found a man to make her question her desire to stay single. She was in the bride business, but getting married seemed like a distant possibility for her own future.

And she was fine with that. Completely fine.

She straightened the silk hem of the gown, studying the finished effect. *Stunning* was the only word to describe the yards of organza and damask that spilled in an elegant line from a single white satin rose and a glittering diamond brooch.

The rose had been the bride's idea. The diamond had been Summer's. The combination was feminine, fresh, and unforgettable. In this gown the anxious bride would be elegant, aristocratic, and flawlessly beautiful.

But Summer had twenty more pieces of lingerie to finish before the wedding, which was less than three weeks away. What she needed was a fairy godmother. Barring that, she would accept some skilled embroidery help.

Neither seemed likely.

She glanced out the window and frowned. It was the warmest December that England had ever known. Winter clothes were still in their boxes. The last of the climbing roses lingered in fragile blooms. Normally the delay of winter would be something to celebrate. But with Christmas so close, people wanted snow and carols and all the charms of winter.

As she rubbed her cramped neck, a light flashed against the leaded glass windows at the rear of her shop.

Quickly she grabbed an alpaca throw and covered the costly gown. Then she went to check the outrageously expensive alarm control panel that she'd had installed the week before.

The bride had recently broken Hollywood's glass ceiling and now commanded ten million dollars per picture. The groom was the son of one of Greece's most prominent families. They were determined to keep the details and location of their ceremony a secret, and Summer was sworn to help them.

As dry leaves blew over the empty sidewalk, Summer studied the wall and saw that the green light on her alarm box was no longer flashing. For some reason the system was not working. She touched the two wires running to the window. Both seemed to be fine.

She would have to check the power box outside behind her shop, where her electrical equipment was mounted against the wall of the historic building.

Sighing, Summer closed the big oak door leading out into the mews. Armed with a flashlight, she traced the crisscrossing wires of red, pink, and blue running above her back door. All of them looked intact.

Wind whipped around the corner as she moved to the back wall that held her secondary control panel. In the beam of her flashlight, she noticed that a nail had worked free on the nearby window frame. It appeared to be pressing two wires out of line.

She pulled a small ladder beneath the window and clambered up for a better look. Flashlight in hand, she struggled to bend the wires back into place, but only managed to break two of her fingernails.

She gnawed at her lip. Maybe she needed a hammer? Or possibly a screwdriver? This was definitely *not* her job, but she wanted the windows secure. Tomorrow she would call the company and have a technician dispatched to deal with the wiring problem.

Her cat jumped up beside her, rubbing against her skirt. Suddenly, he froze.

"Churchill, what's wrong?"

The big cat yowled and then shot between her legs, leaping to the ground. He raced blindly under the ladder and Summer swayed, nearly falling.

Then every thought tumbled from her mind as something caught her shoulders and flung her sideways against the brick wall. Her flashlight was knocked free, plunging her into darkness.

A hard hand locked down over her mouth.

Chapter Two

Summer fought a wave of panic.

She was gripped tightly and shoved down the darkened alley toward her shop's back door. She tried to speak, but her mouth was locked beneath strong fingers. She bit down and felt fabric tear, shredded over hard muscle. Instantly she was shoved against the wall.

"Bad-tempered little thief, aren't you?"

She aimed a right hook into the shadows and connected with taut muscle. Instantly she was bracketed against the cold wall.

"That will get you nowhere, I warn you."

Summer's heart pounded wildly. She was hit by alternating waves of panic and fury. *"Let me go,"* she spat out.

But her angry words were muffled by his hand at her mouth.

Summer heard a watch tick softly near her ear. She heard his muffled curse and then the sound of ripping cloth. He was tearing off her best Armani skirt, she thought wildly. Then he would push her down into the darkness and—

"Irritating female. Now my jacket is ruined. That's the second tuxedo gone this month." He pulled her closer, his hand still locked over her mouth. Darkness vied with moonlight, capturing the sharp planes of his cheeks and jaw.

In the shifting light, Summer saw him more clearly now. He had watchful eyes, the eyes of a man who would miss nothing. If he wasn't planning to assault her, what did he *want*?

Petty cash? Her jewelry? Or did he plan to try stealing the wedding dress?

She coughed hard as her mouth was suddenly freed. But now she was pressed face-first against the wall. "Time for the handcuffs."

"Are you out of your mind?" she sputtered. "I—I triggered the alarm. The police are already on their way." It was a complete lie, but he wouldn't know that.

The man laughed once. "I could use their help. Then I can finish my job and get on with my evening. In case you didn't know it, robbery is considered serious business."

Summer blinked. What *was* he talking about?

He gripped her arm, grunting when she jammed her fist hard into his ribs.

"Give it up. Your crime spree is over. The people of Rye can sleep peacefully tonight." He pushed open her back door. "No tricks. I prefer not to use force unless I have to."

At that moment Churchill raced out of the darkness and shot between her legs. The big cat seemed terrified. Outside in the alley, a low whine filled the air.

A trail of white sparks shot out from the metal security box.

The man muttered, shoving the door closed with his foot. "With an alarm system like that, any criminal in Europe would have free access. Wasted money for whoever bought *that*."

The high-pitched whine grew louder. Summer heard a crack and then the grinding sound of tumblers being thrown in her door.

Blue light shimmered against the wall as a set of heavy metal bars dropped down in place over the windowsill. That feature had been part of her new security package. All the doors and windows were now secure, all the bolts engaged.

The override into high protection mode had been triggered, possibly by the short-circuiting wires in the back panel.

Now she was locked inside her shop with a crazy man.

She took a quick breath and kicked out with her

heel. The man grunted and turned sideways, smoothly avoiding the blow.

Maybe he wanted the gown. Finished or not, it was worth a great deal.

No way. Over her dead *body* would he have that.

She aimed a furious kick at his right knee while she bit his hand. But even when her teeth drew blood, he didn't release her. A heartbeat later she was shoved into her very best reproduction Louis XIV armchair, with her arms caught behind her in what felt like plastic restraints.

The arrogant baboon!

The beam from her commandeered flashlight traveled over her twisting body.

"Funny, you don't look like a common thief."

Her furious answer was trapped beneath his locked fingers while he ran his other hand over her shoulders and chest. "No weapons," he muttered, shining the flashlight around her neat but over-stocked back workroom. Half-finished lace lingerie hung from dress forms beside bolts of damask that shimmered in rainbow colors. "Nothing to steal here but a bunch of silly clothes."

Snarling vainly, Summer kicked him again. Her designs? *Silly clothes?*

Summer wondered why the lights were out. She was certain they had been on when she left the shop earlier. But the status of her lights seemed un-important as she struggled vainly to break free.

The man glanced around. He sidestepped her kicks with infuriating ease. "Probably looking for disposable cash and jewelry." The flashlight picked out an antique cameo and a delicate Venetian glass perfume bottle. He gave an unimpressed grunt. "Mostly trinkets."

He glanced around at the darkened shop, where rhinestones and pearls and two small rubies winked in reflected light from the alley.

"I doubt that alarm system will ever work again," he muttered, as he dug in his pocket.

Summer glared at him in icy fury. He didn't talk like a thief. But of course a thief would never announce who he was. She muttered vainly beneath his clamped fingers and then kicked out again as he ran a hand down her arm. Something cold and sleek and metal brushed her skin.

First a plastic restraint. Now handcuffs. Furious, Summer tried to think what to do next. She forced herself to slump forward, her whole body slack.

"Give up, do you? That should make this easier for both of us. Now I'll just finish with these cuffs and . . ."

When he bent forward, Summer wrenched backward and sent the two of them toppling to the floor. She heard a sharp metallic click, followed by an abrupt curse. The man's hand fell away from her mouth and she dragged in a breath of blessed air.

She was pulled sharply against his chest. Metal clicked against her hand. Summer tried to wriggle free, but the handcuff locked her to him. "I've got places to go, too, Red." His eyes narrowed on the hair tumbling over her shoulders. "I'm going to see you safely under lock and key. Then I'll send an officer to collect you."

She was handcuffed to a crazy man. This was a *nightmare*.

She shoved at his hand, desperate to make him see his mistake. "I *own* this shop." She took a strangled breath. "If you don't release me, you'll be the one headed into custody."

"Oh, that's smashing. A five-year-old could manage a better argument than that. Why don't you stop talking while we wait for the security team to arrive?" He sounded cold and completely bored. Then he looked down at the handcuff. "That's just bloody grand. I hate human bites." He raised their joined hands and Summer saw blood darkening his white cuff.

"You're bleeding."

"Of course I am. You've got one hell of a bite."

She stumbled to her feet. "I'll bite you again if you don't let me—"

He jerked his arm, and the movement sent her sprawling beside him on the floor. A basket full of lace toppled forward into her lap. "Don't you *dare* bleed on my veils. Bloodstains are impossible to get out of antique lace."

She saw him frown and study her worktable. He ran a finger across the unfinished lace veil.

"Don't touch my veil. That lace cost me a fortune."

The callused hands froze. "Say that again."

"What part don't you understand? Don't touch the veil? How about two hundred fifty euros per meter?"

He stared. "These are *your* veils?"

"Of course they're mine. After I add satin roses and freshwater pearls, they'll be worth even more."

In the gloom she saw his eyes narrow. "What kind of lace is that?"

"Why do you care?"

"Answer the question." His voice was cold.

"Alençon. I found them in a tiny shop in Brittany. If you get the lace dirty, it's impossible to clean, and I don't have time to replace them."

He stared at her in the darkness. Moonlight played over his face. A muscle shifted at his jaw. "Alençon lace. Two hundred fifty euros a meter in Brittany."

"That's right."

He looked down at the handcuff and shook his head. "Do you really own this shop?"

"That's what I've been *trying* to tell you."

He took a short, angry breath and said something Summer didn't quite hear.

"Well?"

"Well what?" he muttered.

"I'd like an apology. And then you can remove your wretched handcuff and leave."

She didn't expect an apology, but it didn't hurt to try.

"If you own Lace and Dreams, why were you here so late? And why were you toying with the wires in the security panel out in the alley?" He sounded irritated now.

"I don't think that's any of your business. I don't have a clue who you are." Summer glared at his perfectly cut black jacket and pristine white shirt. Definitely custom made. Bespoke, as the English put it. He probably wore heirloom cuff links under the perfectly cut jacket.

Stiff with fury, she tried to twist sideways, but her wrist caught short on cold metal.

"Nice legs." He studied the skin visible in the moonlight. His irritation had changed. Now he actually seemed . . . amused.

Summer tried to stay calm.

Calm, calm, calm . . .

It wasn't working.

"Forget my legs. Open this handcuff *now*."

"Afraid I can't. I took off the restraint, but the handcuff is not going anywhere. That happens to be my newest prototype. No way for it to be picked, shattered, forced, or bent. It's a new titanium alloy. It only responds to a custom-made key or the code of a remote receiver."

"Then use the key. I want out of this blasted thing." Summer stared at him in disbelief and fury.

"I am *not* staying locked up with you for another second."

His brow rose. "Are you always this irritating?"

"Only when I've been attacked, mauled, and handcuffed by a strange man breaking into my shop." Summer pushed to her feet, hauling him with her.

"Where you going?"

"I have to get out of here. We need to find something to break this stupid cuff."

"It's unbreakable, I told you." He gave a cold laugh. "Not even a blowtorch would work."

She tugged him across the room. "Anything can be broken. Now hold that flashlight up and be quiet."

"Whatever you wish, Your Highness."

"It's Summer O'Neal to you. We sane people on the other side of the Atlantic gave up royalty and titles more than two centuries ago." Summer stalked into the main room of her shop, dragging the man with her.

Light glimmered off elegant gilt side chairs and crystal vases full of fresh flowers. The man next to her gave a low whistle. "Posh. It's all yours?"

"You have a problem with a woman being in charge?"

His gaze roamed slowly over her flushed cheeks. "Not in the slightest."

He was calm and utterly confident. Summer suddenly realized there was a lean, honed body pressing against her thigh and no one else around to protect her. But she wasn't about to give this man the pleasure of getting a rise out of her. "Exactly who are you?"

"Cary Grant in *To Catch a Thief*?" he offered.

"Nowhere close."

He slid a finger appreciatively over a semitransparent chemise of lace and peau de soie embellished with tiny seed pearls.

Summer swatted his hand. "Don't touch the merchandise. And answer my question."

"Daniel St. Pierre, formerly of the London police force."

"And why did you grab me in that hammerlock?"

"I'm no longer with the London police. I'm strictly private security these days. I was on a job." He studied a small mahogany table covered with a soft alpaca throw and shrugged. "I thought you were trying to break in." He looked down, rummaging in his pocket. "Honest mistake."

"You thought I was—" Summer broke off with a strangled oath. "What gave you the right to prowl about and interfere? This is private property, in case you hadn't noticed."

"I noticed." He rummaged some more. "Calm down. I just found the key to my cuffs. You can stop squirming now." He held up a bright square of silver. "They're unbreakable, just the way I said." He slid the key in place and Summer's hand came free.

She winced, rubbing her wrist, surprised when he reached over to massage the skin gently. "Sorry about that. This is still a prototype."

"What's your name again?"

"Dane St. Pierre. I'm doing a favor for a friend. His sister owns a shop around the corner, and I had to check on the local security. I saw you out in the alley and I assumed that you were breaking in."

Summer paced the room, trying to keep her irritation in check. "Well, now you know I *wasn't*. So you can take your prototype handcuff and your expensive tuxedo and leave."

"What about your alarm? It's completely nonfunctional. I saw those sparks. The whole control panel could be shorted out. That's a clear fire risk."

Summer froze. She needed some kind of protection until repairs could be done. "Can you fix it? I would pay you, of course. After you show me some kind of ID."

"Left front pocket of my jacket."

Summer tugged out a sleek leather wallet and opened it to find a laminated card. "R and H Security. That's you?"

He nodded.

"Offices in London, Paris, Singapore, and Dubai?"

"We may close Singapore. Not much business there lately."

Summer had to admit that he seemed like the real thing. "In that case, I could use your help with my security system. And I suppose that I could sew your tuxedo for you."

"You must be good. Well, I did have plans for the night." He cleared his throat. "I could probably be a little late."

Summer gestured to his black satin tuxedo collar. "Bespoke?"

He nodded. "If you are going to do the thing, then do it properly. That's what my father always said."

Summer knew exactly what the finest custom-tailored Italian tuxedo cost: roughly the price of her rent for the next six months.

So he had money. Probably lots of it. And he had style, too. But that was no business of hers. She crossed her arms. "Can you help me? Or should I say *will* you help me? And you can figure out what's wrong with my lights while you're at it."

"Calm down, Red. I'm considering the idea. I'll have to make some calls. But you are clearly in need of help, and what kind of gentleman walks out on a lady in distress?"

Most men did, in Summer's experience.

She tried to ignore the hard line of his shoulders in that exquisite tuxedo and his suddenly charming grin. "Flattery won't get you more money, Mr. St. Pierre. And you owe me for those unforgivable assault tactics. Now, will you help me or not?"

He sighed. "Fine. Let me make two calls and I'll open up that wiring." He dug in one pocket and then the other. "I don't seem to have my cellphone. I had it out in the mews before you decided to channel Bruce Lee."

"*Me?* I was the one being attacked. Let's get the story straight. And don't worry about your phone because you can use mine." Summer reached into the pocket of her skirt. There was nothing.

She tried the other side.

No luck there, either.

"I—I can't find my cellphone, either, but I know I had it when I went outside. That was before the wiring went crazy and Churchill nearly knocked me off the ladder. And before *you* showed up."

"Churchill?"

"My cat. He was terrified."

Dane looked rueful. "I did have a good reason to be suspicious, you must admit. But I'm sorry that things became . . . a bit physical. You're sure the phone isn't on your desk or in the back room?"

Summer shook her head. "I took it outside with me. But we can use the landline instead." She walked to a small alcove with a reproduction French writing desk and picked up the receiver.

Then she closed her eyes.

"Well?"

"Power is out. Not just a problem with the lights, I'm afraid. I didn't notice before. Whatever happened out there must have short-circuited all my power. When I track down the man who sold me this awful, overpriced system—"

She grabbed a trench coat from a peg near the back door. "I'll go find my phone. If I can't locate it, I'll walk over to my neighbor around the corner and phone."

"You'd better take this." He held out her flashlight, smiling.

Was he actually *enjoying* their predicament?

"I'll get my tools from the car and start working."

"Thank you," Summer said stiffly. "I won't be long." She buttoned up her coat and shivered. The temperature was dropping, and she realized they had no heat in the shop.

Irritated, she gripped the metal door latch.

Nothing moved.

She glared down at the security fob that *should* have overridden the locks. Without power, it was absolutely useless. And without a phone, she couldn't summon her overpriced security company for help.

Now they were locked in.

Together. Without any way out.

Chapter Three

She heard him cross the room. He leaned down to look at the lock. "I don't think I understand. You purchased a security system to lock yourself in?"

"It's *only* supposed to trigger when someone tries to cut or override the system. Then it's meant to keep them inside while the police are called automatically. It's not supposed to happen when I'm here and nothing is wrong. That power surge must have reset everything, but I'm not a security expert." She eyed Dane in silence. "You are. Or at least you *say* you are. Why don't you fix it so we can leave?"

"I'm working on it." He glanced at the bolts and then tried the door latch. Nothing moved.

"So?"

"Locked. Just like you said. They managed to

get this part right, because those tumblers are frozen. Too bad they didn't set the rest of the monitoring system up equally well. But what can you expect?"

"I expect a good job."

"Not from that company. They give cheap bids and they hire inexperienced workers. Anyone in the security field could have told you that."

"My business adviser found them for me. He said they were highly recommended. I prefer to do my own research, but things have been so hectic." Summer blew out an angry breath. "I trusted him to make a good decision."

Dane shook his head. "You were fleeced. I doubt the company will be responding to any alerts on the control panel. They have a reputation for being shoddy in their monitoring services, too."

Summer's heart sank. The new alarm system had been crushingly expensive. And if it wasn't even being monitored . . .

She put her hands on her hips and frowned. "So what do we do now?"

He crossed the room and sat down in the Louis XIV chair. "We wait. Somebody will figure it out eventually. Too bad I didn't have more warning. I have a very fine bottle of chilled Château Climens out in the car. That would have gone down very nicely about now."

"Wine? Is that all you can think about?"

"Well, I can think of other things. But I doubt they're appropriate to the discussion."

Summer flushed. He had mentioned having plans for the night. They had to mean meeting a woman. Clearly he had planned to give her a very expensive bottle of wine. Summer had heard of Château Climens and its rich, almost magical sweetness. "For a policeman, you have expensive taste, Mr. St. Pierre."

"Ex-policeman. And it's Viscount Ravenhurst, actually. Twelfth generation. But I don't use the title much. Just call me Dane."

Hysterical laughter built in Summer's chest. She was locked in her shop with a genuine British viscount.

"Despite the manhandling, I suppose I should thank you. I might never have found out about my security company otherwise."

"Not the nicest way to learn." His voice turned rough. "I happen to know that there have been six robberies in this part of Sussex in the last month. Two of them involved armed assault."

"Armed . . . assault?" Summer's pulse lurched. "How come I've heard nothing about—"

"You wouldn't. Generally these things are covered up as long as possible. Crime isn't conducive to tourism. Do you have any idea what percent of local revenues come from tourism here?"

Summer barely heard him. "Six robberies?"

He nodded gravely.

"I saw someone walking past in the mews earlier tonight. A tall figure in a tan coat, no one that I recognized. When I went to check, he was gone. Was that . . . you?"

He looked away. "I'm afraid not."

Fear skittered along Summer's neck. A stranger had been out there in the darkness, watching her. She was glad suddenly for Dane's presence beside her.

She had seen an occasional person walking through the mews for a week now, but she had thought nothing of it beyond shoppers or diners returning home via a shortcut.

Fear sank deep.

"Here, drink this. Don't faint on me now, damn it."

Dane pressed a glass into her hand. The water was cool and she drank all of it in a gulp.

"Better?"

Summer nodded.

"Good. Let's talk about something else." He brushed a row of cut perfume bottles on a shelf lined with black velvet. "How did you get started in the wedding gown business?"

"Why do you want to know?"

"Because you interest me, Ms. O'Neal."

Summer stared at the rim of her goblet. Somehow she found herself telling him about the first hat she had designed. The first bridal commission she'd accepted. How she had struggled for two years in a dingy basement workshop on the fringes of Chinatown in New York City. How she hated the haggling and the impersonality and had jumped at an offer to set up her own design shop here in England with the backing of a banker she had met on a buying tour in Florence.

St. Pierre listened well. He laughed at all the right spots, frowned at the hard times. When she was done, Summer saw that the moon had crossed nearly the whole width of the skylight.

She tried to hide a yawn. "I'm exhausted. I'm not sure I can stay awake much longer."

"Go ahead and sleep." He found a little satin cushion and held it out to her. "This should help."

Summer studied his face in the moonlight. "Sometimes you're rude and arrogant. Then you do something thoughtful like that. Which are you, wonderful or terrible?"

He gave a crooked smile, and the force of it made him look younger and far less cynical. "I suppose that depends whom you ask. Now go to sleep. I'll wake you when a guard arrives to open the door."

Summer tossed and turned, trying to keep their contact minimal, but it was impossible not to feel his warmth. When she was finally settled, he pulled the soft alpaca throw over her shoulders. She caught a scent of his cologne, a mix of smoke and citrus.

"Is this one of your pieces?"

"I made it, but not for sale. Sometimes when I'm tired of sewing, I like to knit. I'm glad to have it tonight because it's cold without the heat on." She sat up and raised the blanket. "You might as well come under, too. That gorgeous tuxedo can't be keeping you very warm."

Dane nestled up beside her and then pulled the soft alpaca blanket over them both.

Summer closed her eyes. It had been a long time since she had felt this relaxed. Though she hated to admit it, some of that feeling had to do with the strong, masculine body curved next to hers.

Not that it meant anything. Not that it was personal. But it was still . . . very pleasant. "Dane?"

"You're supposed to be asleep."

"One more question."

"I'm listening."

"What about *your* work? Who did you say you work for now?"

There was a moment of silence. Then he cleared his throat. "I didn't say. Now go to sleep."

Summer heard thunder. Was it raining?

She opened her eyes and saw pale gray through the skylight. Then she felt a man's body, warm and strong against her back.

Dane St. Pierre.

Despite the chill in the shop, she was wonderfully warm, snuggled against him.

The lights were still off. Suddenly Summer realized that the hammering wasn't thunder at all. It sounded like a truck motor outside in the street. A door slammed loudly and voices moved up the walk.

Had rescuers finally arrived?

Dane was watching her when she sat up. "How long have you been awake?"

"About an hour. I enjoyed watching you sleep. You snore, do you know that?"

"I do *not* snore."

"Just a little. It's rather endearing." He sat up, stretched and straightened his tuxedo, then walked to the door. Voices drifted.

Metal scraped on metal as bolts were drawn back.

The front door opened. A man in a black security suit peered inside. "Allied Security. Who are you?"

"I'm the shop owner," Summer said quickly. "Summer O'Neal. Everything shorted out here last night, and we've been stuck here for hours. Why didn't anyone answer the alert when the alarm system was triggered?"

"First that we knew of it." The uniformed man shot a flashlight across the darkened room and then pulled out a walkie-talkie. "All clear in here. Equipment malfunction. Better send a tech team." He sounded bored.

"I need that control panel fixed this morning."

"You'll have to take that up with my boss," the man said with a shrug.

Dane moved in front of Summer, his eyes hard. "But we both know your president is nowhere in Rye or the country. He's at his house in the south of France with that expensive mistress of his. And we both know that he will never respond to client calls."

The man's eyes narrowed. "I wouldn't know about any of that."

"Unless you want a very nasty and public lawsuit, you'll take out your cellphone and contact him right now. We'll be expecting a tech team here in ten minutes. They will have all this equipment up and running within the hour. Is that understood?"

"Why would I possibly agree to that?"

"If you don't, I'll have to ring your boss's wife. She happens to be a close family friend. You definitely wouldn't like the result of that call."

The man went a little pale, grabbing for his cellphone.

Summer watched in amazement as he barked detailed orders to his dispatcher.

In twenty minutes all the windows and doors were restored to working order. In an hour the outside security panel had been replaced. Every wire was retested, and the power backup was repaired.

All of it had been done under the cold scrutiny of Dane, who looked dangerous and unyielding, noting every detail. Summer was glad for his presence. It was clear that the repair team would have been content with a far-from-satisfactory job.

When the workers finally left, Summer blew out a sigh of relief. "It's almost seven. Why don't you let me buy you breakfast? It's the least I can do to thank you. Without you, I'm sure my system would still be down."

Dane looked thoughtful. "I highly recommend you change your monitoring company. I'll give you a name to call. I also suggest that you upgrade your system to include a remote alarm that you carry in your pocket. Practice using it and don't go anywhere without it. I wasn't exaggerating about those robberies, Summer."

"I know you weren't. And I appreciate the advice." She hesitated. "Why don't you drop off your tux and let me fix it? It's the least I can do."

Dane leaned down and brushed a strand of hair from her cheek. "I'll do that. But I'm afraid I need to take a raincheck on your offer of breakfast. I'm late already, and I have appointments all morning." He held out a card. "Here's my number. Call me if you have any problems . . . or even if you don't."

He turned at the door, and his hand trailed over a satin camisole edged in pink pearls. "Actually, I think we should do this all again. Minus the biting, kicking, and the locked doors, of course." His eyes darkened. "What do you say?"

Summer put a hand on her chest, feeling a little giddy. For a moment she couldn't speak. "I'll think about it."

"Good. Because I definitely like your taste in lingerie, Summer O'Neal."

Then he was gone.

Chapter Four

Summer managed two hours of sleep at home but was back in her studio before noon, measuring beads for the gown and the matching bridal sash. It was detailed and laborious work, and she was relieved that her assistant was going to handle the actual beading.

She had enough to do with six pieces of matched silk charmeuse lingerie and the final embellishing details on the wedding gown. And Summer knew that nothing was final until the bride had her last fitting. Getting married made people emotional, and weddings were tricky business.

Lizzy, her assistant, walked around the adjoining table and stretched. "So tell me about last night. I still don't understand how you were caught inside."

"Something about the alarm malfunctioning from a short. Thankfully, Dane was in the area doing security for a friend. He turned out to be very helpful. *After* he put me in a stranglehold and nearly gave me a heart attack," Summer said dryly. "He recommended a new security company. Someone reliable, thank heavens." Summer glanced into the storage room. "Is the technician almost done back there?"

"Probably another hour. He implied that the previous work was very shoddy. They had to rip everything back to the wall and start over. I think you're lucky that this happened, Summer."

"Except for the discomfort last night, I'd have to agree." Summer rubbed her neck with a sigh, feeling the tug of sore muscles. "I'm walking down the street for a proper latte and a breath of air. Do you want anything?"

"A Prada purse, a million dollars, and a husband." Lizzy's eyes sparkled with mischief. "*Not* necessarily in that order."

Summer bit back a laugh. "I was thinking of something in the hot-beverage line."

"A large chai with cream, in that case."

"By the way, how did your blind date go last night?"

"Don't ask. My brother thought the man was fine. Never let your brother set you up, okay? I mean that, on pain of death."

"That bad?"

"I think I'll just stay single forever."

"Give it time, Lizzy." Summer picked up her sweater. "Someday you'll meet the one man for you and you'll fall blindly."

"You never have." Lizzy's eyes narrowed. "You never talk about it, but something makes me think you've given up on happy ever afters for yourself."

"Not completely. But I'm not very optimistic." Summer stared out the window. "Fortunately, I have good friends who actually made a pact about getting married. We kept a complete list of all our rules."

Lizzy raised an eyebrow. "I can't wait to hear this."

"We were thirteen at the time." Summer laughed. "We called ourselves the Brides Club. The idea was simple. No one gets married until all of the others have questioned the prospective groom and given their approval. But it stuck with us over the years. Everyone takes their duties seriously, believe me. Except . . . well, I couldn't get away to meet one friend's husband in time. I hate that I couldn't be there for her." Summer blew out a breath. "We met at camp in Michigan when we were kids, and we've all stayed in touch. It was hard to do, but it mattered to us. I still remember how wonderful that summer was."

Summer thought of cool, fresh wind whistling through impossibly tall pines. She remembered the warmth of newly found friends far from home and the unquestioning support they had given one another. Why hadn't she stayed in closer touch with the other three? Work was no excuse. Friendship was too precious to lose.

She resolved to contact Annie, Rina, and Sage in the coming week. Maybe she would make a lightning visit back to the States, just as soon as she finished the commission for her current bridal client. Her friend Annie had come through a very hard time and still needed their support.

"You're so lucky. I don't have *any* friends like that." Lizzy sounded wistful. "Just a brother who happens to be clueless."

"You're going to meet all of them. My friend Rina is engaged to the heir to the throne of Markovia. She's a very straightforward person with no taste for luxury or grand fashion, but given the situation, she needs a showstopper bridal gown."

"That's amazing. You never told me."

"It was a recent development that surprised us all. But Rina asked for my help. She needs a world-class gorgeous gown, and you and I are going to give it to her," Summer said proudly. She sketched idly on the notepad near her desk, almost without thinking.

Long flowing lines appeared above a sweeping skirt. A curve of beaded fabric started at the collar, swirled around one shoulder, and ended in a spray of diamonds just above the opposite side of the waist. "I've started working on some ideas for the gown."

Lizzy looked over her shoulder. "It's spooky how you can work up a shape so quickly, especially something complicated like that. So when do I get to meet these friends of yours?"

"The wedding is still in the planning stage. It's a big event for their country, and everything has to be organized carefully. But don't worry, we'll have plenty of time to create an unforgettable gown for Rina."

Lizzy looked worried. "Are you sure? The last few months haven't been much fun, working under this tight deadline."

"I'll watch the calendar on this one," Summer said firmly. "No surprises."

"Speaking of surprises, what should I tell Mr. Tall, Dark, and Dangerous if he appears at the door? Are you going to meet him for coffee?"

"I'm afraid not. Dane is very busy. Besides, it's not personal, Lizzy."

"No? Then why do you smile when you mention his name?"

Summer huffed out a breath. "I do *not* smile. I barely know the man. I'm not sure what he does, but it seems important and he probably has no time for a . . . private life. And that's fine with me. We'll go our separate ways as if the night never happened. I do think I should send him a bottle of champagne as a thank-you. I owe him for recommending a *real* security firm instead of that crew of misfits. All in all, things could be much worse."

Summer lingered over her extra-large cup of coffee at the little teashop down the street. Through the old leaded windows she watched mothers pass with small children as teenagers raced by with excited dogs. Men and women held hands, laughing at some shared memory.

As she sat with her steaming coffee, a father and son struggled up the street, carrying a small, freshly cut tree with great care. The man waved at a laughing woman in an open doorway. Down the block a tall man in an old-fashioned farmer's work smock arranged a pile of handmade balsam fir wreaths. Farther down the street at number 21, the bustling owner laid out red ribbon, holly berries, rustic wooden reindeer, and lengths of cut pine for garlands.

Summer sighed at the comforting scene. Pine scent and wood smoke filled the air. As she watched life pass outside the window in a flow of bright, relentless, beautiful variations, Summer wished she had a piece of that life right now. Running Lace and Dreams was a constant inspiration, but she wondered if Lizzy was right. Maybe she should call Dane for a casual update on the security company that he had referred. They could have coffee . . . just to keep in touch.

No, it was better this way. No commitments that would be broken. He was clearly a busy man, and she was up to her neck with this bridal project.

What was the point?

This was the only *logical* thing to do.

She frowned as she put on her jacket, feeling glum. When was the weather going to change? It was still warm in the afternoon, nothing like it should be at Christmastime. That felt all wrong to her.

When would there be carols and the smell of roasting chestnuts? Best of all, when would she feel the first magic snowflakes brush her face?

Dane's partner held out a cup of coffee and then slid six security reports across the polished wooden desk. "These just came in. Sorry to ask, but I'm up to my neck with that royal job in Mayfair."

"Quite all right, Robert. I'll take care of it. Thanks for the coffee." Dane eyed the cup for a minute. "Is it your usual disgusting, overroasted Italian brand?"

Robert Harrison smiled. "That would be the one. Doesn't seem to bother me."

"Because you have no taste. Still, I suppose this is better than nothing. I can't seem to concentrate today. Probably the effect of having two hours of sleep on a cramped Louis XIV reproduction sofa last night."

"Wearing a tuxedo, no less." Dane's partner cleared his throat. "I hope she was worth it. With beautiful legs and gorgeous—"

Dane cut him off. "She was lovely. And she had a surprising sense of humor about everything. You've heard of Lace and Dreams near the Mermaid Inn? She owns it. I'm sure your wife knows exactly what her lingerie costs. Everything there is handmade."

Her shop was almost as exceptional as she was, Dane thought. Quirky. Elegant. Colorful.

Absolutely unexpected.

"My wife is giddy about that place. She's told me how much she would love something from the shop." His partner toyed with his coffee cup. "Wait a minute, you said this lady owes you a favor after last night. Why don't you call in the debt? Get me something small. I don't know, garters or a slip thing. Whatever women like. My wife would go out of her mind."

"I'm not calling in any favors, not even for you." Dane ignored the pleading look in his partner's eyes.

"Some kind of friend you are." Harrison rubbed his neck. "Her clothes don't come cheap, but it would be worth the cost. When are you going to see her again?"

Dane shrugged. "I'm all backed up here. Maybe tomorrow." *Maybe not at all,* he thought. This was a busy time, and he would be leaving on another security junket in less than two weeks. It was only practical to let the connection go. Although she interested him.

She *more* than interested him.

Hell.

Maybe he could call her shop and see about ordering something. That would be simple enough. And he did owe it to Harrison. They had been working long hours for almost two years since they had begun the company. Dane knew there was endless hard work still to come.

He took another sip of cold coffee, frowning. Last night had been his first evening off duty for weeks. He'd planned to spend it with a beautiful woman who had just come through a messy divorce. Veronica had killer legs and killer looks and was open to an occasional uncomplicated night with him.

But as Dane summoned visions of candlelight and laughter, instead of Veronica he saw creamy skin and vibrant auburn hair. Summer obliterated every other woman from his mind.

He closed his eyes on a curse. First of all, she *wasn't* his type. He liked his women uncomplicated.

Summer was all brittle wit, with an artist's high-strung temperament. She was bossy, too. In fact, she was just the kind of stubborn, independent female who generally set his nerves on edge. Yet his thoughts kept wandering to her long legs and the way her body had fit so perfectly against his while they slept. He wondered how all that wild red hair would feel tangled in his fingers, wrapped around his wrist while he kissed her.

He reached for his coffee cup, frowning when he saw the mark of her teeth on his arm. She did have one wicked bite.

She was volatile. Quirky.

Bossy beyond redemption.

And then Dane laughed.

One hell of a woman.

Chapter Five

At seven o'clock Summer was back at her desk, with all her beads sorted and all her silk cut and freshly pressed. The air smelled lightly of lavender, her favorite fragrance. She had used no water or steam. Simple heat and a nice silk organza pressing cloth did the job best.

She ran a finger over the beads, all counted and labeled, nested in neat plastic containers on her assistant's desk. Now she could finally relax.

She closed her eyes, spinning her cellphone on the desk. After much searching she had found it, out of charge, knocked across the cobblestones under a metal garbage bin. Seeing the phone made her remember all the night's drama. But there had been nice moments, too, like the thoughtful way Dane had rubbed the bruised spot on her wrist.

How he'd covered them both with her alpaca throw. She couldn't forget the sharp intimacy of that moment, though they were strangers.

Suddenly restless, she moved across the room and lifted the soft, cabled alpaca to her face. Did it still hold the faint scent of Dane's body? Something with cinnamon and lemons and a kind of smoky clove smell?

Ridiculous. She was imagining things. And it wasn't like her to be silly and foolish and a day-dreamer. She had always prided herself on being calm and practical.

Quick footsteps tapped outside in the mews. Summer's hands tightened.

She took a jerky breath, gripping her cellphone. The door was locked. No one could get in.

But the bolt turned and the door creaked open. Summer froze, her heart lurching.

It was Dane who stood in the doorway, outlined by slanting sunlight, smiling at her with a question in his eyes as he dangled a small key fob. "I borrowed it from your new security company. Everything okay here, Red?"

Now it is, she thought.

The sight of him left her breathless and a little dizzy. He looked . . . different. She had seen him only in the dark, but here in the full daylight he seemed taller than she had remembered. His face was more rugged, his eyes dark with something that looked like the weight of difficult experiences. Not quite cynicism, but very close.

It annoyed Summer how quickly she felt calmed by his presence. "Everything is perfect. Why shouldn't it be? So did you come to drop off your tuxedo?"

"Actually, I came to apologize for last night. I believe that I owe you for a very uncomfortable evening. And for your ruined skirt." He studied her face thoughtfully. "You look tired."

Was it so obvious? Summer shrugged. "Weddings can be a tiring business, Mr. St. Pierre."

"Dane," he said quietly. "And I do owe you. I'll replace the skirt that was ruined when I . . . strong-armed you into your shop."

"You can't. The style is five years old. It's my favorite, but they don't make it anymore. I was told the style had been retired."

He gave a slow grin. "Perhaps for the general public, but I happen to know someone on the inside. I did a favor for her when an ex-boyfriend was being rather unpleasant. If there are any skirts anywhere, she'll find one. Or she'll see that they pull the old pattern and make you a new one."

"She must be a good friend," Summer said suspiciously. "Maybe even . . . more than a friend?"

"Relax. We're not *that* kind of friends. Now, then, you may want to step away from the door and cover your ears."

"Why?"

"You'll see shortly. Where is your security key fob? You carry it with you, right?"

"Yes, of course, just the way you advised."

"Fine. I'll take that from you." He pressed the button.

Immediately red lights flashed on the wall and an earsplitting electronic howl filled the air. Dane stood calmly, studying his watch.

One minute passed. Three minutes more passed. His smiled faded. When the first truck pulled in and a uniformed man appeared at the door, Dane motioned to the panel.

The man turned it off and spoke into a headset. "Alarm registered. I am on site now. Activity monitored. Accidental alarm triggered. Status is fine."

"On the contrary. This was a test and you failed. That response took four minutes, ten seconds. I checked the traffic patterns, and you should have been here in under three minutes."

The man opened his mouth and then closed it again.

"Shall I report this to your superior?"

"No, sir."

"Then explain why you were a minute and ten seconds late."

"I dropped my cellphone. Sir."

"And will that happen again during an alarm response?" Dane glanced at the man's chest. "Adamson?"

"No, sir. It will not."

"And will anyone else be making the same mistake when they respond to an alarm at this address?"

"Definitely not."

"I happen to know that there's a change in top management set for this company. A few public rumors about bad response times would not do well for any of you."

The man went a little paler.

"Are we clear?"

"Yes, sir. Very clear."

"Fine. I'll be monitoring those response times. Now you can go."

Dane watched the man walk back to his truck. "I think he got the message. First item of business taken care of."

"Are you always this . . . *alpha*?"

"Only when it's necessary. And it's clear to me that you haven't taken any time off to eat. I did a little research about you, Summer O'Neal. I know that you're booked solid for orders of wedding gowns and related garments. I know that your client list is exclusive and very private. And I know that you are expensive and come highly recommended." He touched her chin and tilted it up gently, staring at her face. "That means you work too hard. I'm going to remedy that right now. We're going to dinner. Don't bother to argue."

Summer crossed her arms, hit by a conflicting mix of excitement and irritation and panic. "Despite your charmingly presumptuous command, I can't. There's far too much to do here. And I have one more meeting tonight."

Dane glanced at his watch. "It's almost seven-thirty. Isn't that rather late in the bridal business?"

"We keep late hours, as the client requires. Besides, I'm not hungry."

"Really? When was the last time you ate?"

Summer tried to remember. The day was a blur of missed deliveries, alarm repairs, and tracking down a lost box of seed pearls. Food had been the last thing on her mind. "Lunchtime."

"When you probably had an apple or a banana and a handful of nuts. A cup of coffee to go with them. Am I right?"

It had been *two* cups of coffee. She had had an orange, accompanied by a handful of pistachios. But he was close. Frightfully close. How did he know her so well?

"I had a full meal, thank you very much." She avoided his eyes. "And I'm not ready for dinner." She admitted the offer was tempting. She had thought about him at odd moments all through the day and wondered what he was doing. He was easy to talk to, easy to like. *Dangerously* easy to like.

She frowned at her worktable, wishing it could be magically cleared, with every task finished.

Dane made an irritated sound. "I thought you might say that." He walked out and then returned with a large picnic basket. Immediately, wonderful smells assaulted Summer. The scent of freshly baked bread and roasted chicken mingled in the small room. The perfume of rich dark chocolate drifted and enticed her senses.

This wasn't playing fair. She would die for a piece of that chocolate, whatever it was. But she refused to give in to his arrogance. She turned away.

Then her stomach growled. Very loudly.

"Still not hungry?" He smiled slowly. "Let's see if we can change that."

Chapter Six

More rich smells drifted around Summer in intoxi-cating layers.

The temptation was unbearable. "Okay, I *am* hungry. Actually, I'm ravenous."

Dane laughed. "Nice to hear you admit it."

Summer followed him across the room and into the tiny kitchen. How did he know where every-thing was? And why was he so annoyingly com-fortable in her kitchen?

The man seemed to be comfortable anywhere.

But hunger overtook her irritation. "Something smells amazing. Is that fruity smell oranges? And rosemary?"

"Tuscan chicken stuffed with oranges and rose-mary. Everything marinated and then grilled under hot bricks."

"I'm impressed."

"You should be."

"But I still don't have time to—"

"You can eat. I'll clean up afterward."

Summer just stared at him. How could anyone say *no* to an offer like that?

Dane moved past her. "This is a private recipe from one of the best restaurants in Sussex. My brother's," he added proudly.

"The restaurant or the recipe?"

"Both. Gabe was always the rebellious one in the family." Dane smiled. "He claims that he learned the secret while he was hiking through the hills near Florence one summer. No one else makes chicken quite like this. Don't you have a little patio?" Without skipping a beat, Dane pulled dishes out of the bottom of his basket, arranged them on the table, and then glanced back at Summer, who was still staring at him blankly. "Patio?

"Oh. Right. On the other side of the storeroom."

"Excellent. I thought I saw it last night. Why don't you get the table ready."

"I have to work later, remember?"

"We can fit in time for you to eat."

Summer's stomach rumbled loudly. The roasted chicken had garlic along with the rosemary, she was sure of it.

But she shook her head firmly when Dane pulled out a bottle of wine. "None for me. I really can't."

"Well, you wouldn't deny me a glass, I hope? I'm definitely off duty now."

Summer put her hands on her hips. "What exactly *is* the work you do?"

"A little of this. A little of that."

"Where? For whom?"

"Let's eat first. It would be criminal to let this chicken get cold."

"Cheater," she muttered.

"Pragmatist."

"You're not going to tell me?"

Dane shrugged. "Maybe later. Now hand me that plate."

They ate in a pleasant, comfortable kind of silence. Dane glanced through the open French doors at the bright fabrics and sheer lace, looking thoughtful. "So these things you make. Wedding gowns. Veils and lace lingerie. My partner's wife knows all about them. I gather they're very expensive."

Summer stiffened. She was sensitive on the subject of prices. "They're inexpensive if you calculate the hours of work required and the cost of fine materials. These are one-of-a-kind pieces meant to become heirlooms. And they require techniques that are in danger of vanishing. The work I do is Old World. One of my stitches dates back to a tailor who worked at the time of Elizabeth the First."

"Relax. I'm not questioning your prices or your

authenticity. I can see that these things . . . are special, though I know nothing about fabric or beads. I've never seen anything like this before." His eyes darkened. "Something tells me that your pieces cling in all the right places."

They certainly did. Summer saw to that. She took very careful measurements and put hours of thought into the best way to flatter a woman's figure. Her clients were always thrilled with the finished effect. That was one of the reasons her garments were in such demand. "I like to make my customers look beautiful. I think that I have a skill for it."

"That's what I hear. How many employees do you have in your workshop?"

"Just me and one assistant. Lizzy is a treasure. She's careful, and also very efficient."

"Only the two of you?" Dane frowned. "Why don't you hire more people? Then you wouldn't be up until all hours working."

"I wouldn't be up until all hours like this. Find more help." Summer shrugged. "Skilled seamstresses and embroiderers aren't exactly thick on the ground. I suspect you know something about that if you've ever looked for an experienced butler."

He smiled a little at that. "My father used to rant on that particular topic, so I see your point. But there has to be a better way. You can't do all the work yourself along with sales and business planning."

He'd just hit on a major point of contention between Summer and her assistant, who insisted that Summer needed two more employees so she could focus on building new client relationships. Without new clients, the company had no future, or so Lizzy kept telling her.

Word of mouth was giving Summer all the growth she needed, but that might change overnight. One bad review from a disgruntled client . . .

She shivered at the thought. "It's on my list as soon as this wedding commission is done."

"Move it higher on your list. Exercise is important. Making time for a life is even more crucial. Otherwise, you burn out and bad things begin to happen. Balance is something I'm trying to accomplish myself."

"How is that working out?"

"Mixed success," Dane said dryly. "How about some more chicken?"

Summer held out her plate. "It's wonderful. I can't refuse."

This dinner was exactly what she needed. When Dane St. Pierre showed his nice side, he was nearly irresistible. He asked the right questions and then listened as if it was important. Before she knew it, she was describing her last trip to France, where she had rummaged in the markets in search of antique fabric and satin trims. The strange thing was, he looked like the details fascinated him.

Because he was such a good listener, Summer found herself telling him about studying art history in college, wandering into a museum in San Francisco and seeing a royal gown from the Tudor period. From that moment she had been lost, utterly and completely.

She had gone to work as an intern in London, following that with a year of study in Florence. Her skill had grown, fueled by her creativity. Now she had her own business, which inspired her and motivated her every day.

"The bottom line? I love what I do." Summer looked down ruefully at her hands. "Except when I cut my fingers with my needles and embroidery scissors. Or when my neck throbs after a foot of intricate beading or reverse appliqué."

"Price of success, Red. A massage now and then might help."

Another thing that Lizzy had been telling her.

She glanced down at the plate, where a plump piece of mozzarella was smothered in golden spices. "If you're not going to have that last piece of cheese . . ."

"Be my guest. I like to watch you eat. Better still . . ." Dane lifted the cheese and held it out to her. Summer hesitated. She leaned closer and took a bite from his fingers. Her mouth brushed his thumb and a hot wave of awareness raced through her.

The cheese was ecstasy.

She didn't even want to think about his touch.

She cleared her throat. "Wow. I really need to get the name of that restaurant."

"Why don't I take you next week? My brother has been at me to visit for ages. He would be ecstatic to arrange dinner for us."

"It sounds wonderful." Then Summer thought of her schedule and winced. How could she possibly go anywhere? "I'll have to think about it. But tell me about yourself now. Your brother is a chef. Why did you choose police work?"

"It's not really that interesting."

"Why don't you let me decide. I'd say your job is very important. Possibly dangerous, too?"

"Close," he murmured.

"Are you still in high-profile security work?"

"Now and again."

"Royal protection, too?"

He smiled a little. "You know I can't talk about it."

"So what made you leave the police?"

He poured some wine and studied the glass. "Long hours. Long weeks. Long surveillance. It all takes a toll. Don't get me wrong. We were doing important work and I enjoyed every moment. But after a while it's best for a younger man, someone enthusiastic and excited about the details. Probably someone who is a little naïve."

"And you're not?"

"Not anymore," Dane said dryly. "Goes with the territory."

Summer wondered what kind of jobs had made him tough and laconic. She decided it was none of her business. "So who do you protect now?"

"No details."

"Which means you probably work for some of the same people you guarded before. But I won't ask questions. I see a few of those same people and I know how stressful their lives can be. There can be a dark side to fame because of stalkers. Angry ex-husbands or old lovers. Things the public seldom sees."

Dane steepled his fingers. "True again. I suppose you do see that with your clients. But no more talk about work. Let's just focus on the extraordinary chocolate ganache with raspberries that my brother insisted I bring for dessert. It's a killer. Forget about any hope of calorie counting."

Summer's mouth was already watering. Before she could answer, she heard quiet footsteps echo out in the mews and then a muttered oath. The door creaked.

Dane slid to his feet. He frowned, lifting his raincoat from the side chair.

A weapon? Summer tried to clear her tangled thoughts. In the wake of his sudden arrival and a wonderful dinner, she had forgotten all about her last appointment.

"Dane, it's all right. I'm expecting someone. She has a key."

"Maybe. Or maybe it's someone else." He moved to the door in full protective mode, ignoring her. Leaning down, he glanced out into the darkness.

Then he shook his head with a wry smile. "Coast is clear. I believe your last appointment has just arrived."

Chapter Seven

Dane looked outside again and gave a quiet whistle. "Is that who I *think* it is?"

Summer smiled. "I would have told you sooner, but I was distracted." She glanced at the antique clock above her desk. "I had no idea it was so late. I blame you for that. You're a very good listener." She ran a hand through her hair and crossed to the door. "Why don't you stay? Something tells me you would help put her at ease."

"Flattery? That's playing dirty." Dane swept up their empty dishes and silverware. "Very well. My night is all yours. Any particular orders?"

"Just . . . make her laugh. Marisa is under a lot of pressure and she needs a distraction. Something tells me you're a genius in the distraction department."

"I'm not sure that's a compliment, but I'll give it my best effort."

Summer opened the door and blinked. She took the expensive raincoat that Marisa Lang held out to her. "Rain? Why can't we have some snow? At least a few perfect flakes."

The actress pulled off her dark scarf and propped a pair of sunglasses on her forehead. She was strikingly beautiful at close range. Even without makeup, her skin was luminous and her eyes were an impossible shade of aquamarine.

"No snow in sight. It does spoil the Christmas mood, doesn't it?" The slender blonde turned and saw Dane in a chair at the center of the shop. She stiffened. "I'm sorry, Summer. You didn't tell me you had company. I can come back tomorrow."

"Don't worry. Dane and I were just finishing dinner. It was . . . a surprise."

The woman smiled warmly. "I'm delighted to hear it. We were beginning to wonder if you were ever going to have any personal life."

"*We?*"

"Lizzy and I. We worry about you. You work too hard. Frankly, you can cancel my order for the last three garments. I already have more than I need." She cast a glance at Dane and leaned closer to Summer. Her voice fell to a whisper. "Take some time off and go spend it with *him*. Heavens, what a hunk. Actually, he looks familiar. Do I know him?"

Summer wondered where the actress might have

met Dane. Through his work or through his obligations as a peer of the realm, it was very possible that their paths might have crossed. "I'll introduce you. You don't mind if he stays, do you? He's very discreet."

"I'd love to meet him. I warn you, I'm in matchmaking mode these days. I want *everyone* married and as happy as I am."

"Marisa, meet my friend Dane St. Pierre. His complete title is Viscount Ravenhurst, but he tells me that the lord business isn't what it used to be."

The actress laughed and clapped her hands. "Of course. I *knew* that I had met you. It was a charity ball in Surrey."

He nodded. "I remember that you were caught in a throng of ardent admirers. No fiancé in sight, as I recall."

"That's the night I met Peter." A flush filled Marisa's cheeks. "And you were all alone, as I recall. I wondered at that. I suppose you had recently ended a desperate love affair."

Dane cleared his throat. "Not exactly."

No, he had been working, Summer thought. But clearly Dane wanted to change the subject. He stood up, circling around the heavy linen bag that Summer had hung in the middle of the room. "Is this the final creation? I'll offer you my opinion, if you like. You can choose. Fulsome praise and extravagant lies. Or the absolute truth."

Marisa frowned. "The truth, *please*. I get so little of it these days. That's one of the reasons I love working with Summer. If I choose a fabric or design that's not good for my figure or coloring, she tells me flat out. No drawn-out explanations or evasions. Do you know how rare that is?"

Dane's eyes darkened. "I have a very good notion of how rare that is. I do think that makes her special."

Summer felt her cheeks burn. She turned away, fussing to unzip the linen bag that held the finished gown. "Let's go get you dressed, Marisa. Are you sure Peter isn't lurking somewhere nearby?" Summer smiled. "I know he was wild to get a view of you in the gown. You've been talking about it so much."

"No, Peter is at a business meeting tonight. He wanted to come, but I scheduled it for precisely that reason." Marisa Lang moved gracefully into the dressing room, her face luminous beneath the big chandelier. "I can barely wait to see your magic."

After ten minutes passed, Dane began to grow impatient. Inside the dressing room he heard quiet murmurs, soft questions, and the rustle of heavy silk. There was something very intimate about those sounds.

Summer was good at this business. She knew when to agree and when to question. It was clearly an emotional time for her client, and Marisa was anxious that everything go well. Dane had heard she had a big movie coming up. He'd also heard that her husband-to-be was under pressure from his parents to produce an heir very fast.

The difficulties of modern life in the jet set, he thought.

The dressing room curtain slid back with a flourish. Summer looked out, her eyes gleaming. "Ready?"

"Definitely."

When the bride appeared, a beaded veil covered her famous high cheekbones and fell over her shoulders. The satin gown seemed to float around her, almost as if it were alive. Light danced off the pearls at the bottom of the veil and the intricate folds at Marisa's slender shoulders.

The effect was entrancing. The groom would be struck dumb. Dane was nearly in that condition himself.

If Summer ever made a dress like that for *herself* and wore it, he would be struck deaf and dumb. Especially if she wore it for another man . . .

Where had that thought come from? Dane frowned, realizing that Summer had just asked him a question. "Sorry?"

"What do you think of it?"

The bride turned slowly. "Remember, I asked for the complete and honest truth."

"The truth is that no one will be able to speak

when you walk down that aisle. Maybe even breathe. I'm not feeling too steady, either."

Marisa laughed, but the sound was uncertain. Dane realized this was the moment for some psychology to smooth her nerves. "I'm being absolutely honest. There's something elegant about the way the gown falls into those little folds. Pleats, I guess they're called. They run all the way up to the shoulder. How do you make something like that, Summer?"

"Very slowly. But it is a beautiful effect, especially when they end in that diamond clip at the neckline. Only one diamond. Nothing overwhelming. But it's arresting?"

"I'm afraid they'll have to *arrest* her other suitors. They're going to be frantic."

"You're sure? Both of you? I don't want Peter to be disappointed. All his family will be there, plus journalists from five countries. My parents and my new agent, too, of course."

Summer lifted the veil. "I would never lie. I shouldn't say this, but I've worked with many people, and yet this dress and the way you wear it will be my favorite. Just don't *tell* anyone else."

The actress took a deep breath. She studied herself in the mirror, relying on her own eyes and not the impression of someone else. She spun slowly and gave a surprised laugh. "It is magical, isn't it? Almost what you'd expect a princess to wear." She twirled, and silk rustled as she lifted her arms. "Oh,

Summer, *thank* you. This dress is more than I could imagine. Peter will be so pleased. I'm certain of it. *That's* what I want most."

Summer brushed a hand across her eyes. There was a moment of silent bonding and deep emotion. *Are all brides this way?* Dane wondered.

"You two probably want to be alone to finish up."

But Marisa shook her head. "No, stay. I won't keep you any longer. Clearly you both have better things to do. Help me take this off, can you, Summer? I'll just be a moment. Then I suggest you finish the bottle of wine I saw on the table."

When she swirled back to the dressing room, her laughter drifted in the quiet air.

"She's very honest," Summer said thoughtfully. "Very vulnerable, too. I hope she stays that way."

"Peter's a decent man. I know his family a little. I think they are a good match. She may need to develop a tougher skin, but I suppose being in Hollywood will help that."

"You *know* the groom?"

"Not extremely well. We've worked together on occasion. And no, I can't discuss it."

"Is there anyone you *don't* know?"

Dane gave a slow smile. "No one who matters. But you heard your client. Go help her with the dress, and then I'll walk her to her car. After that, I have something in mind. It's barely nine, you know. That gives us all the time in the world."

Chapter Eight

They argued about sports.

Summer loved football and Dane loved soccer.

They disagreed about movies. Summer loved French films and he loved British classics from Pinewood Studios.

They worked their way through pop music and science fiction novels and independent travel. He loved the Maldives; Summer loved Florence in the winter.

He laughed and told her that two people were never more mismatched, but the energy between them sparked as they talked about everything that mattered along with things of no importance at all. There was a wariness, tinged with an excited kind of expectation that Summer found impossible to resist.

Dane took her hand as they walked up the street. Travel was no problem, he said. They could fit Florence and the Maldives into one trip. It would be easy for her to pack: two silk dresses and a skimpy bathing suit. Top optional.

Summer laughed at his easy banter. He guided them to a little restaurant that happened to be one of Summer's favorites. When he walked inside, the owner greeted Dane by name and guided them to a private table next to the little courtyard with the twinkling Christmas tree lights.

Dane asked about the owner's mother.

The owner asked about Dane's new business.

"You know the owner? This place is not exactly on the standard tourist's map."

"I asked some people I trust." He smiled and reached across the table, putting his hand over Summer's. "And the gentleman in question had already approached our security firm. He's concerned about the local burglaries. We're putting together a monitoring plan for everyone on this street." He frowned. "That will make me feel better about you working so late at night."

"But I didn't ask you to do this. And as for payment—"

"Irrelevant. I intend to set up this monitoring program either way. Now let's change the subject, shall we? I believe that chocolate is your particular weakness."

"Bribery, Lord Ravenhurst?"

"Count on it. I intend to tunnel under all your defenses, Ms. O'Neal. I'll overwhelm your senses with dark chocolate."

"And then?"

"Let's throw out the rule book tonight, shall we? We can see where the journey takes us. No plans and no expectations."

Summer felt giddy and suddenly reckless. "You're a persuasive man."

"So I'm told. It never seemed to matter before." His eyes darkened. "Now it does. I didn't expect how much." He traced her hand, frowning. "Is there a man in your past? Someone important?"

She swallowed hard. "No one current."

"What happened?"

"There were . . . one or two, a long time ago. Nothing serious. No one who mattered."

Dane slid his fingers into hers. "Good. But you mentioned something about a business partner?"

"Percy is just a good friend. He's been wonderful with financial advice in the last year. He was the one who helped me find this space when it came up for lease."

"He bungled your alarm company research." Dane stiffened. "Is he a business partner or a would-be lover?" He winced at the rough tone to his question. Why did her scent suddenly fill his head? Why did the bloody question suddenly *matter* so much?

Summer put down her glass carefully. "Percy

isn't a lover. I don't have those kinds of feelings for him."

Dane could see that clearly now that he had calmed down. Women gave off signals about things like that. There was a sense of being off-limits and already involved. Summer O'Neal had neither. She looked vulnerable, intensely curious, slightly fragile. He found himself wanting to touch her hair and skim her cheek. To see how those full lips would taste if he leaned a little closer.

It was probably a bad idea, but he didn't care if it was.

Summer stared at the little white lights twinkling in the courtyard. "Lately he seems a little more opinionated. More . . . possessive."

"Has he been bothering you?" Dane demanded.

"Not really." Summer frowned. "He has hinted at us having something more. And there's the casual touch, the quick brush of an arm."

"Tell him to go to hell," Dane snapped.

"It's not that easy." Summer ran a hand over her cheek, pushing back a strand of auburn hair. "Percy believed in me when no one else did. He recommended clients. He helped me secure lines of credit and checked my balance sheets."

"I'll just bet he's checked your sheets," Dane muttered. "And now he wants you to think you owe him."

"I do owe him. For his friendship and for his advice . . ." Her voice trailed away.

"So now he wants to collect in bed."

"I didn't say that."

"You didn't have to say it." Dane's voice was grim. "I want to talk to the man."

Actually, Dane wanted to *kill* the man.

Slowly.

Summer looked up in surprise when the owner brought over a bottle in a gleaming silver bucket, and two waiters appeared with dessert.

"You didn't have a chance for wine earlier, so I thought we would try again. It's a remarkable vintage." He nodded his approval of a sample taste and then waited while the owner filled Summer's glass. "I know the man and woman who make this. They're ruthless, opinionated, quirky, and all-around unforgettable. I think you'll like their wine."

"Because I'm ruthless, opinionated, and quirky, too?"

"Because you're *unforgettable,*" Dane said roughly.

Summer tasted the wine and sighed. "Heaven on the tongue. Light and just a little sensual, with layers of oak and plum."

"Well described." Dane raised his glass to her in a silent toast. "The owners would be proud. They live most of the year in the south of France now. I try to visit when I can."

"I haven't been there, but it's high on my list. The Camargue and the white horses. The Roman Viaduct at Nîmes. The Knights Templars' castle at Carcassonne."

"That's quite a list. Carcassonne is well worth a visit."

"You've been there?"

"Three times."

Summer raised an eyebrow. "Work or holiday?"

"A little of both. Have some more wine."

"Are you hoping to make me drunk?"

"Caught," he murmured. "But back to Carcassonne. It's remarkable to sleep in rooms that once rang to the hooves of Knights Templars' mounts. There is history everywhere, down every street and over every hill."

Summer thought about this for a long time. "I love the images you paint."

"I know some small vineyards making wine you will never find outside France. And the markets there are full of local textiles. Lace. Embroidery. Toiles. We should go," Dane said suddenly. "Together. What do you say?"

Summer sighed.

Carcassonne. The south of France.

With Dane.

What a temptation.

"Now, that's purely evil. You know how all of that appeals to my creative side."

"We wouldn't go to work," Dane said slowly. "We would go to live. To eat well, to drink wine that tantalizes and restores. We would feel the history in every stone and wall. When the sky is clear and bright, it seems to go on forever. Just like your eyes."

His voice deepened with emotion, like gravel pouring into cool, deep water.

Summer closed her eyes, dazed and overwhelmed.

It was impossible to think straight. He made her want things she had never considered.

"Let's go." Dane tossed down his napkin and stood up, then moved around to pull out Summer's chair. He reached for his wallet, but the owner appeared by magic, shaking his head.

"Absolutely not. Tonight is my gift. Call it my wish for the beginning of a successful business arrangement."

Summer stood up, feeling a little giddy from the wine and from the sudden emotions that Dane had stirred. She had never felt so alive, with her life so full of possibilities. Maybe it was time to be a little reckless.

But reality was hard to ignore. "I've got seed beads and pleats to finish in the morning," she said slowly. "No dancing until dawn for me."

"A pity." Dane held out her coat and she slipped it on, feeling a frisson of awareness at the press of his hands. His angular face was almost unbearably handsome, and he watched her with all his attention, controlled and intense. How long had it been since a man had looked at her like this?

Dangerous question.

Dangerous territory.

"You'll be done with this job someday, you know." They walked out into the street and Summer felt Dane move closer. Then he slipped his arm through hers. He didn't ask, and she didn't protest. It felt remarkably natural, as if her arm was meant to be nowhere else but held tight against him.

She gave her head a shake. "I didn't plan to drink so much. Catch me if I fall."

"You'll never fall. I'll see to that," he whispered.

Wind gusted up the street and brushed through her hair. Summer shivered a little and felt Dane pull her closer.

She didn't want to speak. She didn't want to ask questions or think about work or make plans for anything at all. The night was too beautiful.

She didn't want it ever to end.

Dane watched light glow in a halo around Summer's face and wondered why she was so beautiful. He felt dizzy when he looked at her. The thought made him frown.

He felt a hit of emotion as Summer brushed against him. Her hair settled on his shoulder and he smelled cinnamon and bergamot. A lethal mix, he decided.

"So what's she like?"

"She?"

"The woman you were going to meet before you appeared last night."

"What makes you think—"

"Oh, be serious. You were dressed to the teeth and carrying a very expensive bottle of vintage wine. You had a lean and hungry look about you. Of course you were meeting a woman." Summer studied his face. "So what is she like?"

What a question, Dane thought. "Veronica is just . . . well, Veronica. What do you care?"

"Simple curiosity, I suppose. I've never been on close terms with a British lord before. Unless you count the oaf who drove his red Jaguar onto my front sidewalk, then collapsed in my tulips."

Dane's mouth twitched. "That would have to be Harry Whitworth. The man never could hold his whisky."

Summer chuckled. "That's the one. But stop trying to change the subject. Is she tall and thin, all blond hair and skinny legs?"

Dane certainly wouldn't describe Veronica as skinny. She had curves in all the right places. But suddenly he didn't want to talk about Veronica. He loosened his tie and slid Summer's hand into the crook of his arm. "Not exactly."

"I suppose she wears see-through lace and wildly expensive French perfume. Something made especially for her. And she probably giggles a lot."

He and Veronica had never talked much, Dane realized. Somehow that bothered him. After all, two people should talk about things, just the way he was talking with Summer. He liked arguing and laughing with her.

"Jealous, Red?"

"In a pig's eye. I'm just curious. So?"

"She sometimes laughs. I can't say I remember."

"You were too busy trying to maneuver your way into her bedroom, I suppose."

Dane didn't tell her that no maneuvering had been necessary. Veronica had always been at least as enthusiastic as he was.

He decided it was time to change the subject. Veronica seemed a dim memory to him already.

Somehow it felt natural for him to cup Summer's cheek and ease her closer against his shoulder.

She sighed and looked up at the sky. "That's the Big Dipper, isn't it?"

Dane chuckled. "We call it the Plow on this side of the Atlantic, Red. In Romania it's known as the Great Wagon."

"Name all the stars and I'll really be impressed."

Dane's head slanted back as he concentrated. "Well, the first star at the end of the bowl is Dubhe, and that's Merak just below it. Phecda and Megrez are next, followed by Alioth. That's Mizar right there at the bend of the handle. Do you see it?"

Summer nodded.

"Alioth has some strange, fluctuating spectral lines. And Mizar is actually two stars. In ancient

Persia sailors tested their eyesight by whether or not they could see Mizar's companion star."

"I guess I'd fail." Summer yawned. "What language was that?"

"Persian. Most of the constellation names that we use today are Persian."

Summer eased closer, sounding sleepy. "Say them again. It's like a poem."

Dane went down the list, smiling as he remembered lazy summer nights as a boy in Norfolk. Life had been simpler then. His greatest adventure was to stare through the gritty lens of a homemade telescope and dream of traveling out into space. He felt Summer relax against him, her head slanting onto his shoulder. When he looked down she was yawning.

Moonlight wreathed her face in silver. She looked vulnerable and very beautiful.

Summer stopped walking. "Thank you for a wonderful evening. You really *didn't* need to bring me dinner. After all, you did arrange for me to have a proper alarm system. I probably owe *you*, if we were really keeping tabs."

"Oh, I'm keeping tabs," Dane said softly. His finger traced her cheek in the moonlight.

"This is where I live," Summer said, her voice unsteady.

"Nice building. Looks old." Dane glanced up at the darkened windows. "I don't think I'll walk you up. Flip the lights on and off inside so I know everything's fine. Then turn the lights off and go to sleep. No work. I'll be watching."

"Bully."

"Call it what you want. You need to rest."

Summer smiled at him crookedly. "I don't have the slightest idea why I'm taking orders from you."

"Because I mean well. You know that."

Summer sighed as his fingers drifted along her cheek. Wind blew up the street. "Snow would make tonight really perfect. Do you think it will *ever* happen this year?"

"It will. Like most of the very good things in life, it will come when you least expect it." Dane's hands trailed over her hair. "Just the way I feel right now. I think the wine has gone to your head as well as mine," he said roughly. "Better go inside. I'll call you tomorrow."

"Dane, you're busy and I'm busy. Is this a good idea?"

"It's the best idea I've ever had. And while we figure out exactly what's happening between us, I'd appreciate it if you'd stopped arguing. *Go.*"

He ran his fingers slowly across her cheek and over her forehead. Then he gave his head a shake. "You take my breath away, Summer O'Neal. But if you stand this close and smile at me like that much longer, I may *not* be responsible for the results."

*   *   *

For a long time Summer lay in the quiet night, watching the stars through her window. She felt restless, struck by conflicting emotions, with the awareness that her life was at a crucial turning point. Everything could change in a moment, if she let it.

If she chose to discover the things that Dane had described. He had made no promises and had never crossed the line of proper behavior, but Summer could read the dark intensity in his eyes. He felt the possibilities just as much as she did. He was offering her adventure and passion, along with the chance to discover her own strengths and desires.

She closed her eyes on a groan, pulling the pillow over her head. She had wedding clothes to finish and her business to think about. But the real problem, always at the back of her mind, was the way her family had slowly, inexorably fallen apart. Her father had traveled more and more until Summer barely remembered who he was.

Her mother's silences had grown. She had become moody and withdrawn. She stopped going out at all.

Finally she had turned cold and angry. She had lashed out at everyone, including Summer, her only daughter. Nothing was her own fault, but she refused to make changes in her life. Everything had frightened Summer's mother, and nothing had pleased her. She was a constant victim in her own eyes, and there had never been laughter in their house, Summer remembered.

She would never allow that to happen to *her*.

Wind gusted up the street. A tree branch tapped at her window. She yawned, closing her eyes. For a moment there almost seemed to be a message in that rhythmic tapping, like a low voice murmuring in her head.

Be brave. Try something new.

That's crazy. Stay right where you are. You'll only get hurt.

Tap, tap.

Tap, tap.

Summer pressed the pillow to her ears, driving out the sound.

It was strange, but she had been certain that Dane meant to kiss her. She had been ready, waiting for him to pull her toward him.

His eyes had been very dark, full of questions, yet open to possibilities.

To her surprise he had simply slid her arm through his and turned, walking up the steps to her apartment in the beautifully restored regency building.

She had so wanted to feel his mouth on hers.

With a sigh, she forced her thoughts away from Dane. She closed her eyes and in her mind she drew out a long strand of thread, knotting it carefully.

She let herself drift into the flow of sewing,

threading her imaginary needle right down into sleep.

Her last thought was to wonder if there was a word for the smoky, swirling shade of green in Dane's eyes whenever he said her name.

Chapter Nine

Dane sat at his desk, twirling a lacquer fountain pen.

He should have been thinking about his budget plan for the security project in Rye. He should have been planning his next trip, which was fast approaching. Instead of that, he was thinking about the way Summer laughed. The way her strong, slender fingers stroked a bolt of silk, appreciating its drape.

He couldn't seem to get her out of his mind. And that had to be a bad thing, didn't it? Especially when he was thinking of reasons to delay his next field planning trip.

Or was it time he faced his future and found the one woman he would be happy to share the rest of his life with?

Dane sat for a long time in the morning sunlight, thinking about constellations and Carcassonne and the way Summer's hair glowed in the sunlight. Then he leaned forward and picked up his phone.

He wished he could see her face in twenty minutes when the delivery arrived.

Summer put down a camisole of embroidered silk when the back door buzzer rang. Before she could move, Lizzy jumped up, stretching her shoulders. "I'll answer it. Maybe it's the ribbon delivery from Paris. They're running three days late." She moved past Summer to the back door, and Summer kept working.

She heard murmurs and then laughter. When Lizzy returned, she had a package in her hands.

"Is that the French silk ribbons?"

Lizzy glanced at the box. "It's not from Paris. The box says Armani. Did you order something?"

Summer frowned. "No." She put her finished camisole in a box lined with tissue paper and then crossed to Lizzy's desk. The box said *Milano*. An Armani label ran across the top.

Lizzy held out a card. "This has your name on it. Looks like a man's handwriting to me. Probably a man who *happens* to be an English lord," she murmured.

Summer cleared her throat. "I don't know what you're talking about." But she carried the envelope around into her office to read privately, because she had a fair idea of the box's source.

Bold black letters raced across thick, creamy paper.

> I think this should replace the one you lost.
> I guessed at the size and the color. I hope I did a decent job.
> Let me take you to dinner the first night you wear it.
>
> > Dane

She opened the box slowly, removing a mound of monogrammed tissue paper. Then she ran her fingers over a beautifully woven skirt of fine herringbone tweed.

It was the most elegant and subtle fabric Summer had ever seen, light and soft against her fingers. And it was the exact style of the skirt she had ruined the night her alarm system had failed.

Dane had pegged it perfectly. She couldn't begin to imagine how many favors he had called in for this. Her experienced eye noticed all the careful seam details and edgings of custom work.

But she wasn't sure she should accept something of this value. Should she? Did it imply more than she was prepared to give?

She realized that Lizzy was standing right behind her, looking into the box. "That's a beautiful skirt. Wait—that's just like the one that got ripped."

"Dane replaced it. I can't imagine how he managed to do it so fast." Carefully, Summer put the skirt back in its box.

Lizzy shook her head. "Armani. Custom. I'd say that sounds serious. Not that anyone's asking *my* opinion." Smiling broadly, Lizzy walked back to her desk, whistling under her breath.

The tune sounded like the "Wedding March."

Summer suppressed an urge to laugh. Dane was a menace. A devastatingly charming and impossible-to-resist *menace*.

But Dane was bound to lose interest in her. Men always preferred the excitement of pursuit. She wasn't sultry or experienced, the kind of woman that dropped a man in his tracks and made him change his life overnight. And really, what did they have in common?

With a sigh, Summer put the box on the shelf above her worktable. Then she told herself to forget all about the ruggedly attractive Englishman with eyes that made her feel young and reckless and impossibly beautiful.

Her cellphone chimed fifteen minutes later with a text message from Dane.

Have dinner with me. I'll pick you up at your
flat.

There was a delay. Then she heard the beep of a
second text.

I believe I already mentioned that you work
too hard. But not tonight.
And it would please me very much if you wore
the skirt.

Summer sighed. She had another row of hand-
beading to finish. Why couldn't she concentrate?

Lizzy walked around and pulled the fabric from
her hands. "I'll finish this. You've spent too much
time in this lonely workshop already. Go enjoy a
night out with your lord."

Summer put away her phone and grumbled.
"When did *you* get so smart?"

"I've always been smart. You've just never noticed before. I've finished my sleeve, so now I'll finish yours. I'm better at beading than you are,
anyway."

It was true. Lizzy was much better at beading.
Summer was efficient, but she preferred garment
structure, embroidery, and actual designing. Wasn't
it true that you were always better at the things you
loved most?

She pulled out her phone and frowned down at
the screen. She bit her lip.

What to say?

Lizzy sighed and rolled her eyes. "Stop thinking. Text him back and then go home and get ready. Wear the red knit dress that gives you an hourglass figure. He'll melt at one glance."

"He wants me to wear his skirt."

"Wow. That sounds serious to me."

Summer paced and took a deep breath, floating on a wave of excitement. Maybe he *was* different. Maybe this could actually last.

She typed in her answer quickly, before she could change her mind.

That would be nice. I'll see you at eight. By the way, the skirt is gorgeous.
How can I possibly thank you?

Instantly another text shot back.

I'm sure we can think of something.

Summer flushed and then laughed out loud.

At twenty minutes after seven, Summer left for home. Lizzy was still locking up, but she insisted that Summer go ahead.

And it was time she finally started to delegate responsibility.

Tonight would be her first real test.

Halfway home, Summer remembered that she had left her cashmere sweater on her desk, folded in a bag with her best embroidery needles. She wanted to wear the sweater because it matched her new skirt perfectly.

Damn and blast.

She spun around, running back up the street. If she was very fast, she could grab her bag, lock up again, and still have time to be ready when Dane arrived.

The lights were out in the workshop when she turned the corner. Wind blew up the street and she heard a cat howl in the distance. She had left Churchill at home that morning and she wanted to get back to feed him.

She glanced around, saw the street was empty, and moved to the alarm. Quickly she punched in the code. Her hand slid into her pocket, where she kept her new security fob.

Everything was quiet.

She opened the door, flipped on the lights, and moved to her desk, relieved to see the bag right where she had left it.

"Got you," she muttered.

Lizzy had left a finished silk slip on her desk, covered with exquisite beadwork. Summer had been very lucky the day she found Lizzy, fresh out of design school and one year's experience at a workshop in Paris. Very, very lucky.

Maybe this delegating responsibility would be easier than she had expected.

She moved back to the door and turned off the lights.

A hard hand slammed down over her throat and shoved her back against the wall.

Chapter Ten

He must have been waiting inside the shop, Summer thought blindly. She began to fight, kicking backward as the man gripped her arm and yanked it behind her back. She felt something sharp dig at her neck.

"Stop fighting. You're going to open the safe for me. One more move and I'll use this knife."

Summer swallowed hard. Her hand slid into her pocket and traced the remote security fob.

"Whatever you want. I—I promise."

He didn't answer. Summer felt his hands shaking. He was panicked, and that was not a good sign.

She felt the alarm fob. She had practiced with it, even in the dark. She knew what button to push.

The bigger one with the raised center was the duress button and would send out a silent alert.

The man jerked at her arm, but she twisted away and pressed the alarm button hard. She knew that a silent alarm had just gone out.

She cleared her throat, trying to relax. "The safe—it's in the storeroom. The room next to the back hallway."

"Show me. And don't do anything stupid."

She nodded, fighting down her fear as he pushed her in front of him. "There's a key. I'll go find it."

He shook his head. "You have a passcode. I know that. Use the code and forget about the key. Remember, nothing suspicious. Nothing to attract attention."

"Of course." Summer was trying to estimate the lapsed time. Someone should be here within three minutes. She had to stay calm until then.

She frowned when she heard a click and realized that he had turned off the lights. He would attract less attention that way.

"I can't see."

A small flashlight came on, casting a shielded, pinpoint beam in front of her. "Stop talking and open the safe."

How long had he been watching her shop to learn these details?

But she didn't argue. He seemed unstable, glancing out the front windows, and she didn't know what might set him off.

Muttering, he pushed her toward the back wall. "Open your safe."

Her hands shook as she reached up and found the small framed painting that covered her safe. She pulled the painted canvas away from the wall and studied the metal doors, pretending to work at remembering the numbers.

"*Hurry up.*"

No more delays. It was too dangerous.

Summer tapped in the string of numbers on the safe, and her heart sank as the door slid open. They didn't keep much money here, only petty cash. Deposits were made on a daily basis at the bank, though most of their payments came electronically or via credit card. But they had received a shipment of pearls and a few gems in connection with Marisa Lang's wedding commission. Right now there was almost twenty thousand dollars' worth of gems and textiles inside the safe. Some of the vintage lace panels and antique tapestry pieces were worth nearly a thousand dollars each.

She blinked back tears. The loss would be devastating.

"Move over." The man shoved her sideways with one hand against her neck, the knife resting close to her skin as he reached in and knocked all the items from the safe into a bag.

In the penlight beam Summer saw that he was wearing a ski mask. She couldn't see any details of his face. He pulled her around and ran his beam across the room. "Now open the other safe. The one underneath your desk, where you keep the really expensive jewels."

"I don't have another safe. There isn't—"

The knife jabbed at her skin. "*Shut up.* I know you have one. Find it."

He must have confused this with a different shop, Summer thought desperately. But he would never believe that. "Fine. I'll open it. Just—just don't hurt me."

She took a deep breath and crossed toward the sewing table in the back room. They did have a locked tapestry box where she kept some of her oldest lace samples. She leaned down, then pretended to reach under the box. "The lock is hidden," she explained in a shaky voice.

The lid opened. The man in the mask ran his light across layers of neatly folded fabric and grabbed a large rhinestone brooch, shoving it into his bag. It wasn't worth half of what one piece of her best lace cost, Summer thought angrily. "That's it? Where is the set of matched emeralds?"

He *definitely* had her confused with someone else. "I don't . . . that is, we sold them. A customer who came in today liked them. She bought them all."

The man cursed. He swept the box off the table and dumped all the contents onto the floor. When he bent down to dig through the fabric, Summer's hand slid onto the table. In silence she found her biggest, sharpest rotary cutter.

She swung around quickly, moving toward the door. The man came after her, but stopped when the beam of his penlight played across the razor-sharp blade she was holding in front of her. He wasn't going to take her lace or her petty cash or anything else in the shop.

He gave a low, ugly laugh. "You want to fight me? That's a damn stupid idea."

Behind her Summer heard a click. The back door slid open. She caught a smoke-and-cloves scent. Relief swirled up in a rush.

"On the contrary. Her fighting you is an amazing and unforgettable sight. Especially when you consider that she's armed herself with a fabric cutter. What a woman." Dane moved closer. He sounded cold, absolutely in control. "I, on the other hand, am equipped with a Beretta 92S, and right now it is aimed at your forehead. Be absolutely clear: I will shoot if you don't drop the knife. I will not miss."

His voice was cold with command.

After a moment Summer's attacker cursed. Then he did exactly as Dane had ordered.

Dane didn't look at Summer, his eyes locked on the man across the room. But he took a step closer to her. "Did he hurt you?"

"N-No. I'm fine."

"Lucky for him," Dane said harshly. He gestured for the man to move toward the front door. "Turn around and put your hands flat on the wall, out where I can see them."

Summer dragged in a raw breath when the man finally obeyed.

In a blur, she realized it was over. Dane was here and she was safe. So was her shop. Her legs shook as she collapsed in the chair beside her desk.

It was all chaos, a storm of voices and police, along with the arrival of all her neighboring shop owners. Everyone offered her sympathy and support. When Lizzy arrived, looking pale and frightened, Dane calmed her down, murmuring answers to her questions. He had insisted that a medic examine Summer, explaining that you didn't always know you had been wounded during the adrenaline rush of an attack.

Summer wasn't physically harmed beyond a small knife cut at her shoulder. The medic had cleaned that up and bandaged it carefully, then pronounced her safe to go home.

She had helped Lizzy lock up, while Dane kept a watchful eye over them both. But the thought of going into her empty apartment made her shiver.

Lizzy had gone now. They were alone in front of Summer's shop.

"I have a rental in Hastings. Why don't you come back home with me?" Dane said gruffly.

Summer shook her head. "I don't want to be inside. It feels . . . claustrophobic. Do you have your car nearby?"

He nodded.

"Would you mind taking me for a ride?" She felt his arm slide around her. "Now."

"Whatever you want, Red. Name the place."

Summer leaned in to him, bringing her hand up to grip his waist, drinking in his warmth and feeling stronger. "A long ride. Up to Fairlight and then down to the water. Would you mind terribly?"

His hand tightened on hers. He took a harsh breath. "Mind? I'd drive you all the way to China if you asked me."

The moon was rising as he turned onto the coast road. Wind brushed through the tall grass that bordered the marsh. Clouds raced above a three-quarter moon. Seabirds cried, whirling over the restless grass, where sheep dotted the level ground by the sea.

Summer focused on every detail, listening to the muffled hammer of the waves in the distance. She prayed this would distract her, helping her forget the night's fear and ugliness.

Dane parked at the highest curve in the road, where she had a view of the water. And then he pulled her into his arms, his hands gentle at her shoulders. They didn't need to talk. That touch was enough.

As Dane stared at her without moving, Summer had the sudden sense of falling. There were shadows in those keen eyes along with fierce questions. His thigh was slanted against hers, his breath warm on her face.

She felt the kiss brush her lips. Faint as moonlight.

Summer realized she was flowing against him, shaping her mouth to his. She tried not to think about wedding vows and fine gowns as Dane's hands slid into her hair, easing her closer. He seemed to know just where to touch, just how to stroke her skin. Her head fell back and he planted gentle kisses along her neck.

This I desire, she thought blindly.

This is the best kind of belonging.

His fingers opened, feathering against the curve of her breast.

Then the Englishman pulled away with a curse. He straightened her sweater awkwardly. "Sorry. Punch me if you like."

Summer blinked. Punch him? What she wanted was to kiss him again, to tug off that tie and find the heat beneath his elegant shirt. She wanted . . . *him.*

She'd never known this kind of wanting before.

Heat filled her cheeks. "I don't know what came

over me. When you touch me . . . I forget to breathe." She looked away.

Dane slid his palm across her flushed cheek. "Don't look away, Summer. I know exactly what came over us. You're an incredible woman. One minute you're all sparks and the next minute you're all dreams and laughter. You make a man want . . . forever. I'd like to work on that."

He turned her so that she was sheltered against his shoulder.

Forever, she thought.

That sounded perfect to her.

I want a commitment, Dane thought. For the first time in his life, forever seemed like a wonderful idea.

But he wouldn't get it. Not with Summer or any other woman. In his line of work, *forever* was measured in hours and minutes. Strange that it had never bothered him before. But now with moonlight gilding Summer's cheeks and her perfume tormenting his senses, forever mattered intensely.

Wind raced up from the sea. Already the stars were fading. Gray light filtered through the sky.

Dane studied their linked hands. "I didn't want to tell you, but I have to leave. I can't postpone the trip any longer," he said tightly. "I'll be gone a week. Maybe when I get back, we could . . ."

Her face was still. All ivory. He expected a flat denial. Or at the very least a protest.

"Yes," she said breathlessly.

He wanted to kiss her again, to feel the curve of her breast against his palm. Belatedly, her answer sank in. "Yes, what?"

"When you get back. We could . . ." She looked at his mouth as if she couldn't tear her gaze away. As if she yearned to touch him.

Dane traced her mouth. "Christmas Eve. I'll meet you at the teashop on the corner," he said roughly. "Promise."

She took a deep breath and nodded. "Will it be dangerous, wherever you're going?"

He didn't answer.

She smiled crookedly. "No, don't tell me. Say it will be fast cars, sandy beaches, and clever women. Just lie."

He kissed her instead. Hard and fierce. When she slanted her head back, meeting his mouth, the kiss turned slow and gently searching. It gave and it took without claims or conditions until time seemed to stop.

Gravel whirled up. A seabird cried in its lonely flight down to the water.

Dane sighed and pulled away. "I'll have a friend I trust look in on you while I'm gone."

"You don't have to."

"Like hell I don't."

She touched his jaw gently. "Bully."

"Pragmatist." He smoothed her hair. "Don't look at me like that, or I'll kiss you again. And if I kiss you now, I'm not sure I could stop." His eyes darkened. "Remember. Christmas Eve. I'll be there."

Chapter Eleven

Summer's first postcard arrived two days later. She was finishing a lace peignoir with a matching ivory jacket. Churchill was curled up beside her, asleep on the sunny window ledge.

Summer's heart gave a little lurch as she turned over the heavy vellum card.

No fast cars, the card read, above a big slanting *D*.

The postmark was from Normandy. Summer closed her eyes, shivering in the rush of memories. The feel of his hands. The heat of his lips.

Stay safe, St. Pierre, she thought fiercely.

The second card came at the end of the week after she finished sewing a row of pink pearls onto a fine shantung evening tunic.

No *sandy beaches,* the second card read.

Summer smiled at the big slanting *D*. This time the postmark showed Milan.

She tucked away the card along with the first, in a box lined with black velvet, trying not to feel her heart race.

At her front door a plainclothes officer paced back and forth. He and a second man had taken up a silent presence on the morning of Dane's departure. The white cat nestled closer, nudging her hand and purring loudly. Summer looked at the calendar on her desk. December 24 was outlined with a bright red circle.

There had been a moment in a back street in Singapore when Dane had seen her face in a crowd, smelled her scent. Then she was gone, as unreal as the smoke drifting over the cramped stalls.

His face was tense when the financial delegation approached the Daimlers parked at the curb in front of him. Harrison shifted uneasily beside him. A dim sum vendor bumped down the slanting sidewalk, bamboo steamers shaking.

Harrison said, "It's time to move." As he spoke, two men trotted out of the alley, paper bags shoved beneath their arms. When the first bullet hit and he fell, Dane was thinking of Summer's smile.

*   *   *

She waited for another card. Waited and waited.

But no card came.

More days passed. Her bridal commission was complete, the last gown packed in tissue with sprigs of lavender.

But instead of celebrating, Summer paced the quiet workroom while the white cat studied her with polite curiosity. She clenched her fists and muttered with each step. She was angry . . . and very frightened.

When she saw the officer outside, she cornered him. "Have you heard anything from Dane—Lord Ravenhurst?"

A shadow passed over his eyes. "There was . . . an incident."

The officer looked away.

"Was he hurt?" she whispered.

His face closed down. He studied the cars passing on the narrow street and would tell her nothing more.

Suddenly, the afternoon sunlight seemed thin and cold.

She was at the teashop two hours before noon on the twenty-fourth.

Dane didn't come.

Summer tried to be calm and optimistic, fighting the dark uncertainty that had been growing inside her all week.

Sunlight faded into lavender. Streetlights came on and twilight gathered over the tile roofs. And he did not come.

Summer smoothed the sleeve of her flowing jacket. Since he had left, she had finished this new piece. It was her best work, its sheer silk clinging like a kiss. This gown was for Dane. She prayed he would be here to see it.

Cold air raked her shoulders, making her shiver. The twenty-fourth of December was fading fast.

Why didn't he come?

She thought about Marisa's face when she had arrived for her finished gown and veil. She had been luminous, vibrant. Summer had outdone herself, stirred by thoughts of a man with too many shadows in his eyes.

She looked down at her cold tea through a blur of tears. Beside it, a cup of eggnog was untouched.

Something brushed her shoulder, not the wind. She spun, gasping.

He looked gaunt and there were new lines at his eyes. Summer saw the white sling at his arm.

She swayed to her feet. "Oh, Dane, you're—"

"Fine," he whispered hoarsely. He drew her awkwardly to his chest. "I was afraid you wouldn't be here." His voice tightened. His mouth was whisky and silk, his hands a promise of paradise.

Summer's pulse hammered at the sweet shock of contact.

"I like what you're wearing." He gave her a

crooked smile as he eased her into the curve of his good arm. "But it's giving me all sorts of bad ideas."

"Good," Summer whispered. "That was the plan." She closed her eyes and kissed him for the sheer, blinding pleasure of it, letting her heart race.

He was back. He was safe.

He brushed her lips with his.

Summer sighed. "I can't feel my toes when you do that."

"Good. I plan on doing a whole lot of it." His eyes narrowed. "You don't have anything against weddings, do you?"

"Other people's?"

"Your own. As in you and me." He took a slow breath. "As in forever and ever, Ms. O'Neal. With me."

When he kissed her again, Summer tried to ignore the slam of her heart against her ribs. "Is this a proposal?"

"I think it is." His eyes were very serious as he slid a strand of hair from her cheek. "Yes, it's definitely a proposal. I know it's too soon, too crazy. But I've never felt remotely like this before."

Summer felt a wave of bubbles glide up through her stomach and lodge against her heart. "Dane," she whispered.

"You don't have to give me an answer now. I'll understand if you want to wait until we—"

"Yes," Summer whispered. She didn't need another second to think about it.

"So what do we do now?" Dane whispered, his lips to her cheek. "Send up smoke signals? Call in the cavalry?"

"We have some mulled cider. Then some eggnog. Well spiked, too." Summer smiled shakily. "No sense in letting it go to waste."

"None for me. Something tells me I'm going to need all my wits tonight. I want to touch you, Summer. And I want to remember every sweet detail of your laughter."

She hesitated. "But your arm."

He leaned down and whispered in her ear. "I'll be very inventive."

"Will you?" Summer chuckled when she clicked the circle of metal down over his wrist. Outside in the street, white flakes drifted down slowly.

Dane blinked. "What the—"

"Caught, Lord Ravenhurst. I brought my handcuffs just in case. Do you have a problem with a woman who takes charge?"

His smile was sin itself. "Not in the slightest. Read me my rights and then take me away."

Snow swirled over the roof of the teashop. "You have the right to remain silent," Summer whispered against his jaw. "Whatever you say may be used against you."

"Is that a promise?"

The teashop owner smiled at them. Lizzy, sitting

at a nearby table with her brother, gave a big wink. The white flakes grew, thick and bright, until the air was a shimmering cloud.

"I love you." Dane's voice was grave. "That's for the record, Summer. And that's forever."

Suddenly white satin and vintage lace didn't seem like a bad idea to Summer. Commitment could be a very sweet thing. Just as long as she had the right man beside her.

Acknowledgments

To Debbie Macomber, consummate writer and storyteller, master knitter, world-class plotter, and the very best friend a person could ever imagine. Thank you for all your generosity, your gift of laughter, your courage, and your wonderful spirit. I adore Christmas, too, so this story is for you.

Thanks also to the unforgettable ladies of the Tuesday-night knitting club. We have laughed and shared and learned and grown together. It is a blessing to know and knit with each one of you—Amanda, Denise, Caroline, Celia, Chris, Lynette, Sara, and Stacy. You light my step. Long may the laughter continue.

Rye is one of my favorite towns in England, full of fog-swept streets, half-timbered houses, and the full and wonderful weight of history around every corner. I saw it in August and imagined it in December. It is breathtaking in all seasons.

Dane is a descendant of a character from one of my earliest books. For more information on my hauntingly suspenseful Draycott Abbey series and new contemporary Brides Club books, please visit me online at christinaskye.com.

Tea is ready, along with a sunny spot for knitting! Enjoy the patterns and all of my favorite recipes.

Happy reading,
Christina

About the Author

CHRISTINA SKYE loves the power of the written word. This *New York Times* bestselling author of thirty-six novels and eight novellas still writes longhand. Usually when her characters refuse to behave. She came to writing late. Once she realized that she could not become the heir to a small European mountain kingdom, writing seemed like the next best thing. She is a pushover for Harris tweed, Scottish cashmere, Shanghai street dumplings, French macarons, and dark chocolate. Not always in that order. She loves to cook, knit on big needles, drink tea, collect vintage scarves, and uncover odd historical tidbits that she can weave into her stories.

After receiving her doctorate in classical Chinese literature, she traveled nonstop for six years, then turned her hand to fiction. In 1990 she sold her first novel in six days. Since then she has written five different series for six different publishers. She has appeared on *ABC World News,* Travel News Network, the *Arthur Frommer Show, Geraldo,* Voice of America, *Looking East,* and *Good Morning, Arizona.*

In 2013 her contemporary romance, *The Accidental Bride,* was chosen as one of the ten best romance novels of the year by prestigious *Booklist* magazine. "Rich with realistically complex characters and subtle wit, the latest addition to Skye's Summer Island series is as warm and comforting as a well-knit afghan. Skye perfectly captures the feel and appeal of small-town life, and this sweetly satisfying romance is an excellent read-alikes suggestion for fans of Debbie Macomber's Cedar Cove series or Robyn Carr's Virgin River books" (John Charles, *Booklist*).

The book also received a reviewer's choice award from *Romantic Times* magazine.

She is currently at work on a new adult paranormal series and five more books in her popular Summer Island contemporary series, set on the ruggedly beautiful Oregon coast.

For recipes, contests, knitting tips, and new book excerpts, visit her online at christinaskye.com.

Savor the magic of the season with
#1 *New York Times* bestselling author
Debbie Macomber's newest Christmas novel

DASHING
THROUGH THE SNOW

Filled with warmth, humor, the promise of love,
and a dash of unexpected adventure.

Continue reading for a sneak peek

Coming soon from Ballantine

Chapter One

"What? Are you kidding?" Ashley Davison couldn't believe what she was hearing. The reservation clerk for Highland Airlines glanced up nervously. "I'm sorry, but I can't sell you a ticket to Seattle. If you'd kindly step aside and wait a few minutes—"

"Can't or won't?" Ashley cut in, growing more frustrated and worried by the minute. She drew in a deep breath in an effort to control her patience. The woman behind the desk, whose name tag identified her as Stephanie, was clearly having a bad day. Getting upset with her, Ashley realized, wasn't going to help the situation. She made a determined effort to lower her voice and remain cool-headed.

"I . . . I can't. I'm sorry . . ."

Ashley refused to take no for an answer. Surprising her mother by flying home for Christmas was too important. "I understand getting a ticket to Seattle three days before Christmas is pushing my luck," she said, doing her best to appear calm and composed. "If I'd been able to book a seat sooner, I would have. Getting Christmas off from work was a complete surprise. I attend graduate school and I also work at a diner. I hated to miss the holidays with my mother, but I didn't have any choice. She's a widow and my brother lives in Texas and can't get home for Christmas, so there's only me." Perhaps if the reservation clerk knew her story, she might reconsider the *can't sell you a ticket* part of this discussion.

"Then my boss decided to close the diner between Christmas and New Year's for renovations after the refrigeration unit broke, and then he decided he may as well get a new deep fryer, too, so it just made sense to close down. All this happened at the very last minute, and because he felt so bad he gave me a Christmas bonus so I could fly home."

"I'm so sorry . . ." Stephanie said again, looking nervous. "If you'd kindly move aside and wait a few minutes."

"I haven't seen my mother since last August," Ashley continued, refusing to give up easily. "I wanted to surprise her. It would mean the world to both of us to be together over the holidays. Would you please look again? I'll take any seat, any time of the day or night."

Stephanie didn't so much as glance down at her

computer screen with even a pretense of trying to accommodate her. "I can't . . . I wish I could, but I can't."

Ashley couldn't help wonder what was up with this *can't* business. That made it all the more nonsensical.

"You *can't*," she repeated. "There must be more of an explanation than that. It just doesn't make sense."

The reservation clerk frowned. Her eyes roamed about the area as if she was looking for someone. That, too, was irritating. It was as if she was seeking a replacement or someone to rescue her.

"I believe you have your answer," the man behind her in line said impatiently. He shifted from one foot to the other, letting Ashley know he didn't appreciate her arguing with the clerk.

Ashley whirled around and confronted him face-to-face. "In case anyone forgot to mention it, this is Christmas. How about a little peace on earth and goodwill toward men? Be patient. I'll be finished as soon as possible and then you can talk to Stephanie, but for now it's my turn."

In response, he rolled his eyes.

Ashley returned her attention to the woman at the counter. "If you *can't* find me a seat on a plane to Seattle, I'd be willing to fly standby."

Stephanie shook her head.

"All the flights to Seattle are already booked?" The man next in line blurted out the question.

Stephanie's eyes widened as if she, too, was surprised he'd jumped into their conversation. "I . . . didn't say that. I'll speak to you directly in just a moment," she said.

"Excuse me?" Ashley flared, forgetting her resolve to remain calm and collected. This was too much. With her hands on her hips, she stared down at the other woman. "This is discrimination. Just because he's a man and good-looking you can dredge up a seat for him, but not for me?" This was outrageous. Ashley had never heard of such a thing. Where was a television crew when you needed one? This would make a juicy piece for the six-o'clock news.

Seeing that the line was getting long and the Grinch behind her wasn't the only one with a short fuse, Ashley decided to drop the entire matter.

"Okay, fine, have it your way, but I think this is just plain wrong." With that, she grabbed hold of her suitcase and with all the dignity she could muster started to walk away, feeling more stressed with each step.

"Miss, miss," the airline employee called after her. "If you'd kindly wait a few minutes I'm sure we could resolve this."

"No way," Ashley refused. "As you've repeatedly said, you *can't* sell me a ticket." With that, she headed out of the airport with her dignity in shreds.

Ashley hadn't expected it would be easy to catch a last-minute flight. She'd already tried to find an available seat online, without luck. For reasons she couldn't understand she kept getting booted off the website. That was the reason she'd decided to come directly to the airport and try her chances there.

Naturally, flying home was her first option. But other modes of transportation were also possibilities. She could always try the bus or travel by train, if there was even one scheduled. The most expedient way to make the trip would be to drive. Unfortunately, her fifteen-year-old hand-me-down car wasn't in the best of shape and she was afraid of it breaking down along the way. To top it off, snow was predicted. Under normal circumstances, snow close to Christmas would be ideal, but not in an aging vehicle. If she could afford . . .

Ashley stopped mid-step. Why hadn't she thought of this earlier? She could always rent a car! The solution was right in front of her, the answer obvious. She should have thought about it long before now. And really there was no better place to rent a car than in an airport.

Perfect.

Reversing direction, Ashley headed toward the car rental agencies, traveling down the escalator, rolling her suitcase behind her. When she reached the rental area, all of the agencies displayed signs that stated all their cars had been rented. All but one. Ashley made her way to that counter.

The longer she waited in line, the more she fumed about the airline clerk who'd insisted she

couldn't sell her a seat. The nerve. And then to basically reassure the man in line behind her that
there were seats available. That was discrimination
of the worst kind, even if the guy was eye candy.
Stephanie was clearly looking to do him a favor,
which only served to irritate Ashley more. Truth be
told, she'd noticed him, too. Hard not to, really. He
was tall and stood with military precision, his dark
appearance lean and strong. She suspected he was
either military or former military. He gave that impression.

The line for the car rental agency slowly crept
forward. As luck would have it, the very man who'd
been so annoying at the airline counter came to
stand behind her again.

It gave Ashley satisfaction to see he hadn't been
any more successful with Stephanie in obtaining a
seat than she had.

"So Stephanie couldn't sell you a seat, either,"
she said, trying hard not to gloat.

"All she had available was standby," he grumbled, fingering his cell.

Ashley would have gladly accepted a chance for
a standby flight. It wouldn't have mattered how
long she had to wait. "Not good enough for you, I
suppose."

He glanced her way and frowned, his look darkening. "I can't take the chance. I need to be in Seattle."

"I do, too," she insisted. "It's almost Christmas."

"This is for a job interview."

"A job?" Ashley echoed. "And you have to be there right before Christmas?"

Instead of answering, he returned his attention to his phone, frowning once again. Apparently he wasn't interested in making conversation with her. Fine. Whatever. That being the case, she wasn't interested in talking to him, either.

Turning back around, Ashley noticed that the line had progressed forward and that it was her turn next.

When the agent became available, she reached the counter and offered the man a warm smile, hoping not to have the same experience as she had with the clerk from the airline. "Merry Christmas."

The man looked harried and tired. Ashley didn't blame him. It was a hectic time of year.

"Merry Christmas," he returned without a lot of enthusiasm.

"I need to rent a car," she said, stating the obvious. "I'm headed to Seattle."

The agent looked down at his computer screen. "This is your lucky day. You have the last car in the entire lot and my guess is it's the last vehicle in the entire airport."

"I'll take it," she said, beaming him a smile.

"Excuse me," the man behind her said. "Did I

just hear you say that this is the last car you have available?"

It was all Ashley could do not to revel in her good luck and his lack of fortune. "And it's all mine." She couldn't resist rubbing it in. She was about to suggest he use his power-schmoozing techniques on the ticket agent upstairs again, but didn't. This car was hers. There was no need to taunt him any more than she already had.

"I'm sorry, sir, but I'm afraid it's all we have."

Ashley narrowed her eyes and glared at the handsome stranger.

"Okay, fine," he said, none too pleased. "Then I say we share it. That makes perfect sense, seeing that we both want to get to Seattle."

"It's not happening." Did Mr. *GQ* think she was stupid? Others might be influenced by his good looks and his charm, but not her. "For all I know, you could be a serial killer."

"Don't be ridiculous," he countered. "It's the perfect solution. I need to get to Seattle and so do you."

"I am not sharing this car with you!" Better safe than sorry.

"Miss," the agent interrupted. "If you're going to rent the car I'll need your credit card and driver's license."

"I fully intend to rent this car," Ashley said, glancing at the arrogant man standing next to her.

She slapped her driver's license and credit card on the countertop and whirled around to face him.

"You're unbelievable," she told him, letting him know she wouldn't be pushed around. Some people might be taken in by this alpha male, but not her. It took more than a pretty face to win her over. "I'd be crazy to consider traveling with a complete stranger."

"Come on," he pleaded. "I'll pay for the car, accept all the responsibility, and you can ride for free."

"Oh sure. That's what you say now."

"It's a workable solution," the agent suggested. "It's a long drive to Seattle, and you'd both get what you want."

Ashley hesitated. It would be nice to save the money. And it was a good distance. Still . . .

"You'll pay all the expenses?" she asked the other man, eyeing him again, gauging his serial-killer potential.

"Gladly."

"Rental fee, insurance, gas? *Everything?*" If she agreed, she'd use her Christmas bonus for spending money.

"I'll pay for *everything*," he reiterated.

Still, she wasn't sure she should trust him. "How do I know I can trust you?" she asked, eyes narrowing as she studied him. Sure, he looked decent enough, clean cut and all, but she'd seen enough true-crime shows on television to realize the killer was often the charming, handsome man no one suspected.

"You want references?" He made it sound like a big joke.

"Yes."

"Okay, fine." He exhaled as if completely put out, as if she was the one being unreasonable. "Who do you want to talk to? Will my mother do? What about my sister?"

"What about your wife?" If there was dirt to be had, the wife would be in the know. Besides, it made sense to alert the unsuspecting wife that he was about to travel with her.

"I'm not married."

"Okay, your girlfriend."

"I'm not involved at the moment." Just the way he spoke told her his patience was wearing thin. Too bad. She wasn't about to team up with someone she didn't know without a whole lot of assurances.

"Yeah, right." Men this good-looking never stayed out of relationships for long.

"Come on, lady, you have nothing to lose."

"I don't think so," she said.

"Miss Davison?" the agent said, returning her credit card and identification.

"Yes?"

"If I were you, I'd reconsider."

"You really should," Mr. Tall, Dark, and Handsome reiterated. "I'm taking on the responsibility and you'll ride for free. That's the deal. Take it or leave it."

Ashley hesitated and looked to the agent. "You really think I should do this?"

The agent nodded.

Ashley inhaled and did her best to size up the other man.

"Dash Sutherland," he said, and extended his hand. "If you want to talk to my mother, then I'd be happy to call her. You'll find I'm no evil threat to you or anyone else. We both need to get to Seattle and this is a viable solution."

Ashley had to admit she was tempted; still, she wasn't sure. "We'll drive straight through?"

"Whatever you want."

She chewed on her lower lip, indecision gripping her.

"Having a companion will make the drive easier," he said, encouraging her.

Ashley sighed. What tempted her most was the idea that he was willing to pick up all the expenses. And despite everything, she found herself attracted to him, which she wasn't entirely happy about.

"What more can I say to convince you?" he asked, growing impatient.

"Miss." The rental car clerk focused his gaze on her. "Take his offer."

Ashley studied the agent, not understanding why he was siding with this stranger. "Why do you care?"

The clerk met her look head-on. "Because I can't rent a car to anyone under twenty-five."

"Ah . . ." Ashley swallowed hard.

A smile slowly took over Dash's features as understanding came. "And you're not twenty-five, are you?"

Countdown to Christmas

Debbie Macomber's
Mrs. Miracle

Debbie Macomber's
Mr. Miracle

Debbie Macomber's
Call Me Mrs. Miracle

16 All New Premieres

Holiday Movies - All Day! All Night! | Starting November 1

AVAILABLE ON DVD + DIGITAL HD!

Based on the bestselling book series by the
#1 NEW YORK TIMES bestselling author
Debbie Macomber

The Heart of TV